SLEEPSIDE

THE COLLECTED FANTASIES OF GREG BEAR

SLEEPSIDE

THE COLLECTED FANTASIES OF GREG BEAR

GREG BEAR

ibooks, inc.
new york
www.ibooks.net

DISTRIBUTED BY SIMON & SCHUSTER, INC.

A Publication of ibooks, inc.

ibooks, inc.
24 West 25th Street
New York, NY 10010

The ibooks World Wide Web Site Address is:
http://www.ibooks.net

ISBN 0-7434-9805-4
First ibooks, inc. printing October 2004
10 9 8 7 6 5 4 3 2 1

Printed in the U.S.A.

CONTENTS

ON LOSING THE TAINT
OF BEING A CANNIBAL
An Introduction by Greg Bear

I'm reminded of the line delivered by Joseph Bologna in the motion picture comedy, *The Big Bus*. His character, Dan Torrance, once drove a bus through Donner Pass, and of course got snowed in. Desperation quickly set in among the passengers, and some odd recipes were resorted to. Torrance pleads that he did not know what was in the soup, adding, "One lousy foot, and they call you a cannibal for the rest of your life!"

Writing science fiction is one of those odd activities, like being a cannibal, that marks you permanently, even should you later become a vegan.

The odd relationship most people have with science—awed fascination, not infrequently dismay and distrust, and guilty dependence—guarantees a mixed reaction among the reading public: "You actually *enjoy* science? Writing about it, making it up? How *interesting*."

Their tone of voice tells you that you are now marked forever in their minds.

Science fiction explores the outer limits of the current Western paradigm, science; its playground is all that we know about the universe, and what we imagine we might eventually know.

Many of us, at one time or another, enjoy playing with previous paradigms—mind over matter, magic, dream logic, and so on. Literature does not play favorites; excellent stories have been written in all these areas.

A science fiction writer who writes fantasy, however,

is regarded by some as an odd bird indeed. Write science fiction, become well known for it, and—well, your fantasy stories become almost *invisible*. All those times when you *weren't* a cannibal—simply forgotten.

Yet most of the great science fiction writers have written a great deal of fantasy, and I have, as well. But prejudices and snobbery on both sides of the fence have grown in the past ten or fifteen years.

I've never thought of my fantasy stories as dabbling or slumming. They represent an important part of my writing. Some of my very finest work is fantasy. The first novel I ever finished—an early version of what would later be published as *The Infinity Concerto* and *The Serpent Mage*—was fantasy. My second published novel, *Psychlone*, is a ghost story, heavily influenced by Stephen King. In real life I've even gone hunting ghosts in a world-famous hotel, just like Carnacki, though without his spectacular success.

I love fantasy.

Perhaps by gathering some of my fantasy in one volume, I can convince the world that I've had at least a few moments when I was not a cannibal.

But I won't bet on it.

Being a writer of science fiction is just so *odd*.

Thank goodness.

Webster

Dry.

It lingered in the air, a dead and sterile word made for whispers. Vultures fanned her hair with feather-duster wings. Up the dictionary's page ran her lean finger, wrapped in skin like pink parchment, and she found *Andrews, Roy Chapman,* digging in the middle of the Gobi, lifting fossil dinosaur eggs cracked and unhatched from their graves.

She folded the large, heavy book on her finger. The compressed pages gripped it with a firm, familiar pressure.

With her other hand, Miss Abigail Coates explored her face, vacant of any emotion she was willing to reveal. She did not enjoy her life. Her thin body gave no pleasure, provoked no surprise, spurred no uncontrollable passion. She took no joy in the bored pain of people in the streets. She felt imprisoned by the sun that shed a revealing, bleaching light on city walls and pavement, its dust-filled shafts stealing into her small apartment.

Miss Coates was fifty and, my God the needle in her throat when she thought of it, she had never borne a child; not once had she shared her bed with a man.

There had been, long ago, a lonely, lifeless love with a boy five years younger than she. She had hoped he would blunt the needle pain in her throat; he had begged to be given the chance. But she had spurned him. *I shall use my love as bait and let men pay the toll.* That had been her excuse, at any rate, until the first flush of her youth had faded. Even after that, even before she had felt *dry,* she had never found the right man.

"*Pitiful,*" she said with a sigh, and drew herself up from the overstuffed chair in her small apartment, standing straight and lean at five feet seven inches. *I weep inside, then read the dear Bible and the even more dear dictionary. They tell me weeping is a sin. Despair is the meanest of my sins—my few sins.*

She looked around the dry, comfortable room and shielded her eyes from the gloom of the place where she slept, as if blinded by shadow. The place wasn't a bedroom because in a *bedroom* you slept with a man or men and she had none. Her eyes moved up the door frame, nicked in one corner where clumsy movers had knocked her bed against the wood, twenty years ago; down to the worn carpet that rubbed the bottoms of her feet like raw canvas. To the chair behind her, stuffing poking from its middle. To the wallpaper, chosen by someone else, stained with water along the cornice from an old rain. And finally she looked down at her feet, toes frozen in loose, frayed nylons, toenails thick and well-manicured; all parts of her body looked after but the core, the soul.

She went into the place where she slept and lay down. The sheets caressed her, as they were obliged to do, wrinkles and folds in blankets rubbing her thighs, her breasts. The pillow accepted her peppery hair, and in the dark, she ordered herself to sleep.

The morning was better. There was a whole day ahead. Something might happen.

Afternoon passed like a dull ache. In the twilight she fixed her pale dinner of potatoes and veal.

In the dark, she sat in her chair with the two books at her feet and listened to the old building crack and groan as it settled in for the night. She stared at the printed flowers on the wallpaper that someone must have once thought pretty.

The morning was fine. The afternoon was hot and sticky

and she took a walk, wearing sunglasses. She watched all the young people on this fine Saturday afternoon. *They hold hands and walk in parks. There, on that bench; she'll be in trouble if she keeps that up.*

She went back to the patient apartment that always waited, never judging, ever faithful and unperturbed.

The evening passed slowly. She became lazy with heat. By midnight a cool breeze fluttered the sun-browned curtains in the window and blew them in like the dingy wings of street birds.

Miss Coates opened her dictionary, looking for comfort, and found words she wanted, but words she didn't need. They jumped from the pages and would not leave her alone. She didn't think them obscene; she was not a prude. She loved the sounds of all words, and these words were marvelous, too, when properly entrained with other words. They could be part of rich stories, rich lives. The sound of them made her tremble and ache.

The evening ended. Again, she could not cry. Sadness was a moist, dark thing, the color of mud.

She had spent her evenings like this, with few variations, for the past five years.

The yellow morning sunlight crept across the ironing board and over her fanciest dress, burgundy in shadows, orange in the glare. "I need a lover," she told herself firmly. But one found lovers in offices and she didn't work; in trains going to distant countries, and she never left town. "I need common sense, and self-control. That part of my life is over. I need to stop thinking like a teenager." But the truth was, she had no deficiency of self-control. It was her greatest strength.

It had kept her away from danger so many times.

Her name, Coates, was not in the dictionary. There was *coati, coatimundi, coat of arms, coat of mail,* and then *coauthor,* Miss Coauthor, partner and lover to a handsome writer. They would *collaborate, corroborate, celebrate.*

Celibate.

She shut the book.

She drew the curtains on the window and slowly tugged the zipper down the back of her dress with the practiced flourish of a crochet hook. Her fingers rubbed the small of her back, nails scraping. She held her chin high, eyes closed to slits.

A lone suitor came through the dark beyond the window to stroke her skin—a stray breeze, neither hot nor cool. Sweat lodged in the cleft between her breasts. She was proud of her breasts; they were small but still did not sag when she removed her bra. She squatted and marched her hands behind her to sit and then lie down on the floor. Spreading her arms against the rough carpet, Miss Coates pressed her chin into her clavicle and peered at her breasts, boyish against the prominent ribs. Untouched. Unspoiled goods.

She cupped them in both hands. She became a thin crucifixion with legs straight and toes together. Her head lay near the window. She looked up to see the curtains fluttering silently like her lips. Mouth open. Tongue rubbing the backs of her teeth. She smoothed her hands to her stomach and let them rest there, curled on the flat warmth.

My stomach doesn't drape. I am not so undesirable. No flab, few wrinkles. My thighs are not dimpled with gross flesh.

She rolled over and propped herself on one elbow to refer to the dictionary, then the Bible.

Abigail Coates mouthing a word: *Lover.*

The dictionary sat tightly noncommittal in buckram, the Bible silent in black leather.

5

She gently pushed the Bible aside. For all its ancient sex and betrayal and the begetting of desert progeny, it would do nothing for her. She pulled the dictionary closer. "Help me," she said. "Book of all books, massive thing I can hardly lift, every thought lies in you, all human possibilities. Everything I feel, everything that *can* be felt, lies waiting to be described in combinations of the words you contain. You hold all possible lives, people and places I've never seen, things dead and things unborn. Haven of ghosts, home of tyrants, birthplace of saints."

She knew she would have to be audacious. What she was about to do would be proof of her finally having cracked, like those dinosaur eggs in the Gobi; dead and sterile and cracked.

"Surely you can make a man. Small word, little effort. You can even *tell* me how to make a man from you." She could almost imagine a man rising from the open book, spinning like a man-shaped bird cage filled with light.

The curtains puffed.

"Go," she said. She crossed her legs in a lotus next to the thick book and waited for the dust of each word, the microscopic, homeopathic bits of ink, each charged with the shape of a letter, to sift between the fibers of the paper and combine.

Dry magic. The words smelled sweet in the midnight breeze. *Dead bits of ink, charged with thought, arise.*

Veni

Her tongue swelled with the dryness of the ink. She unfolded and lay flat on her stomach to let the rough carpet mold her skin with crossword puzzle lines, upon which the right words could be written, her life solved.

Miss Coates flopped the dictionary around to face her, then threw its clumps of pages open to the middle. Her finger searched randomly on the page and found a word.

She gasped. *Man,* it said, clear as could be next to her immaculate, colorless nail. Man! She moved her finger and sucked in her breath.

"There *is* a man in you!" she told the book and laughed. It was a joke, that's all; she was not that far gone. Still grinning, she rubbed her finger against the inside of her cheek and pressed the dampness onto the word. "Here," she said. "A few of my cells." She was clever, she was scientific, she was brilliant! "Clone *them.*" Then she thought that possibility through and said, "But don't make him look like me or think like me. Change him with your medical words, *plastic surgery* and *eugenics* and *phenotype.*"

The page darkened under the press of her finger. She swung the dictionary shut and returned to her lotus.

As my trunk rises from the flower of my legs and the seat of my womb, so, man, arise from the book of all books.

Would it thunder? Only silence. The dictionary trembled and the Bible looked dark and somber. The yellow bulb in the shaded lamp sang like a dying moth. The air grew heavy. *Don't falter,* she told herself. *Don't lose faith, don't drop the flower of your legs and the seat of your womb. A bit of blood? Or milk from unsucked breasts? Catalysts... Or, God forbid, something living, a* fly *between the pages, the heart of a bird, or*—she shuddered, ill with excitement, with a kind of belief—*the clear seed of a dead man.*

The book almost lifted its cover. It *breathed.*

"That was it," she whispered in awe. "The words know what to do."

Frost clung to its brown binding. The dictionary sucked warmth from the air. The cover flew back. The pages riffled, flew by, flapped spasmodically, and two stuck together, struggling, bulging...and then splitting.

A figure flew up, arms spread, and twirled like an ice skater. It sucked in dust and air and heat, sucked sweat from her skin, and turned dry emptiness into damp flesh.

"Handsome!" she cried. "Make him handsome and rugged and kind, and smart as I am, if not smarter. Make him like a father but not my father and like a son and a lover especially a lover, warm, and give him breath that melts my lips and softens my hair like steam from jungles. He should like warm dry days and going to lakes and fishing, but no—he should like reading to me more than fishing, and he should like cold winter days and ice-skating with me he could if you will allow me to suggest he could be brown-haired with a shadow of red and his cheeks rough with fresh young beard I can watch grow and he should—"

His eyes! They flashed as he spun, molten beacons still undefined. She approved of the roughed-in shape of his nose. His hair danced and gleamed, dark brown with a hint of red. Arms, fingers, legs, crawled with words. An ant's nest of dry ink *foot*s crawled over his feet, tangling with *heel*s and *ankle*s and *toe*s. *Arm*s and *leg*s fought for dominance up the branches and into the trunk, where *torso* and *breast*s and other words fought them back. The battle of words went on for minutes, fierce and hot.

Then—what had been a dream, a delusion, suddenly became magic. The words spun, blurred, became real flesh and real bone.

His breasts were firm and square and dark-nippled. The hair on his chest was dark and silky. He was still spinning. She cried out, staring at his groin.

Clothes?

"Yes!" she said. "I have no clothes for men."

A suit, a pink shirt with cuff links and pearl decorations. His eyes blinked and his mouth opened and closed. His head drooped and a moan flew out like a whirled weight cut loose from a string.

"Stop!" she shouted. "Please stop, he's finished!"

The man stood on the dictionary, knees wobbly, threatening to topple. She jumped up from the floor to catch him, but he fell away from her and collapsed on the carpet beside the chair. The book lay kicked and sprawled by his feet, top pages wrinkled and torn.

Miss Coates stood over the man, hands fluttering at her breasts. He lay on his side, chest heaving, eyes closed. Her wide gaze darted from point to point on his body, lower lip held by tiny white teeth. After a few minutes, she was able to look away from the man. She squinted more closely at the dictionary, frowned, then bent to riffle through the pages. Every page was blank. The dictionary had given everything it had.

"I am naked," she told herself, stretching out her hands, using the realization to shock herself to sensibility. She went into the place where she slept to put on some clothes. Away from the man, she wondered what she would call him. He probably did not have a name, not a Christian name at any rate. It seemed appropriate to call him by a name like everyone else, even if she had raised him from paper and ink, from a dictionary.

"Webster," she said, nodding sharply at the obvious. "I'll call him Webster."

She returned to the living room and looked at the man. He seemed to be resting peacefully. How could she move him to a more comfortable place? The couch was too small to hold his ungainly body; he was very tall. She measured him with the tape from her sewing kit. Six feet two inches. His eyes were still shut; what color were they? She squatted beside him, face flushed, thinking thoughts she warned herself she must not think, not yet.

She wore her best dress, wrapped in smooth dark burgundy, against which her pale skin showed to best advantage. It was one o'clock in the morning, however, and she was exhausted. "You seem comfortable where you are," she told the man, who did not move. "I'll leave you on the floor."

Abigail Coates went into her bedroom to sleep. Tired as she was, she could not just close her eyes and drift off. She felt like shouting for joy and tears dampened the pillow and moistened her pepper hair.

In the darkness, *he* breathed. Dreaming, did he cause the words to flow through her drowsing thoughts? Or was it simply his breath filling the house with the odor of printer's ink?

In the night, *he* moved. Shifting an arm, a leg, sending atoms of words up like dust. His eyes flickered open, then closed. He moaned and was still again.

Abigail Coates's neck hair pricked with the first rays of morning and she awoke with a tiny shriek, little more than a high-pitched gasp. She rolled from her stomach onto her back and pulled up the sheet and bedspread.

Webster stood in the doorway, smiling. She could barely see him in the dawn light. Her eyelids were gummy with sleep. "Good morning, Regina," he said.

Regina Abigail Coates. Everyone had called her Abbie, when there had been friends to call her anything. No one had ever called her Regina.

"Regina," Webster repeated. "It reminds one of queens and Canadian coins."

How well he spoke. How full of class.

"Good morning," she said feebly. "How are you?" She suppressed an urge to giggle. *Why are you?* "How...do you feel?"

A ghost of a smile. He nodded politely, unwilling to

complain. "As well as could be expected." He walked into her room and stopped at the foot of her bed, like a ghost her father had once told her about. "I'm well-dressed. Too much so, I think. It's uncomfortable."

Her heart was a little piston in her throat, pushing up the phlegm that threatened to choke her.

He walked around to her side of the bed, just as the ghost once had.

"You brought me out. Why?"

She stared up at his bright green eyes, like drops of water raised from the depths of an ocean trench. His hand touched her shoulder, lingered on the strap of her night-gown. One finger slipped under the strap and tugged it up a quarter of an inch. "This is the distance between OP and OR," he murmured.

She felt the pressure of the cloth beneath her breast.

"Why?" he asked again. His breath sprinkled words over her face and hair. He shook his head and frowned. "Why do I feel so obliged to..." He pulled down the blind and closed the drapes and she heard the soft fall and hiss of rayon dropped onto a chair. In the darkness, a knee pressed the edge of her bed. A finger touched her neck and lips covered hers and parted them. A tongue explored.

He tasted of ink.

In the early morning hours, Regina Abigail Coates gave a tiny, squeezed-in scream.

Webster sat in the overstuffed chair and watched her leave the apartment. She shut the door and leaned against the wall, not knowing what to think or feel. "Of course," she whispered to herself, as if there were no wind or strength left in her. "Of course he doesn't like the sun."

She walked down the hallway, passed the doors of neighbors with whom she had not even a nodding acquaintance, and descended the stairs to the first floor. The street was filled with cars passing endlessly back and forth. Tugging out wrinkles from her dress, she stepped into the sunlight and faced the world, the new Regina Coates, *debutante*.

"*I know* what all you other women know," she said softly, with a shrill triumph. "All of you!" She looked up and noticed the sky, perhaps for the first time in twenty years; rich with clouds scattered across a bright blue sheet, demanding of her, *Breathe deeply*. She was part of the world, the real world.

Webster still sat in the chair when she returned with two bags of groceries. He was reading her Bible. Her face grew hot and she put down the bags and snatched it quickly from his hands. She could not face his querying stare, so she lay the book on a table, out of his reach, and said, "You don't want that."

"Why?" he asked. She picked up the bags again by their doubled and folded paper corners, taking them one in each hand into the kitchen and opening the old refrigerator to stock the perishables.

"When you're gone," Webster said, "I feel as if I fade. Am I real?"

She glanced up at the small mirror over the sink. Her shoulders twitched and a shudder ran up her back. *I am very far gone now*.

Regina brought in the afternoon newspaper and he held his hand out with a pleading expression; she handed it across, letting it waver for a moment above a patch of worn carpet, teasing him with a frightened, uncertain smile. He took it, spread it eagerly, and rubbed his fingers over the pages. He turned the big sheets slowly, seeming to absorb more than read. She fixed them both a snack but Webster refused to eat. He sat across from her at the small table, face placid, and for the moment, that was more than enough. She sat at her table, ate her small trimmed sandwich and drank her glass of grapefruit juice. Glancing at him from all sides—he did not seem to mind, and it made his outline sharper—she straightened up the tiny kitchen.

What was there to say to a man between morning and night? She had expected that a man made of words would be full of conversation, but Webster had very little experience. While all the right words existed in him, they had yet to be connected. Or so she surmised. Still, his very presence gratified her. He made her as real as she had made him.

He refused dinner, even declining to share a glass of wine with her after (she had only one glass).

"I expect there should be some awkwardness in the early days," she said. "Don't you? Quiet times when we can just sit and be with each other. Like today."

Webster stood by the window, touched a finger to his lips, leaving a smudge, and nodded. He agreed with most things she said.

"Let's go to bed," she suggested primly.

In the dark, when her solitude had again been sundered and her brow was sprinkled with salty drops of exertion, he lay next to her, and—

He *moved*.

He *breathed*.

But he did not sleep.

Regina lay with her back to him, eyes wide, staring at the flowers on the ancient wallpaper and a wide trapezoid of streetlight glare transfixing a small table and its vase. She felt ten years—no, twenty!—sliding away from her, and yet she couldn't tell him how she felt, didn't dare turn and talk. The air was full of him. Full of words not her

13

own, unorganized, potential. She breathed in a million random thoughts, deep or slight, complex or simple, eloquent or crude. Webster was becoming a generator. Kept in the apartment, his substance was reacting with itself; shut away from experience, he was making up his own patterns and organizations, subtle as smoke.

Even lying still, waiting for the slight movement of air through the window to cool him, he worked inside, and his breath filled the air with potential.

Regina was tired and deliciously filled, and that satisfaction at least was hers. She luxuriated in it and slept.

In the morning, she lay alone in the bed. She flung off the covers and padded into the living room, pulling down her rucked-up nightgown, shivering against the morning chill. He stood by the window again, naked, not caring if people on the streets looked up and saw. She stood beside him and gently enclosed his upper arm with her fingers, leaned her cheek against his shoulder, a motion that came so naturally she surprised herself with her own grace. "What do you want?" she asked.

"No," he said tightly. "The question is, what do *you* want?"

"I'll get us some breakfast. You *must* be hungry by now."

"No. I'm not. I don't know what I am or how to feel."

"I'll get some food," she continued obstinately, letting go of his arm. "Do you like milk?"

"No. I don't know."

"I don't want you to become ill."

"I don't get ill. I don't get hungry. You haven't answered my question."

"I love you," she said, with much less grace.

"You don't love me. You need me."

"Isn't that the same thing?"

"Not at all."

"Shall we get out today?" she asked airily, backing away, realizing she was doing a poor imitation of some actress in the movies. Bette Davis, her voice light, tripping.

"I can't. I don't get sick, I don't get hungry. I don't go places."

"You're being obtuse," she said petulantly, hating that tone, tears of frustration rising in her eyes. *How must I behave? Is he mine, or am I his?*

"*Obtuse, acute, equilateral, isosceles, vector, derivative, sequesential, psych-integrative, mersauvin powers...*" He shook his head, grinning sadly. "That's the future of mathematics for the next century. It becomes part of psychology. Did you know that? All numbers."

"Did you think that last night?" she asked. She cared nothing for mathematics; what could a man made of words know about numbers?

"Words mix in blood, my blood is made of words.... I can't stop thinking, even at night. Words are numbers, too. Signs and portents, measures and relations, variables and qualifiers."

"You're flesh," she said. "I gave you substance."

"You gave me existence, not substance."

She laughed harshly, caught herself, forced herself to be demure again. Taking his hand, she led him back to the chair. She kissed him on the cheek, a chaste gesture considering their state of undress, and said she would stay with him all day, to help him orient to his new world. "But tomorrow, we have to go out and buy you some more clothes."

"Clothes," he said softly, then smiled as if all was well. She leaned her head forward and smiled back, a fire radiating from her stomach through her legs and arms. With a soft step and a skip she danced on the carpet, hair swinging. Webster watched her, still smiling.

"And while you're out," he said, "bring back another dictionary."

"Of course. We can't use *that* one anymore, can we? The same kind?"

"Doesn't matter," he said, shaking his head.

The uncertainty of Webster's quiet afternoon hours became a dull, sugarcoated ache for Regina Coates. She tried to disregard her fears—that he found her a disappointment, inadequate; that he was weakening, fading—and reasoned that if she was his *mistress,* she could make him do or be whatever she wished. Unless she did not know what to wish. Could a man's behavior be wished for, or must it simply be experienced?

At night the words again poured into her, and she smiled in the dark, lying beside the warmth of the shadow that smelled of herself and printer's ink, wondering if they should be taking precautions. She was a late fader in the biological department and there was a certain risk....

She grinned savagely, thinking about it. All she could imagine was a doctor holding up a damp bloody thing in his hands and saying, "Miss Coates, you're the proud mother of an eight-ounce... *Thesaurus.*"

"Abridged?" she asked wickedly.

She shopped carefully, picking for him the best clothes she could afford, in a wide variety of styles, dipping into her savings to pay the bill. For herself she chose a new dress that showed her slim waist to advantage and hid her thin thighs. She looked girlish, summery. That was what she wanted. She purchased the dictionary and looked through gift shops for something else to give him. "Something witty and interesting for us to do." She settled on a game of Scrabble.

Webster was delighted with the dictionary. He regarded the game dubiously, but played it with her a few times. "An appetizer," he called it.

"Are you going to eat the book?" she asked, half in jest. "No," he said.

She wondered why they didn't argue. She wondered why they didn't behave like a normal couple, ignoring her self-derisive inner voice crying out, *Normal!?*

My God, she said to herself after two weeks, staring at the hard edge of the small table in the kitchen. *Creating men from dictionaries, making love until the bed is damp—at my age! He still smells like ink. He doesn't sweat and he refuses to go outside. Nobody sees him but me. Me. Who am I to judge whether he's really there?*

What would happen to Webster if I were to take a gun and put a hole in his stomach, above the navel? A man with a navel, not born of woman, is an abomination—isn't he?

If he spoke to her simply and without emotion just once more, or twice, she thought she would try that experiment and see.

She bought a gun, furtive as a mouse but a respectable citizen, for protection, a small gray pistol, and hid it in her drawer. She thought better of it a few hours after, shuddered in disgust, and removed the bullets, flinging them out of the apartment's rear window into the dead garden in the narrow courtyard below.

On the last day, when she went shopping, she carried the empty gun with her so he wouldn't find it—although he showed no interest in snooping, which would at least have been a sign of caring. The bulge in her purse made her nervous.

She did not return until dinnertime. *The apartment is not my own. It oppresses me. He oppresses me.* She walked

17

quietly through the front door, saw the living room was empty, and heard a small sound from behind the closed bedroom door. The light flop of something stiff hitting the floor.

"Webster?" Silence. She knocked lightly on the door. "Are you ready to talk?"

No reply.

He makes me mad when he doesn't answer. I could scare him, force him react to me in some way. She took out the pistol, fumbling it, pressing its grip into her palm. It felt heavy and formidable.

The door was locked. Outraged that she should be closed out of her own bedroom, she carried the revolver into the kitchen and found a hairpin in a drawer, the same she had used months before when the door had locked accidentally. She knelt before the door and fumbled, teeth clenched, lips tight.

With a small cry, she pushed the door open.

Webster sat with legs crossed on the floor beside the bed. Before him lay the new dictionary, opened almost to the back. "Not now," he said, tracing a finger along the rows of words.

Regina's mouth dropped open. "What are you looking at?" she asked, tightening her fingers on the pistol. She stepped closer, looked down, and saw that he was already up to VW.

"I don't know," he said. He found the word he was looking for, reached into his mouth with one finger and scraped his inner cheek. Smeared the wetness on the page.

"No," she said. Then, "Why...?"

There were tears on his cheeks. The man of dry ink was crying. Somehow that made her furious.

"I'm not even a human being," he said.

She hated him, hated this weakness; she had never liked

weak men. He adjusted his lotus position and gripped the edges of the dictionary with both hands. "Why can't you find a human being for yourself?" he asked, looking up at her. "I'm nothing but a dream."

She held the pistol firmly to her side. "What are you doing?"

"Need," he said. "That's all I am. Your hunger and your need. Do you know what I'm good for, what I can do? No. You'd be afraid if you did. You keep me here like some commodity."

"I wanted you to go out with me," she said tightly.

"What has the world done to you that you'd want to create me?"

"You're going to make a woman from that thing, aren't you?" she asked. "Nothing worthwhile has ever happened to me. Everything gets taken away the moment I..."

"Need," he said, raising his hands over the book. "You cannot love unless you need. You cannot love the real. You must change the thing you love to please yourself, and damn anyone if he should question what hides within you."

"You *thing*," she breathed, lips curled back. Webster looked at her and at the barrel of the gun she now pointed at him and laughed.

"You don't need that," he told her. "You don't need something real to kill a dream. All you need is a little sunlight."

She lowered the gun, dropped it with a thud on the floor, then lifted her eyebrows and smiled around gritted teeth. She pointed the index finger of her left hand and her face went lax. Listlessly, she whispered, "Bang."

The smell of printer's ink became briefly more intense, then faded on the warm breeze passing through the apartment. She kicked the dictionary shut.

19

How lonely it was going to be, in the dark with only her own sweat.

The White Horse Child

When I was seven years old, I met an old man by the side of the dusty road between school and farm. The late afternoon sun had cooled, and he was sitting on a rock, hat off, hands held out to the gentle warmth, whistling a pretty song. He nodded at me as I walked past. I nodded back. I was curious, but I knew better than to get involved with strangers. Nameless evils seemed to attach themselves to strangers, as if they might turn into lions when no one but a little kid was around.

"Hello, boy," he said.

I stopped and shuffled my feet. He looked more like a hawk than a lion. His clothes were brown and gray and russet, and his hands were pink like the flesh of some rabbit a hawk had just plucked up. His face was brown except around the eyes, where he might have worn glasses; around the eyes he was white, and this intensified his gaze. "Hello," I said.

"Was a hot day. Must have been hot in school," he said.

"They got air conditioning."

"So they do, now. How old are you?"

"Seven," I said. "Well, almost eight."

"Mother told you never to talk to strangers?"

"And Dad, too."

"Good advice. But haven't you seen me around here?"

I looked him over."No."

"Closely. Look at my clothes. What color are?"

His shirt was gray, like the rock he was sitting on. The cuffs, where they peeped from under a russet jacket, were white. He didn't smell bad, but he didn't look particularly clean. He was smooth-shaven, though. His hair was white, and his pants were the color of the dirt below the rock. "All kinds of colors," I said.

"But mostly I partake of the landscape, no?"

"I guess so," I said.

"That's because I'm not here. You're imagining me, at least part of me. Don't I look like somebody you might have heard of?"

"Who are you supposed to look like?" I asked.

"Well, I'm full of stories," he said. "Have lots of stories to tell little boys, little girls, even big folk, if they'll listen."

I started to walk away.

"But only if they'll listen," he said. I ran. When I got home, I told my older sister about the man on the road, but she only got a worried look and told me to stay away from strangers. I took her advice. For some time afterward, into my eighth year, I avoided that road and did not speak with strangers more than I had to.

The house that I lived in, with the five other members of my family and two dogs and one beleaguered cat, was white and square and comfortable. The stairs were rich dark wood overlaid with worn carpet. The walls were dark oak paneling up to a foot above my head, then white plaster, with a white plaster ceiling. The air was full of smells—bacon when I woke up, bread and soup and dinner when I came home from school, dust on weekends when we helped clean.

Sometimes my parents argued, and not just about money, and those were bad times; but usually we were happy. There was talk about selling the farm and the house and going to Mitchell where Dad could work in a computerized feed-mixing plant, but it was only talk.

It was early summer when I took to the dirt road again. I'd forgotten about the old man. But in almost the same way, when the sun was cooling and the air was haunted by lazy bees, I saw an old woman. Women strangers are less malevolent than men, and rarer. She was sitting on the gray rock, in a long green skirt summer-dusty, with a daisy-colored shawl and a blouse the precise hue of cottonwoods seen in a late hazy day's muted light. "Hello, boy," she said.

"I don't recognize you, either," I blurted, and she smiled.

"Of course not. If you didn't recognize him, you'd hardly know me."

"Do you know him?" I asked. She nodded. "Who was he? Who are you?"

"We're both full of stories. Just tell them from different angles. You aren't afraid of us, are you?"

I was, but having a woman ask the question made all the difference. "No," I said. "But what are you doing here? And how do you know—?"

"Ask for a story," she said. "One you've never heard of before." Her eyes were the color of baked chestnuts, and she squinted into the sun so that I couldn't see her whites. When she opened them wider to look at me, she didn't have any whites.

"I don't want to hear stories," I said softly.

"Sure you do. Just ask."

"It's late. I got to be home."

"I knew a man who became a house," she said. "He didn't like it. He stayed quiet for thirty years, and watched all the people inside grow up, and be just like their folks, all nasty and dirty and leaving his walls to flake, and the bathrooms were unbearable. So he spit them out one morning, furniture and all, and shut his doors and locked them."

"What?"

"You heard me. Upchucked. The poor house was so

disgusted he changed back into a man, but he was older and he had a cancer and his heart was bad because of all the abuse he had lived with. He died soon after."

I laughed, not because the man had died, but because I knew such things were lies. "That's silly," I said.

"Then here's another. There was a cat who wanted to eat butterflies. Nothing finer in the world for a cat than to stalk the grass, waiting for black-and-pumpkin butterflies. It crouches down and wriggles its rump to dig in the hind paws, then it jumps. But a butterfly is no sustenance for a cat. It's practice. There was a little girl about your age—might have been your sister, but she won't admit it—who saw the cat and decided to teach it a lesson. She hid in the taller grass with two old kites under each arm and waited for the cat to come by stalking. When it got real close, she put on her mother's dark glasses, to look all bug-eyed, and she jumped up flapping the kites. Well, it was just a little too real, because in a trice she found herself flying, and she was much smaller than she had been, and the cat jumped at her. Almost got her, too. Ask your sister about that sometime. See if she doesn't deny it."

"How'd she get back to be my sister again?"

"She became too scared to fly. She lit on a flower and found herself crushing it. The glasses broke, too."

"My sister did break a pair of Mom's glasses once."

The woman smiled.

"I got to be going home."

"Tomorrow you bring me a story, okay?"

I ran off without answering. But in my head, monsters were already rising. If she thought I was scared, wait until she heard the story I had to tell! When I got home my oldest sister, Barbara, was fixing lemonade in the kitchen. She was a year older than I but acted as if she were grown-up. She was a good six inches taller, and I could beat her if I got in a lucky punch, but no other way—so her power over me was awesome. But we were usually friendly.

"Where you been?" she asked, like a mother.

"Somebody tattled on you," I said.

Her eyes went doe-scared, then wizened down to slits. "What're you talking about?"

"Somebody tattled about what you did to Mom's sunglasses."

"I already been whipped for that," she said nonchalantly. "Not much more to tell."

"Oh, but I know more."

"Was *not* playing doctor," she said. The youngest, Sue-Ann, weakest and most full of guile, had a habit of telling the folks somebody or other was playing doctor. She didn't know what it meant—I just barely did—but it had been true once, and she held it over everybody as her only vestige of power.

"No," I said, "but I know what you were doing. And I won't tell anybody."

"You don't know nothing," she said. Then she accidentally poured half a pitcher of lemonade across the side of my head and down my front. When Mom came in I was screaming and swearing like Dad did when he fixed the cars, and I was put away for life plus ninety years in the bedroom I shared with younger brother Michael. Dinner smelled better than usual that evening, but I had none of it. Somehow I wasn't brokenhearted. It gave me time to think of a scary story for the country-colored woman on the rock.

School was the usual mix of hell and purgatory the next day. Then the hot, dry winds cooled and the bells rang and I was on the dirt road again, across the southern hundred acres, walking in the lees and shadows of the big cottonwoods. I carried my Road-Runner lunch pail and my pencil box and one book—a handwriting manual I hated so much I tore pieces out of it at night, to shorten its lifetime and I walked slowly, to give my story time to gel.

She was leaning up against a tree, not far from the rock. Looking back, I can see she was not so old as a boy of eight years thought. Now I see her lissome beauty and grace, despite the dominance of gray in her reddish hair, despite the crow's-feet around her eyes and the smile-haunts around her lips. But to the eight-year-old she was simply a peculiar crone. And he had a story to tell her, he thought, that would age her unto graveside.

"Hello, boy," she said.

"Hi." I sat on the rock.

"I can see you've been thinking," she said.

I squinted into the tree shadow to make her out better. "How'd you know?"

"You have the look of a boy that's been thinking. Are you here to listen to another story?"

"Got one to tell, this time," I said.

"Who goes first?"

It was always polite to let the woman go first, so I quelled my haste and told her she could. She motioned me to come by the tree and sit on a smaller rock, half-hidden by grass. And while the crickets in the shadow tuned up for the evening, she said, "Once there was a dog. This dog was a pretty usual dog, like the ones that would chase you around home if they thought they could get away with it—if they didn't know you or thought you were up to something the big people might disapprove of. But this dog lived in a graveyard. That is, he belonged to the caretaker. You've seen a graveyard before, haven't you?"

"Like where they took Grandpa."

"Exactly," she said. "With pretty lawns, and big white-and-gray stones, and for those who've died recently, smaller gray stones with names and flowers and years cut into them. And trees in some places, with a mortuary nearby made of brick, and a garage full of black cars, and a place behind the garage where you wonder what goes on." She knew the place, all right. "This dog had a pretty good life. It was his job to keep the grounds clear of animals at night. After the gates were locked, he'd be set loose, and he wandered all night long. He was almost white, you see. Anybody human who wasn't supposed to be there would think he was a ghost, and they'd run away.

"But this dog had a problem. His problem was, there were rats that didn't pay much attention to him. A whole gang of rats. The leader was a big one, a good yard from nose to tail. These rats made their living by burrowing under the ground in the old section of the cemetery."

That did it. I didn't want to hear any more. The air was a lot colder than it should have been, and I wanted to get home in time for dinner and still be able to eat it. But I couldn't go just then.

"Now the dog didn't know what the rats did, and just like you and I, probably, he didn't much care to know. But it was his job to keep them under control. So one day he made a truce with a couple of cats that he normally tormented and told them about the rats. These cats were scrappy old toms, and they'd long since cleared out the competition of other cats, but they were friends themselves. So the dog made them a proposition. He said he'd let them use the cemetery anytime they wanted, to prowl or hunt in or whatever, if they would put the fear of God into a few of the rats. The cats took him up on it. 'We get to do whatever we want,' they said, 'whenever we want, and you won't bother us.' The dog agreed.

"That night the dog waited for the sounds of battle. But they never came. Nary a yowl." She glared at me for emphasis. "Not a claw scratch. Not even a twitch of tail in the wind." She took a deep breath, and so did I. "Round about midnight the dog went out into the graveyard. It was very dark, and there wasn't wind or bird or speck of star to relieve the quiet and the dismal inside-of-a-box-camera blackness. He sniffed his way to the old part of the graveyard and met with the head rat, who was sitting on a slanty, cracked wooden grave marker. Only his eyes and a tip of tail showed in the dark, but the dog could smell him. 'What happened to the cats?' he asked. The rat shrugged his haunches. 'Ain't seen any cats,' he said. 'What did you think—that you could scare us out with a couple of cats? Ha. Listen—if there had been any cats here tonight, they'd have been strung and hung like meat in a shed, and my young'uns would have grown fat on—'"

"No-o-o!" I screamed, and I ran away from the woman and the tree until I couldn't hear the story anymore.

"What's the matter?" she called after me. "Aren't you going to tell me your story?" Her voice followed me as I ran.

It was funny. That night, I wanted to know what happened to the cats. Maybe nothing had happened to them. Not knowing made my visions even worse—and I didn't sleep well. But my brain worked like it had never worked before.

The next day, a Saturday, I had an ending—not a very good one in retrospect—but it served to frighten Michael so badly he threatened to tell Mom on me.

"What would you want to do that for?" I asked. "Cripes, I won't ever tell you a story again if you tell Mom!"

Michael was a year younger and didn't worry about the future. "You never told me stories before," he said, "and everything was fine. I won't miss them."

He ran down the stairs to the living room. Dad was smoking a pipe and reading the paper, relaxing before checking the irrigation on the north thirty. Michael stood at the foot of the stairs, thinking. I was almost down to grab him and haul him upstairs when he made his decision and headed for the kitchen. I knew exactly what he was considering—that Dad would probably laugh and call him a little scaredy-cat. But Mom would get upset and do me in proper.

She was putting a paper form over the kitchen table to mark it for fitting a tablecloth. Michael ran up to her and hung on to a pants leg while I halted at the kitchen door, breathing hard, eyes threatening eternal torture if he so much as peeped. But Michael didn't worry about the future much.

"Mom," he said.

"Cripes!" I shouted, high-pitching on the i. Refuge awaited me in the tractor shed. It was an agreed-upon hiding place. Mom didn't know I'd be there, but Dad did, and he could mediate.

It took him a half hour to get to me. I sat in the dark behind a workbench, practicing my pouts. He stood in the shaft of light falling from the unpatched chink in the roof. Dust motes maypoled around his legs. "Son," he said. "Mom wants to know where you got that story."

Now, this was a peculiar thing to be asked. The question I'd expected had been, "Why did you scare Michael?" or maybe, "What made you think of such a thing?" But no. Somehow she had plumbed the problem, planted the words in Dad's mouth, and impressed upon him that father-son relationships were temporarily suspended.

"I made it up," I said.

"You've never made up that kind of story before."

"I just started."

He took a deep breath. "Son, we get along real good, except when you lie to me. We know better. Who told you that story?"

This was uncanny. There was more going on than I could understand—there was a mysterious adult thing happening. I had no way around the truth. "An old woman," I said.

Dad sighed even deeper. "What was she wearing?"

"Green dress," I said.

"Was there an old man?"

I nodded.

"Christ," he said softly. He turned and walked out of the shed. From outside he called me to come into the house. I dusted off my overalls and followed him. Michael sneered at me.

"'Locked them in coffins with old dead bodies,'" he mimicked. "Phhht! You're going to get it."

The folks closed the folding door to the kitchen with both of us outside. This disturbed Michael, who'd expected instant vengeance. I was too curious and worried to take my revenge on him, so he skulked out the screen door and chased the cat around the house. "Lock you in a coffin!" he screamed.

Mom's voice drifted from behind the louvered doors. "Do you hear that? The poor child's going to have nightmares. It'll warp him."

"Don't exaggerate," Dad said.

"Exaggerate what? That those filthy people are back? Ben, they must be a hundred years old now! They're trying to do the same thing to your son that they did to your brother...and just look at *him!* Living in sin, writing for those hell-spawned girlie magazines."

"He ain't living in sin, he's living alone in an apartment in New York City. And he writes for all kinds of places."

"They tried to do it to you, too! Just thank God your aunt saved you."

"Margie, I hope you don't intend—"

"Certainly do. She knows all about them kind of people. She chased them off once, she can sure do it again!"

All hell had broken loose. I didn't understand half of it, but I could feel the presence of Great Aunt Sybil Danser. I could almost hear her crackling voice and the shustle of her satchel of Billy Grahams and Zondervans and little tiny pamphlets with shining light in blue offset on their covers.

I knew there was no way to get the full story from the folks short of listening in, but they'd stopped talking and were sitting in that stony kind of silence that indicated Dad's disgust and Mom's determination. I was mad that nobody was blaming me, as if I were some idiot child not capable of being bad on my own. I was mad at Michael for precipitating the whole mess.

And I was curious. Were the man and woman more than a hundred years old? Why hadn't I seen them before, in town, or heard about them from other kids? Surely I wasn't the only one they'd seen on the road and told stories to. I decided to get to the source. I walked up to the louvered doors and leaned my cheek against them. "Can I go play at George's?"

"Yes," Mom said. "Be back for evening chores."

George lived on the next farm, a mile and a half east. I took my bike and rode down the old dirt road going south.

They were both under the tree, eating a picnic lunch from a wicker basket. I pulled my bike over and leaned it against the gray rock, shading my eyes to see them more clearly.

"Hello, boy," the old man said. "Ain't seen you in a while."

I couldn't think of anything to say. The woman offered me a cookie, and I refused with a muttered, "No, thank you, ma'am."

"Well then, perhaps you'd like to tell us your story."

"No, ma'am."

"No story to tell us? That's odd. Meg was sure you had a story in you someplace. Peeking out from behind your ears maybe, thumbing its nose at us."

The woman smiled ingratiatingly. "Tea?"

"There's going to be trouble," I said.

"Already?" The woman smoothed the skirt in her lap and set a plate of nut bread into it. "Well, it comes sooner or later, this time sooner. What do you think of it, boy?"

"I think I got into a lot of trouble for not much being bad," I said. "I don't know why."

"Sit down, then," the old man said. "Listen to a tale, then tell us what's going on."

I sat down, not too keen about hearing another story but out of politeness. I took a piece of nut bread and nibbled on it as the woman sipped her tea and cleared her throat. "Once there was a city on the shore of a broad blue sea. In the city lived five hundred children and nobody else, because the wind from the sea wouldn't let anyone grow old. Well, children don't have kids of their own, of course, so when the wind came up in the first year the city never grew any larger."

"Where'd all the grown-ups go?" I asked. The old man held his fingers to his lips and shook his head.

"The children tried to play all day, but it wasn't enough. They became frightened at night and had bad dreams. There was nobody to comfort them because only grown-ups are really good at making nightmares go away. Now, sometimes nightmares are white horses that come out of the sea, so they set up guards along the beaches and fought them back with wands made of blackthorn. But there was another kind of nightmare, one that was black and rose out of the ground, and those were impossible to guard against. So the children got together one day and decided to tell all the scary stories there were to tell, to prepare themselves for all the nightmares. They found it was pretty easy to think up scary stories, and every one of them had a story or two to tell. They stayed up all night spinning yarns about ghosts and dead things, and live things that shouldn't have been, and things that were neither. They talked about death and about monsters that suck blood, about things that live way deep in the earth and long, thin things that sneak through cracks in doors to lean over the beds at night and speak in tongues no one could understand. They talked about eyes without heads, and vice versa, and little blue shoes that walk across a cold empty white room, with no one in them, and a bunk bed that creaks when it's empty, and a printing press that produces newspapers from a city that never was. Pretty soon, by morning, they'd told all the scary stories. When the black horses came out of the ground the next night, and the white horses from the sea, the children greeted them with cakes and ginger ale, and they held a big party. They also invited the pale sheet-things from the clouds, and everyone ate hearty and had a good time. One white horse let a little boy ride on it and took him wherever he wanted to go. So there were no more bad dreams in the city of children by the sea."

I finished the piece of bread and wiped my hands on my crossed legs. "So that's why you tried to scare me," I said.

She shook her head. "No. I never have a reason for telling a story, and neither should you."

"I don't think I'm going to tell stories anymore," I said. "The folks get too upset."

"Philistines," the old man said, looking off across the fields.

"Listen, young man. There is nothing finer in the world than the telling of tales. Split atoms if you wish, but splitting an infinitive—and getting away with it—is far nobler. Lance boils if you wish, but pricking pretensions is often cleaner and always more fun."

"Then why are Mom and Dad so mad?"

The old man shook his head. "An eternal mystery."

"Well, I'm not so sure," I said. "I scared my little brother pretty bad, and that's not nice."

"Being scared is nothing," the old woman said. "Being bored, or ignorant—now that's a crime."

"I still don't know. My folks say you have to be a hundred years old. You did something to my uncle they didn't like, and that was a long time ago. What kind of people are you, anyway?"

The old man smiled. "Old, yes. But not a hundred."

"I just came out here to warn you. Mom and Dad are bringing out my great aunt, and she's no fun for anyone. You better go away." With that said, I ran back to my bike and rode off, pumping for all I was worth. I was between a rock and a hard place. I loved my folks but I itched to hear more stories. Why wasn't it easier to make decisions?

That night I slept restlessly. I didn't have any dreams, but I kept waking up with something pounding at the back of my head, like it wanted to be let in. I scrunched my face up and pressed it back.

At Sunday breakfast, Mom looked across the table at me and put on a kind face. "We're going to pick up Auntie Danser this afternoon, at the airport," she said.

My face went like warm butter.

"You'll come with us, won't you?" she asked. "You always did like the airport."

"All the way from where she lives?" I asked.

"From Omaha," Dad said.

I didn't want to go, but it was more a command than a request. I nodded, and Dad smiled at me around his pipe.

"Don't eat too many biscuits," Mom warned him. "You're putting on weight again."

"I'll wear it off come harvest. You cook as if the whole crew was here, anyway."

"Auntie Danser will straighten it all out," Mom said, her mind elsewhere. I caught the suggestion of a grimace on Dad's face, and the pipe wriggled as he bit down on it harder.

The airport was something out of a TV space movie. It went on forever, with stairways going up to restaurants and big smoky windows that looked out on the screaming jets, and crowds of people, all leaving, except for one pear-shaped figure in a cotton print dress with fat ankles and glasses thick as headlamps. I knew her from a hundred yards.

When we met, she shook hands with Mom, hugged Dad as if she didn't want to, then bent down and gave me a smile. Her teeth were yellow and even, sound as a horse's. She was the ugliest woman I'd ever seen. She smelled of lilacs. To this day lilacs take my appetite away.

She carried a bag. Part of it was filled with knitting,

part with books and pamphlets. I always wondered why she never carried a Bible just Billy Grahams and Zonder-vans. One pamphlet fell out, and Dad bent to pick it up.

"Keep it, read it," Auntie Danser instructed him. "Do you good." She turned to Mom and scrutinized her from the bottom of a swimming pool. "You're looking good. He must be treating you right."

Dad ushered us out the automatic doors into the dry heat. Her one suitcase was light as a mummy and probably just as empty. I carried it, and it didn't even bring sweat to my brow. Her life was not in clothes and toiletry but in the plastic knitting bag.

We drove back to the farm in the big white station wagon. I leaned my head against the cool glass of the rear seat window and considered puking. Auntie Danser, I told myself, was like a mental dose of castor oil. Or like a visit to the dentist. Even if nothing was going to happen her smell presaged disaster, and like a horse sniffing a storm, my entrails worried.

Mom looked across the seat at me—Auntie Danser was riding up front with Dad—and asked, "You feeling okay? Did they give you anything to eat? Anything funny?"

I said they'd given me a piece of nut bread. Mom went, "Oh, Lord."

"Margie, they don't work like that. They got other ways." Auntie Danser leaned over the backseat and goggled at me. "Boy's just worried. I know all about it. These people and I have had it out before."

Through those murky glasses, her flat eyes knew me to my young pithy core. I didn't like being known so well. I could see that Auntie Danser's life was firm and predict-able, and I made a sudden commitment I liked the man and woman. They caused trouble, but they were the exact opposite of my great aunt. I felt better, and I gave her a reassuring grin. "Boy will be okay," she said. "Just a colic of the upset mind."

Michael and Barbara sat on the front porch as the car drove up. Somehow a visit by Auntie Danser didn't bother them as much as it did me. They didn't fawn over her, but they accepted her without complaining—even out of adult earshot. That made me think more carefully about them. I decided I didn't love them any the less, but I couldn't trust them, either. The world was taking sides, and so far on my side I was very lonely. I didn't count the two old people on my side, because I wasn't sure they were—but they came a lot closer than anybody in my family.

Auntie Danser wanted to read Billy Graham books to us after dinner, but Dad snuck us out before Mom could gather us together—all but Barbara, who stayed to listen. We watched the sunset from the loft of the old wood barn, then tried to catch the little birds that lived in the rafters. By dark and bedtime I was hungry, but not for food. I asked Dad if he'd tell me a story before bed.

"You know your mom doesn't approve of all that fairy-tale stuff," he said.

"Then no fairy tales. Just a story."

"I'm out of practice, son," he confided. He looked very sad. "Your mom says we should concentrate on things that are real and not waste our time with make-believe. Life's hard. I may have to sell the farm, you know, and work for that feed-mixer in Mitchell."

I went to bed and felt like crying. A whole lot of my family had died that night, I didn't know exactly how, or why. But I was mad.

I didn't go to school the next day. During the night I'd had a dream, which came so true and whole to me that I had to rush to the stand of cottonwoods and tell the old people. I took my lunch box and walked rapidly down the road.

They weren't there. On a piece of wire bradded to the biggest tree they'd left a note on faded brown paper. It was in a strong feminine hand, sepia-inked, delicately scribed with what could have been a goose-quill pen. It said: "We're at the old Hauskopf farm. Come if you must."

Not "Come if you can." I felt a twinge. The Hauskopf farm, abandoned fifteen years ago and never sold, was three miles farther down the road and left on a deep-rutted fork. It took me an hour to get there.

The house still looked deserted. All the white paint was flaking, leaving dead gray wood. The windows stared. I walked up the porch steps and knocked on the heavy oak door. For a moment I thought no one was going to answer. Then I heard what sounded like a gust of wind, but inside the house, and the old woman opened the door. "Hello, boy," she said. "Come for more stories?"

She invited me in. Wildflowers were growing along the baseboards, and tiny roses peered from the brambles that covered the walls. A quail led her train of inch-and-a-half fluffball chicks from under the stairs, into the living room. The floor was carpeted, but the flowers in the weave seemed more than patterns. I could stare down and keep picking out detail for minutes. "This way, boy," the woman said. She took my hand. Hers was smooth and warm, but I had the impression it was also hard as wood.

A tree stood in the living room, growing out of the floor and sending its branches up to support the ceiling. Rabbits and quail and a lazy-looking brindle cat stared at me from tangles of roots. A wooden bench surrounded the base of the tree. On the side away from us, I heard someone breathing. The old man poked his head around and smiled at me, lifting his long pipe in greeting. "Hello, boy," he said.

"The boy looks like he's ready to tell us a story, this time," the woman said.

"Of course, Meg. Have a seat, boy. Cup of cider for you? Tea? Herb biscuit?"

"Cider, please," I said.

The old man stood and went down the hall to the kitchen. He came back with a wooden tray and three steaming cups of mulled cider. The cinnamon tickled my nose as I sipped.

"Now. What's your story?"

"It's about two hawks," I said, and then hesitated.

"Go on."

"Brother hawks. Never did like each other. Fought for a strip of land where they could hunt."

"Yes?"

"Finally, one hawk met an old crippled bobcat that had set up a place for itself in a rockpile. The bobcat was learning itself magic so it wouldn't have to go out and catch dinner, which was awful hard for it now. The hawk landed near the bobcat and told it about his brother, and how cruel he was. So the bobcat said, 'Why not give him the land for the day? Here's what you can do.' The bobcat told him how he could turn into a rabbit, but a very strong rabbit no hawk could hurt."

"Wily bobcat," the old man said, smiling.

"'You mean, my brother wouldn't be able to catch me?' the hawk asked. 'Course not,' the bobcat said. 'And you can teach him a lesson. You'll tussle with him, scare him real bad—show him what tough animals there are on the land he wants. Then he'll go away and hunt somewheres else.' The hawk thought that sounded like a fine idea. So he let the bobcat turn him into a rabbit, and he hopped back to the land and waited in a patch of grass. Sure enough, his brother's shadow passed by soon, and then he heard a swoop and saw the claws held out. So he filled himself with being mad and jumped up and practically bit all the tail feathers off his brother. The hawk just flapped up and rolled over on the ground, blinking and gawking with his beak wide. 'Rabbit,' he said, 'that's not natural. Rabbits don't act that way.'

"'Round here they do,' the hawk-rabbit said. 'This is a tough old land, and all the animals here know the tricks of escaping from bad birds like you.' This scared the brother hawk, and he flew away as best he could and never came back again. The hawk-rabbit hopped to the rockpile and stood up before the bobcat, saying, 'It worked real fine. I thank you. Now turn me back, and I'll go hunt my land.' But the bobcat only grinned and reached out with a paw and broke the rabbit's neck. Then he ate him, and said, 'Now the land's mine and no hawks can take away the easy game.' And that's how the greed of two hawks turned their land over to a bobcat."

The old woman looked at me with wide baked-chestnut eyes and smiled. "You've got it," she said. "Just like your uncle. Hasn't he got it, Jack?"

The old man nodded and took his pipe from his mouth. "He's got it fine. He'll make a good one."

"Now, boy, why did you make up that story?"

I thought for a moment, then shook my head. "I don't know," I said. "It just came up."

"What are you going to do with the story?"

I didn't have an answer for that question, either.

"Got any other stories in you?"

I considered, then said, "Think so."

A car drove up outside, and Mom called my name. The old woman stood and straightened her dress. "Follow me," she said. "Go out the back door, walk around the house. Return home with them. Tomorrow, go to school like you're supposed to do. Next Saturday, come back, and we'll talk some more."

"Son? You in there?"

I walked out the back and came around to the front of the house. Mom and Auntie Danser waited in the station wagon. "You aren't allowed out here. Were you in that house?" Mom asked. I shook my head.

My great aunt looked at me with her glassed-in flat eyes and lifted the corners of her lips a little. "Margie," she said, "go have a look in the windows."

Mom got out of the car and walked up the porch to peer through the dusty panes. "It's empty, Sybil."

"Empty, boy, right?"

"I don't know," I said. "I wasn't inside."

"I could hear you, boy," she said. "Last night. Talking in your sleep. Rabbits and hawks don't behave that way. You know it, and I know it. So it ain't no good thinking about them that way, is it?"

"I don't remember talking in my sleep," I said.

"Margie, let's go home. This boy needs some pamphlets read into him."

Mom got into the car and looked back at me before starting the engine. "You ever skip school again, I'll strap you black and blue. It's real embarrassing having the school call, and not knowing where you are. Hear me?"

I nodded.

Everything was quiet that week. I went to school and tried not to dream at night and did everything boys are supposed to do. But I didn't feel like a boy. I felt something big inside, and no amount of Billy Grahams and Zondervans read at me could change that feeling.

I made one mistake, though. I asked Auntie Danser why she never read the Bible. This was in the parlor one evening after dinner and cleaning up the dishes. "Why do you want to know, boy?" she asked.

"Well, the Bible seems to be full of fine stories, but you don't carry it around with you. I just wondered why."

"Bible is a good book," she said. "The only good book. But it's difficult. It has lots of camouflage. Sometimes—" She stopped. "Who put you up to asking that question?"

"Nobody," I said.

"I heard that question before, you know," she said. "Ain't the first time I been asked. Somebody else asked me, once."

I sat in my chair, stiff as a ham.

"Your father's brother asked me that once. But we won't talk about him, will we?"

I shook my head.

Next Saturday I waited until it was dark and everyone was in bed. The night air was warm, but I was sweating more than the warm could cause as I rode my bike down the dirt road, lamp beam swinging back and forth. The sky was crawling with stars, all of them looking at me. The Milky Way seemed to touch down just beyond the road, like I might ride straight up it if I went far enough.

I knocked on the heavy door. There were no lights in the windows and it was late for old folks to be up, but I knew these two didn't behave like normal people. And I knew that just because the house looked empty from the outside didn't mean it was empty within. The wind rose up and beat against the door, making me shiver. Then it opened. It was dark for a moment, and the breath went out of me. Two pairs of eyes stared from the black. They seemed a lot taller this time. "Come in, boy," Jack whispered.

Fireflies lit up the tree in the living room. The brambles and wildflowers glowed like weeds on a sea floor. The carpet crawled, but not to my feet. I was shivering in earnest now, and my teeth chattered.

I only saw their shadows as they sat on the bench in front of me. "Sit," Meg said. "Listen close. You've taken the fire, and it glows bright. You're only a boy, but you're just like a pregnant woman now. For the rest of your life you'll be cursed with the worst affliction known to humans. Your skin will twitch at night. Your eyes will see things in the dark. Beasts will come to you and beg to be ridden. You'll never know one truth from another. You might starve, because few will want to encourage you. And if you do make good in this world, you might lose the gift and search forever after, in vain. Some will say the gift isn't special. Beware them. Some will say it is special, and beware them, too. And some—"

There was a scratching at the door. I thought it was an animal for a moment. Then it cleared its throat. It was my great aunt.

"Some will say you're damned. Perhaps they're right. But you're also enthused. Carry it lightly and responsibly."

"Listen in there. This is Sybil Danser. You know me. Open up."

"Now stand by the stairs, in the dark where she can't see," Jack said. I did as I was told. One of them—I couldn't tell which—opened the door, and the lights went out in the tree, the carpet stilled, and the brambles were snuffed.

Auntie Danser stood in the doorway, outlined by star glow, carrying her knitting bag. "Boy?" she asked. I held my breath. "And you others, too."

The wind in the house seemed to answer. "I'm not too

late," she said. "Damn you, in truth, damn you to hell! You come to our towns, and you plague us with thoughts no decent person wants to think. Not just fairy stories, but telling the way people live and why they shouldn't live that way! Your very breath is tainted! Hear me?" She walked slowly into the empty living room, feet clonking on the wooden floor. "You make them write about us and make others laugh at us. Question the way we think. Condemn our deepest prides. Pull out our mistakes and amplify them beyond all truth. What right do you have to take young children and twist their minds?"

The wind sang through the cracks in the walls. I tried to see if Jack or Meg was there, but only shadows remained.

"I know where you come from, don't forget that! Out of the ground! Out of the bones of old wicked Indians! Shamans and pagan dances and worshiping dirt and filth! I heard about you from the old squaws on the reservation. Frost and Spring, they called you, signs of the turning year. Well, now you got a different name! Death and demons, I call you, hear me?"

She seemed to jump at a sound, but I couldn't hear it. "Don't you argue with me!" she shrieked. She took her glasses off and held out both hands. "Think I'm a weak old woman, do you? You don't know how deep I run in these communities! I'm the one who had them books taken off the shelves. Remember me? Oh, you hated it—not being able to fill young minds with your pestilence. Took them off high school shelves and out of lists—burned them for junk! Remember? That was me. I'm not dead yet! Boy, where are you?"

"Enchant her," I whispered to the air. "Magic her. Make her go away. Let me live here with you."

"Is that you, boy? Come with your aunt, now. Come with, come away!"

"Go with her," the wind told me. "Send your children this way, years from now. But go with her."

I felt a kind of tingly warmth and knew it was time to get home. I snuck out the back way and came around to the front of the house. There was no car. She'd followed me on foot all the way from the farm. I wanted to leave her there in the old house, shouting at the dead rafters, but instead I called her name and waited.

She came out crying. She knew.

"You poor sinning boy," she said, pulling me to her lilac bosom.

Richie by the Sea

The storm had spent its energy the night before. A wild, scattering squall had toppled the Thompson's shed and the last spurt of high water had dropped dark drift across the rocks and sand. In the last light of day the debris was beginning to stink and attract flies and gulls. There were knots of seaweed, floats made of glass and cork, odd bits of boat wood, foam plastic shards and a whale. The whale was about forty feet long. It had died during the night after its impact on the ragged rocks of the cove. It looked like a giant garden slug, draped across the still pool of water with head and tail hanging over.

Thomas Harker felt a tinge of sympathy for the whale, but his house was less than a quarter-mile south and with the wind in his direction the smell would soon be bothersome.

The sheriff's jeep roared over the bluff road between the cove and the university grounds. Thomas waved and the sheriff waved back. There would be a lot of cleaning-up to do.

Thomas backed away from the cliff edge and returned to the path through the trees. He'd left his drafting table an hour ago to stretch his muscles and the walk had taken longer than he expected; Karen would be home by now, waiting for him, tired from the start of the new school year.

The cabin was on a broad piece of property barely thirty yards from the tideline, with nothing but grass and sand and an old picket fence between it and the water. They had worried during the storm, but there had been no flooding. The beach elevated seven feet to their property and they'd come through remarkably well.

Thomas knocked sand from his shoes and hung them on two nails next to the back door. In the service porch he removed his socks and dangled them outside, then draped them on the washer. He had soaked his shoes and socks and feet during an incautious run near the beach. Wriggling his toes, he stepped into the kitchen and sniffed. Karen had popped homemade chicken pies into the oven. Walks along the beach made him ravenous, especially after long days at the board.

He looked out the front window. Karen was at the gate, hair blowing in the evening breeze and knit sweater puffing out across her pink and white blouse. She turned, saw Thomas in the window and waved, saying something he couldn't hear.

He shrugged expressively and went to open the door. He saw something small on the porch and jumped in surprise. Richie stood on the step, smiling up at him, eyes the color of the sunlit sea, black hair unruly.

"Did I scare you, Mr. Harker?" the boy asked.

"Not much. What are you doing here this late? You should be home for dinner."

Karen kicked her shoes off on the porch. "Richie! When did you get here?"

"Just now. I was walking up the sand hills and wanted to say hello." Richie pointed north of the house with his long, unchildlike fingers. "Hello." He looked at Karen with a broad grin, head tilted.

"No dinner at home tonight?" Karen asked, totally vulnerable. "Maybe you can stay here." Thomas winced and raised his hand.

"Can't," Richie said. "Everything's just late tonight. I've got to be home soon. Hey, did you see the whale?"

"Yeah," Thomas said. "Sheriff is going to have a fun time moving it."

"Next tide'll probably take it out," Richie said. He looked between them, still smiling broadly. Thomas guessed his age at nine or ten but he already knew how to handle people.

"Tide won't be that high now," Thomas said.

"I've seen big things wash back before. Think he'll leave it overnight?"

"Probably. It won't start stinking until tomorrow."

Karen wrinkled her nose in disgust.

"Thanks for the invitation anyway, Mrs. Harker." Richie put his hands in his shorts' pockets and walked through the picket fence, turning just beyond the gate. "You got any more old clothes I can have?"

"Not now," Thomas said. "You've taken all our castoffs already."

"I need more for the rag drive," Richie said. "Thanks anyway."

"Where does he live?" Thomas asked after closing the door.

"I don't think he wants us to know. Probably in town. Don't you like him?"

"Of course I like him. He's only a kid."

"You don't seem to want him around." Karen looked at him accusingly.

"Not all the time. He's not ours, his folks should take care of him."

"They obviously don't care much."

"He's well-fed," Thomas said. "He looks healthy and he gets along fine."

They sat down to dinner. Wisps of Karen's hair still took the shape of the wind. She didn't comb it until after the table was cleared and Thomas was doing the dishes. His eyes traced endless circuit diagrams in the suds. "Hey," he shouted to the back bathroom. "I've been working too much."

"I know," Karen answered. "So have I. Isn't it terrible?"

"Let's get to bed early," he said. She walked into the kitchen wrapped in a terry-cloth bathrobe, pulling a snarl out of her hair. "Must get your sleep," she said.

He aimed a snapped towel at her retreating end but missed. Then he leaned over the sink, rubbed his eyes and looked at the suds again. No circuits, only a portrait of Richie. He removed the last plate and rinsed it.

The next morning Thomas awoke to the sound of hammering coming from down the beach. He sat up in bed to receive Karen's breezy kiss as she left for the University, then hunkered down again and rolled over to snooze a little longer. His eyes flew open a few minutes later and he cursed. The racket was too much. He rolled out of the warmth and padded into the bathroom, wincing at the cold tiles. He turned the shower on to warm, brought his mug out to shave and examined his face in the cracked mirror. The mirror had been broken six months ago when he'd slipped and jammed his hand against it after a full night poring over the circuit diagrams in his office. Karen had been furious with him and he hadn't worked that hard since. But there was a deadline from Peripheral Data on his freelance designs and he had to meet it if he wanted to keep up his reputation.

In a few more months, he might land an exclusive contract from Key Business Corporation, and then he'd be designing what he wanted to design—big computers, mighty beasts. Outstanding money.

The hammering continued and after dressing he looked out the bedroom window to see Thompson rebuilding his shed. The shed had gone unused for months after Thompson had lost his boat at the Del Mar trials, near

San Diego. Still, Thompson was sawing and hammering and reconstructing the slope-roofed structure, possible planning on another boat. Thomas didn't think much about it. He was already at work and he hadn't even reached the desk in his office. There was a whole series of TTL chips he could move to solve the interference he was sure would crop up in the design as he had it now.

By nine o'clock he was deeply absorbed. He had his drafting pencils and templates and mechanic's square spread across the paper in complete confusion. He wasn't interrupted until ten.

He answered the door only half-aware that somebody had knocked. Sheriff Varmanian stood on the porch, sweating. The sun was out and the sky clearing for a hot, humid day.

"Hi, Tom."

"Al," Thomas said, nodding. "Something up?"

"I'm interrupting? Sorry—"

"Yeah, my computers won't be able to take over your job if you keep me here much longer. How's the whale?"

"That's the least of my troubles right now." Varmanian's frizzy hair and round wire-rimmed glasses made him look more like an anarchist than a sheriff. "The whale was taken out with the night tide. We didn't even have to bury it." He pronounced "bury" like it was "burry" and studiously maintained a midwestern twang.

"Something else, then. Come inside and cool off?"

"Thanks. We've lost another kid—the Cooper's four-year-old, Kile. He disappeared last night around seven and no one's seen him since. Anybody see him here?"

"No. Only Richie was here. Listen, I didn't hear any tide big enough to sweep the whale out again. We'd need another storm to do that. Maybe something freak happened and the boy was caught in it...a freak tide?"

"There isn't any funnel in Placer Cove to cause that. Just a normal rise and the whale was buoyed up by gases, that's my guess. Cooper kid must have gotten lost on the bluff road and come down to one of the houses to ask for help—that's what the last people who saw him think. So we're checking the beach homes. Thompson didn't see anything either. I'll keep heading north and look at the flats and tide pools again, but I'd say we have another disappearance. Don't quote me, though."

"That's four?"

"Five. Five in the last six months."

"Pretty bad, Al, for a town like this."

"Don't I know it. Coopers are all upset, already planning funeral arrangements. Funerals when there aren't any bodies. But the Goldbergs had one for their son two months ago, so I guess precedent has been set."

He stood by the couch, fingering his hat and looking at the rug. "It's damned hard. How often does this kid, Richie, come down?"

"Three or four times a week. Karen's motherly toward him, thinks his folks aren't paying him enough attention."

"He'll be the next one, wait and see. Thanks for the time, and say hello to the wife for me."

Thomas returned to the board but had difficulty concentrating. He wondered if animals in the field and bush mourned long over the loss of a child. Did gazelles grieve when lions struck? Karen knew more about such feelings than he did; she'd lost a husband before she met him. His own life had been reasonably linear, uneventful.

How would he cope if something happened, if Karen were killed? Like the Coopers, with a quick funeral and burial to make things certain, even when they weren't?

What were they burying?

Four years of work and dreams.

After lunch he took a walk along the beach and found his feet moving him north to where the whale had been. The coastal rocks in this area concentrated on the northern edge of the cove. They stretched into the water for a mile before ending at the deep water shelf. At extreme low tide two or three hundred yards of rocks were exposed. Now, about fifty feet was visible and he could clearly see where the whale had been. Even at high tide the circle of rock was visible. He hadn't walked here much lately, but he remembered first noticing the circle three years before, like a perfect sandy-bottomed wading pool.

Up and down the beach, the wrack remained, dark and smelly and flyblown. But the whale was gone. It was obvious there hadn't been much wave action. Still, that was the easy explanation and he had no other.

After the walk he returned to his office and opened all the windows before setting pencil to paper. By the time Karen was home, he had finished a good portion of the diagram from his original sketches. When he turned it in, Peripheral Data would have little more to do than hand it to their drafting department for smoothing.

Richie didn't visit them that evening. He came in the morning instead. It was a Saturday and Karen was home, reading in the living room. She invited the boy in and offered him milk and cookies, then sat him before the television to watch cartoons.

Richie consumed TV with a hunger that was fascinating. He avidly mimicked the expressions of the people he saw in the commercials, as if memorizing a store of emotions, filling in the gaps in his humanity left by an imperfect upbringing.

Richie left a few hours later. As usual, he had not touched the food. He wasn't starving.

"Think he's adopting us?" Thomas asked.

"I don't know. Maybe. Maybe he just needs a couple of friends like you and me. Human contacts, if his own folks don't pay attention to him."

"Varmanian thinks he might be the next one to disappear." Thomas regretted the statement the instant it was out, but Karen didn't react. She put out a lunch of beans and sausages and waited until they were eating to say something. "When do you want to have a child?"

"Two weeks from now, over the three-day holiday," Thomas said.

"No, I'm serious."

"You've taken a shine to Richie and you think we should have one of our own?"

"Not until something breaks for you," she said, looking away. "If Key Business comes through, maybe I can take a sabbatical and study child-rearing. Directly. But one of us has to be free full time."

Thomas nodded and sipped at a glass of iced tea. Behind her humor she was serious. There was a lot at stake in the next few months—more than just money. Perhaps their happiness together. It was a hard weight to carry. Being an adult was difficult at times. He almost wished he could be like Richie, free as a gull, uncommitted.

A line of dark clouds schemed over the ocean as afternoon turned to evening. "Looks like another storm," he called to Karen, who was typing in the back bedroom.

"So soon?" she asked by way of complaint.

He sat in the kitchen to watch the advancing front. The warm, fading light of sunset turned his face orange and painted an orange square on the living room wall. The square had progressed above the level of the couch when the doorbell rang.

It was Gina Hammond and a little girl he didn't recognize. Hammond was about sixty with thinning black hair and a narrow, wizened face that always bore an irritated scowl. A cigarette was pinched between her fingers, as usual. She explained the visit between nervous stammers which embarrassed Thomas far more than they did her.

"Mr. Harker, this is my grand-daughter Julie." The girl, seven or eight, looked up at him accusingly. "Julie says she's lost four of her kittens. Th-th-that's because she gave them to your boy to play with and he-he never brought them back. You know anything about them?"

"We don't have any children, Mrs. Hammond."

"You've got a boy named Richie," the woman said, glaring at him as if he were a monster.

Karen came out of the hallway and leaned against the door jamb beside Thomas. "Gina, Richie just wanders around our house a lot. He's not ours."

"Julie says Richie lives here—he told h-h-her that—and his name is Richie Harker. What's this all about i-i-if he isn't your boy?"

"He took my kittens!" Julie said, a tear escaping to slide down her cheek.

"If that's what he told you—that we're his folks—he was fibbing," Karen said. "He lives in town, closer to you than to us."

"He brought the kittens to the beach!" Julie cried. "I saw him."

"He hasn't been here since this morning," Thomas said. "We haven't seen the kittens."

"He stole 'em!" The girl began crying in earnest.

"I'll talk to him next time I see him," Thomas promised. "But I don't know where he lives."

"H-h-his last name?"

"Don't know that, either."

Mrs. Hammond wasn't convinced. "I don't like the idea of little boys stealing things that don't belong to them."

"Neither do I, Mrs. Hammond," Karen said. "We told you we'd talk to him when we see him."

"Well," Mrs. Hammond said. She thanked them beneath her breath and left with the blubbering Julie close behind.

The storm hit after dinner. It was a heavy squall and the rain trounced over the roof as if the sky had feet. A leak started in the bathroom, fortunately right over the tub, and Thomas rummaged through his caulking gear, preparing for the storm's end when he could get up on the roof and search out the leak.

A small tool shed connected with the cabin through the garage. It had one bare light and a tiny four-paned window which stared at Thomas's chest-level into the streaming night. As he dug out his putty knife and caulking cans, the phone rang in the kitchen and Karen answered it. Her voice came across as a murmur under the barrage of rain on the garage roof. He was putting all his supplies into a cardboard box when she stuck her head through the garage door and told him she'd be going out.

"The Thompsons have lost their power," she said. "I'm going to take some candles to them on the beach road. I should be back in a few minutes, but they may want me to drive into town and buy some lanterns with them. If they do, I'll be back in an hour or so. Don't worry about me!"

Thomas came out of the shed clutching the box. "I could go instead."

"Don't be silly. Give you more time to work on the sketches. I'll be back soon. Tend the leaks."

Then she was out the front door and gone. He looked through the living room window at her receding lights and felt a gnaw of worry. He'd forgotten a rag to wipe the putty knife. He switched the light back on and went through the garage to the shed.

Something scraped against the wall outside. He bent down and peered out the four-paned window, rubbing where his breath fogged the glass. A small face stared back at him. It vanished almost as soon as he saw it.

"Richie!" Thomas yelled. "Damn it, come back here!"

Some of it seemed to fall in place as Thomas ran outside with his go-aheads and raincoat on. The boy didn't have a home to go to when he left their house. He slept some-place else, in the woods perhaps, and scavenged what he could. But now he was in the rain and soaked and in danger of becoming very ill unless Thomas caught up with him. A flash of lightning brought grass and shore into bright relief and he saw the boy running south across the sand, faster than seemed possible for a boy his age. Thomas ran after with the rain slapping him in the face.

He was halfway toward the Thompson house when the lightning flashes decreased and he couldn't follow the boy's trail. It was pitch black but for the lights coming from their cabin. The Thompson house, of course, was dark.

Thomas was soaked through and rain ran down his neck in a steady stream. Sand itched his feet and burrs from the grass caught in his cuffs, pricking his ankles.

A close flash printed the Thompsons' shed in silver against the dark. Thunder roared and grumbled down the beach.

That was it, that was where Richie stayed. He had fled to the woods only after the first storm had knocked the structure down.

He lurched through the wind-slanted strikes of water until he stood by the shed door. He fumbled at the catch and found a lock. He tugged at it and the whole thing slid free. The screws had been pried loose. "Richie," he said, opening the door. "Come on. It's Tom."

The shed waited dry and silent. "You should come home with me, stay with us." No answer. He opened the door wide and lightning showed him rags scattered everywhere, rising to a shape that looked like a man lying on his back with a blank face turned to Thomas. He jumped, but it was only a lump of rags. The boy didn't seem to be there. He started to close the door when he saw two pale points of light dance in the dark like fireflies. His heart froze and his back tingled. Again the lightning threw its dazzling sheets of light and wrapped the inside of the shed in cold whiteness and inky shadow.

Richie stood at the back, staring at Thomas with a slack expression.

The dark closed again and the boy said, "Tom, could you take me someplace warm?"

"Sure," Tom said, relaxing. "Come here." He took the boy into his arms and bundled him under the raincoat. There was something lumpy on Richie's back, under his sopping T-shirt. Thomas's hand drew back by reflex. Richie shied away just as quickly and Thomas thought, *He's got a hunch or scar, he's embarrassed about it.*

Lurching against each other as they walked to the house, Thomas asked himself why he'd been scared by what he first saw in the shed. A pile of rags. "My nerves are shot," he told Richie. The boy said nothing.

In the house he put Richie under a warm shower—the boy seemed unfamiliar with bathtubs and shower heads—and put an old Mackinaw out for the boy to wear. Thomas brought a cot and sleeping bag from the garage into the living room. Richie slipped on the Mackinaw, buttoning it with a curious crabwise flick of right hand over left, and climbed into the down bag, falling asleep almost immediately.

Karen came home an hour later, tired and wet. Thomas pointed to the cot with his finger at his lips. She looked at it, mouth open in surprise, and nodded.

In their bedroom, before fatigue and the patter of rain lulled them into sleep, Karen told him the Thompsons were nice people. "She's a little old and crotchety, but he's a bright old coot. He said something strange, though. Said when the shed fell down during the last storm he found a dummy inside it, wrapped in old blankets and dressed in cast-off clothing. Made out of straw and old sheets, he said."

"Oh." He saw the lump of rags in the lightning and shivered.

"Do you think Richie made it?"

He shook his head, too tired to think.

Sunday morning, as they came awake, they heard Richie playing outside. "You've got to ask about the kittens," Karen said. Thomas agreed reluctantly and put his clothes on.

The storm had passed in the night, having scrubbed a clear sky for the morning. He found Richie talking to the sheriff and greeted Varmanian with a wave and a yawned "Hello."

"Sheriff wants to know if we saw Mr. Jones yesterday," Richie said. Mr. Jones—named after Davy Jones—was an old beachcomber frequently seen waving a metal detector around the cove. His bag was always filled with metal junk of little interest to anybody but him.

"No, I didn't," Thomas said. "Gone?"

"Not hard to guess, is it?" Varmanian said grimly. "I'm

starting to think we ought to have a police guard out here."

"Might be an idea." Thomas waited for the sheriff to leave before asking the boy about the kittens. Richie became huffy, as if imitating some child in a television commercial. "I gave them back to Julie," he said. "I didn't take them anywhere. She's got them now.

"Richie, this was just yesterday. I don't see how you could have returned them already."

"You don't trust me, do you, Mr. Harker?" Richie asked. The boy's face turned as cold as sea-water, as hard as the rocks in the cove.

"I just don't think you're telling the truth."

"Thanks for the roof last night," Richie said softly. "I've got to go now." Thomas thought briefly about following after him, but there was nothing he could do. He considered calling Varmanian's office and telling him Richie had no legal guardian, but it didn't seem the right time.

Karen was angry with him for not being more decisive. "That boy needs someone to protect him! It's our duty to find out who the real parents are and tell the sheriff he's neglected."

"I don't think that's the problem," Thomas said. He frowned, trying to put things together. More was going on than was apparent.

"But he would have spent the night in the rain if you hadn't brought him here."

"He had that shed to go back to. He's been using the rags we gave him for—"

"That shed is cold and damp and no place for a small boy!" She took a deep breath to calm herself. "What are you trying to say, under all your evasions?"

"I have a feeling Richie can take care of himself."

"But he's a small *boy*, Tom."

"You're pinning a label on him without thinking how...without looking at how he can take care of himself, what he can do. But okay, I tell Varmanian about him and the boy gets picked up and returned to his parents—"

"What if he doesn't have any? He told Mrs. Hammond we were his parents."

"He's got to have parents somewhere, or legal guardians! Orphans just don't have the run of the town without somebody finding out. Say Varmanian turns him back to his parents—what kind of parents would make a small boy, as you call him, want to run away?"

Karen folded her arms and said nothing.

"Not very good to turn him back then, hm? What we should do is tell Varmanian to notify the parents, if any, if they haven't skipped town or something, that we're going to keep Richie here until they show up to claim him. I think Al would go along with that. If they don't show, we can contest their right to Richie and start proceedings to adopt him."

"It's not that simple," Karen said, but her eyes were sparkling. "The laws aren't that cut and dried."

"Okay, but that's the start of a plan, isn't it?"

"I suppose so."

"Okay." He pursed his lips and shook his head. "That'd be a big responsibility. Could we take care of a boy like Richie now?"

Karen nodded and Thomas was suddenly aware how much she wanted a child. It stung him a little to see her eagerness and the moisture in her eyes.

"Okay. I'll go find him." He put on his shoes and started out through the fence, turning south to the Thompson's shed. When he reached the wooden building he saw the door had been equipped with a new padlock and the latch screwed in tight. He was able to peek in through a chink in the wood—whatever could be said about Thompson as a boatbuilder, he wasn't much of a carpenter—and scan the inside. The pile of rags was gone. Only a few loose pieces remained. Richie, as he expected, wasn't inside.

Karen called from the porch and he looked north. Richie was striding toward the rocks at the opposite end of the cove. "I see him," Thomas said as he passed the cabin. "Be back in a few minutes."

He walked briskly to the base of the rocks and looked for Richie. The boy stood on a boulder, pretending to ignore him. Hesitant, not knowing exactly how to say it, Thomas told him what they were going to do. The boy looked down from the rock.

"You mean, you want to be my folks?" A smile, broad and toothy, slowly spread across his face. Everything was going to be okay.

"That's it, I think," Thomas said. "If your parents don't contest the matter."

"Oh, I don't have any folks," Richie said. Thomas looked at the sea-colored eyes and felt sudden misgivings.

"Might be easier, then," he said softly.

"Hey, Tom? I found something in the pools. Come look with me? Come on!" Richie was pure small-boy then, up from his seat and down the rock and vanishing from view like a bird taking wing.

"Richie!" Thomas cried. "I haven't time right now. Wait!" He climbed up the rock with his hands and feet slipping on the slick surface. At the top he looked across the quarter-mile stretch of pools, irritated. "Richie!"

The boy ran like a crayfish over the jagged terrain. He turned and shouted back, "In the big pool! Come on!" Then he ran on.

Tom followed, eyes lowered to keep his footing. "Slow down!" He looked up for a moment and saw a small flail of arms, a face turned toward him with the smile frozen in surprise, and the boy disappearing. There was a small cry and a splash. "Richie!" Thomas shouted, his voice cracking. He'd fallen into the pool, the circular pool where the whale had been.

He gave up all thought of his own safety and ran across the rocks, slipping twice and cracking his knees against a sharp ridge of granite. Agony shot up his legs and fogged his vision. Cursing, throwing hair out of his eyes, he crawled to his feet and shakily hobbled over the loose pebbles and sand to the edge of the round pool.

With his hands on the smooth rock rim, he blinked and saw the boy floating in the middle of the pool, face down. Thomas groaned and shut his eyes, dizzy. There was a rank odor in the air; he wanted to get up and run. This was not the way rescuers were supposed to feel. His stomach twisted. There was no time to waste, however. He forced himself over the rim into the cold water, slipping and plunging head first. His brow touched the bottom. The sand was hard and compact, crusted. He stood with the water streaming off his head and torso. It was slick like oil and came up to his groin, deepening as he splashed to the middle. It would be up to his chest where Richie floated.

Richie's shirt clung damply, outlining the odd hump on his back. *We'll get that fixed,* Thomas told himself. *Oh, God, we'll get that fixed, let him be alive and it'll work out fine.*

The water splashed across his chest. Some of it entered his mouth and he gagged at the fishy taste. He reached out for the boy's closest foot but couldn't quite reach it. The sand shifted beneath him and he ducked under the surface, swallowing more water. Bobbing up again, kicking to keep his mouth clear, he wiped his eyes with one hand

and saw the boy's arms making small, sinuous motions, like the fins of a fish.

Swimming away from Thomas.

"Richie!" Thomas shouted. His wet tennis shoes, tapping against the bottom, seemed to make it resound, as if it were hollow. Then he felt the bottom lift slightly until his feet pressed flat against it, fall away until he treaded water, lift again...

He looked down. The sand, distorted by ripples in the pool, was receding. Thomas struggled with his hands, trying to swim to the edge. Beneath him waited black water like a pool of crude oil, and in it something long and white, insistent. His feet kicked furiously to keep him from ducking under again, but the water swirled.

Thomas shut his mouth after taking a deep breath. The water throbbed like a bell, drawing him deeper, still struggling. He looked up and saw the sky, gray-blue above the ripples. There was still a chance. He kicked his shoes off, watching them spiral down. Heavy shoes, wet, gone now, he could swim better.

He spun with the water and the surface darkened. His lungs ached. He clenched his teeth to keep his mouth shut. There seemed to be progress. The surface seemed brighter. But three hazy-edged triangles converged and he could not fool himself any more, the surface was black and he had to let his breath out, hands straining up.

He touched a hard rasping shell.

The pool rippled for a few minutes, then grew still. Richie let loose of the pool's side and climbed up the edge, out of the water. His skin was pale, eyes almost milky.

The hunger had been bad for a few months. Now they were almost content. The meals were more frequent and larger—but who knew about the months to come? Best to take advantage of the good times. He pulled the limp dummy from its hiding place beneath the flat boulder and dragged it to the pool's edge, dumping it over and jumping in after. For a brief moment he smiled and hugged it; it was so much like himself, a final lure to make things more certain. Most of the time, it was all the human-shaped company he needed. He arranged its arms and legs in a natural position, spread out, and adjusted the drift of the Mackinaw in the water. The dummy drifted to the center of the pool and stayed there.

A fleshy ribbon thick as his arm waved in the water and he pulled up the back of his shirt to let it touch him on the hump and fasten. This was the best time. His limbs shrank and his face sunk inward. His skin became the color of the rocks and his eyes grew large and golden. Energy—food—pulsed into him and he felt a great love for this clever other part of him, so adaptable.

It was mother and brother at once, and if there were times when Richie felt there might be a life beyond it, an existence like that of the people he mimicked, it was only because the mimicry was so fine.

He would never actually leave.

He couldn't. Eventually he would starve; he wasn't very good at digesting.

He wriggled until he hugged smooth against the rim, with only his head sticking out of the water. He waited.

"Tom!" a voice called, not very far away. It was Karen.

"Mrs. Harker!" Richie screamed. "Help!"

Sleepside Story

Oliver Jones differed from his brothers as wheat from chaff. He didn't grudge them their blind wildness; he loaned them money until he had none, and regretted it, but not deeply. His needs were not simple, but they did not hang on the sharp signs of dollars. He worked at the jobs of youth without complaining, knowing there was something better waiting for him. Sometimes it seemed he was the only one in the family able to take cares away from his momma, now that Poppa was gone and she was lonely even with the two babies sitting on her lap, and his younger sister Yolanda gabbing about the neighbors.

The city was a puzzle to him. His older brothers Denver and Reggie believed it was a place to be conquered, but Oliver did not share their philosophy. He wanted to make the city part of him, sucked in with his breath, built into bones and brains. If he could dance with the city's music, he'd have it made, even though Denver and Reggie said the city was wide and cruel and had no end; that its four quarters ate young men alive, and spat back old people. Look at Poppa, they said; he was forty-three and he went to the fifth quarter, Darkside, a bag of wearied bones; they said, take what you can get while you can get it.

This was not what Oliver saw, though he knew the city was cruel and hungry.

His brothers and even Yolanda kidded him about his faith. It was more than just going to church that made them rag him, because they went to church, too, sitting superior beside Momma. Reggie and Denver knew there was advantage in being seen at devotions. It wasn't his music that made them laugh, for he could play the piano hard and fast as well as soft and tender, and they all liked to dance, even Momma sometimes. It was his damned sweetness. It was his taste in girls, quiet and studious; and his honesty.

On the last day of school, before Christmas vacation, Oliver made his way home in a fall of light snow, stopping in the old St. John's churchyard for a moment's reflection by his father's grave. Surrounded by the crisp, ancient slate gravestones and the newer white marble, worn by the city's acid tears, he thought he might now be considered grown-up, might have to support all of his family. He left the churchyard in a somber mood and walked between the tall brick and brownstone tenements, along the dirty, wet black streets, his shadow lost in Sleepside's greater shade, eyes on the sidewalk.

Denver and Reggie could not bring in good money, money that Momma would accept; Yolanda was too young and not likely to get a job anytime soon, and that left him, the only one who would finish school. He might take in more piano students, but he'd have to move out to do that, and how could he find another place to live without losing all he made to rent? Sleepside was crowded.

Oliver heard the noise in the flat from half a block down the street. He ran up the five dark, trash-littered flights of stairs and pulled out his key to open the three locks on the door. Swinging the door wide, he stood with hand pressed to a wall, lungs too greedy to let him speak.

The flat was in an uproar. Yolanda, rail-skinny, stood in the kitchen doorway, wringing her big hands and wailing. The two babies lurched down the hall, diapers drooping and fists stuck in their mouths. The neighbor widow Mrs. Diamond Freeland bustled back and forth in a useless dither. Something was terribly wrong.

"What is it?" he asked Yolanda with his first free breath. She just moaned and shook her head. "Where's Reggie

69

and Denver?" She shook her head less vigorously, meaning they weren't home. "Where's Momma?" This sent Yolanda into hysterics. She bumped back against the wall and clenched her fists to her mouth, tears flying. "Something happen to Momma?"

"Your momma went uptown," Mrs. Diamond Freeland said, standing flatfooted before Oliver, her flower print dress distended over her generous stomach. "What are you going to do? You're her son."

"Where uptown?" Oliver asked, trying to control his quavering voice. He wanted to slap everybody in the apartment. He was scared and they weren't being any help at all.

"She we-went sh-sh-shopping!" Yolanda wailed. "She got her check today and it's Christmas and she went to get the babies new clothes and some food."

Oliver's hands clenched. Momma had asked him what he wanted for Christmas, and he had said, "Nothing, Momma. Not really." She had chided him, saying all would be well when the check came, and what good was Christmas if she couldn't find a little something special for each of her children? "All right," he said. "I'd like sheet music. Something I've never played before."

"She must of taken the wrong stop," Mrs. Diamond Freeland said, staring at Oliver from the corners of her wide eyes. "That's all I can figure."

What happened?"

Yolanda pulled a letter out of her blouse and handed it to him, a fancy purple paper with a delicate flower design on the borders, the message handwritten very prettily in gold ink fountain pen and signed. He read it carefully, then read it again.

To the Joneses.

Your momma is uptown in My care. She came here lost and I tried to help her but she stole something very valuable to Me she shouldn't have. She says you'll come and get her. By you she means her youngest son Oliver Jones and if not him then Yolanda Jones her eldest daughter. I will keep one or the other here in exchange for your momma and one or the other must stay here and work for Me.

Miss Belle Parkhurst

969 33rd Street

"Who's she, and why does she have Momma?" Oliver asked.

"I'm not going!" Yolanda screamed.

"Hush up," said Mrs. Diamond Freeland. "She's that whoor. She's that uptown whoor used to run the biggest cathouse."

Oliver looked from face to face in disbelief.

"Your momma must of taken the wrong stop and got lost," Mrs. Diamond Freeland reiterated. "That's all I can figure. She went to that whoor's house and she got in trouble."

"I'm not going!" Yolanda said. She avoided Oliver's eyes. "You know what she'd make me do."

"Yeah," Oliver said softly. "But what'll she make *me* do?

Reggie and Denver, he learned from Mrs. Diamond Freeland, had come home before the message had been received, leaving just as the messenger came whistling up

71

the outside hall. Oliver sighed. His brothers were almost never home; they thought they'd pulled the wool over Momma's eyes, but they hadn't. Momma knew who would be home and come for her when she was in trouble.

Reggie and Denver fancied themselves the hottest dudes on the street. They claimed they had women all over Sleepside and Snowside; Oliver was almost too shy to ask a woman out. He was small, slender, and almost pretty, but very strong for his size. Reggie and Denver were cowards. Oliver had never run from a true and worthwhile fight in his life, but neither had he started one.

The thought of going to Miss Belle Parkhurst's establishment scared him, but he remembered what his father had told him just a week before dying. "Oliver, when I'm gone—that's soon now, you know it—Yolanda's flaky as a bowl of cereal and your brothers...well, I'll be kind and just say your momma, she's going to need you. You got to turn out right so as she can lean on you."

The babies hadn't been born then.

"Which train did she take?"

"Down to Snowside," Mrs. Diamond Freeland said. "But she must of gotten off in Sunside. That's near Thirty-third."

"It's getting night," Oliver said.

Yolanda sniffed and wiped her eyes. Off the hook. "You going?"

"Have to," Oliver said. "It's Momma."

Said Mrs. Diamond Freeland, "I think that whoor got something on her mind."

On the line between dusk and dark, down underground where it shouldn't have mattered, the Metro emptied of all the day's passengers and filled with the night's.

Sometimes day folks went in tight-packed groups on

the Night Metro, but not if they could avoid it. Night Metro was for carrying the lost or human garbage. Everyone ashamed or afraid to come out during the day came out at night. Night Metro also carried the zeroes—people who lived their lives and when they died no one could look back and say they remembered them. Night Metro—especially late—was not a good way to travel, but for Oliver it was the quickest way to get from Sleepside to Sunside; he had to go as soon as possible to get Momma.

Oliver descended the four flights of concrete steps, grinding his teeth at the thought of the danger he was in. He halted at the bottom, grimacing at the frightened knots of muscle and nerves in his back, repeating over and over again, "It's Momma. It's Momma. No one can save her but me." He dropped his bronze cat's-head token into the turnstile, *clunk-chunking* through, and crossed the empty platform. Only two indistinct figures waited trackside, heavy-coated though it was a warm evening. Oliver kept an eye on them and walked back and forth in a figure eight on the grimy foot-scrubbed concrete, peering nervously down at the wet and soot under the rails. Behind him, on the station's smudged white tile walls hung a gold mosaic trumpet and the number 7, the trumpet for folks who couldn't read to know when to get off. All Sleepside stations had musical instruments.

The Night Metro was run by a different crew than the Day Metro. His train came up, clean and silver-sleek, without a spot of graffiti or a stain of tarnish. Oliver caught a glimpse of the driver under the SLEEP-SIDE/CHASTE RIVER/SUNSIDE-46th destination sign. The driver wore or had a bull's head and carried a prominent pair of long gleaming silver scissors on his Sam Browne belt. Oliver entered the open doors and took a smooth handgrip even though the seats were mostly empty. Somebody standing was somebody quicker to run.

There were four people on his car: two women—one young, vacant, and not pretty or even very alive-looking, the other old and muddy-eyed with a plastic daisy-flowered shopping bag—and two men, both sunny blond and chunky, wearing shiny-elbowed business suits. Nobody looked at anybody else. The doors shut and the train grumbled on, gathering speed until the noise of its wheels on the tracks drowned out all other sound and almost all thought.

There were more dead stations than live and lighted ones. Night Metro made only a few stops congruent with Day Metro. Most stations were turned off, but the only people left standing there wouldn't show in bright lights anyway. Oliver tried not to look, to keep his eyes on the few in the car with him, but every so often he couldn't help peering out. Beyond I-beams and barricades, single orange lamps and broken tiled walls rushed by, platforms populated by slow smudges of shadow.

Some said the dead used the Night Metro, and that after midnight it went all the way to Darkside. Oliver didn't know what to believe. As the train slowed for his station, he pulled the collar of his dark green nylon windbreaker up around his neck and rubbed his nose with one finger. Reggie and Denver would never have made it even this far. They valued their skins too much.

The train did not move on after he disembarked. He stood by the open doors for a moment, then walked past the lead car on his way to the stairs. Over his shoulder, he saw the driver standing at the head of the train in his little cabin of fluorescent coldness, the eyes in the bull's head sunk deep in shade. Oliver felt rather than saw the starlike pricks in the sockets, watching him. The driver's left hand tugged on the blades of the silver shears.

"What do you care, man?" Oliver asked softly, stopping for an instant to return the hidden stare. "Go on about your work. We all got stuff to do."

The bull's nose pointed a mere twitch away from Oliver, and the hand left the shears to return to its switch. The train doors closed. The silver side panels and windows and lights picked up speed and the train squealed around a curve into darkness. He climbed the two flights of stairs to Sunside Station.

Summer night lay heavy and warm on the lush trees and grass of a broad park. Oliver stood at the head of the Metro entrance and listened to the crickets and katydids and cicadas sing songs unheard in Sleepside, where trees and grass were sparse. All around the park rose dark-windowed walls of high marble and brick and gray stone hotels and fancy apartment buildings with gable roofs.

Oliver looked around for directions, a map, anything. Above the Night Metro, it was even possible ordinary people might be out strolling, and he could ask them if he dared. He walked toward the street and thought of Momma getting this far and of her being afraid. He loved Momma very much. Sometimes she seemed to be the only decent thing in his life, though more and more often young women distracted him as the years passed, and he experienced more and more secret fixations.

"Oliver Jones?"

A long white limousine waited by the curb. A young, slender woman in violet chauffeur's livery, with a jaunty black and silver cap sitting atop exuberant hair, cocked her head coyly, smiled at him, and beckoned with a white-leather-gloved finger. "Are you Oliver Jones, come to rescue your momma?"

He walked slowly toward the white limousine. It was bigger and more beautiful than anything he had ever seen before, with long ribbed chrome pipes snaking out from under the hood and through the fenders, stand-alone golden headlights, and a white tonneau roof made of real leather. "My name's Oliver," he affirmed.

"Then you're my man. Please get in." She winked and held the door open.

When the door closed, the woman's arm—all he could see of her through the smoky window glass—vanished. The driver's door did not open. She did not get in. The limousine drove off by itself. Oliver fell back into the lush suede and velvet interior. An electronic wet bar gleamed silver and gold and black above a cool white-lit panel on which sat a single crystal glass filled with ice cubes. A spigot rotated around and waited for instructions. When none came, it gushed fragrant gin over the ice and rotated back into place.

Oliver did not touch the glass.

Below the wet bar, the television set turned itself on. Passion and delight sang from the small, precise speakers. "No," he said. "No!"

The television shut off.

He edged closer to the smoky glass and saw dim streetlights and cab headlights moving past. A huge black building trimmed with gold ornaments, windows outlined with red, loomed on the corner, all but three of its windows dark. The limousine turned smoothly and descended into a dark underground garage. Lights throwing huge golden cat's eyes, tires squealing on shiny concrete, it snaked around a slalom of walls and pillars and dusty limousines and came to a quick stop. The door opened.

Oliver stepped out. The chauffeur stood holding the

door, grinning, and doffed her cap. "My pleasure," she said.

The car had parked beside a big wooden door set into hewn stone. Fossil bones and teeth were clearly visible in the matrix of each block in the walls. Glistening ferns in dark ponds flanked the door. Oliver heard the car drive away and turned to look, but he did not see whether the chauffeur drove this time or not.

He walked across a wood plank bridge and tried the black iron handle on the door. The door swung open at the suggestion of his fingers. Beyond, a narrow red-carpeted staircase with rosebush-carved maple banisters ascended to the upper floor.

The place smelled of cloves and mint and, somehow, of what Oliver imagined dogs or horses must smell like—a musty old rug sitting on a floor grate. (He had never owned a dog and never seen a horse without a policeman on it, and never so close he could smell it.) Nobody had been through here in a long time, he thought. But everybody knew about Miss Belle Parkhurst and her place. And the chauffeur had been young. He wrinkled his nose; he did not like this place.

The dark wood door at the top of the stairs swung open silently. Nobody stood there waiting; it might have opened by itself. Oliver tried to speak, but his throat itched and closed. He coughed into his fist and shrugged his shoulders in a spasm. Then, eyes damp and hot with anger and fear and something more, he moved his lips and croaked, "I'm Oliver Jones. I'm here to get my momma."

The door remained unattended. He looked back into the parking garage, dark and quiet as a cave; nothing for him there. Then he ascended quickly to get it over with and passed through the door into the ill-reputed house of Miss Belle Parkhurst.

*　　*　　*

The city extends to the far horizon, divided into quarters by roads or canals or even train tracks, above or underground; and sometimes you know those divisions and know better than to cross them, and sometimes you don't. The city is broader than any man's life, and it is worth more than your life not to understand why you are where you are and must stay there.

The city encourages ignorance because it must eat.

The four quarters of the city are Snowside, Cokeside where few sane people go, Sleepside, and Sunside. Sunside is bright and rich and hazardous because that is where the swell folks live. Swell folks don't tolerate intruders. Not even the police go into Sunside without an escort. Toward the center of the city is uptown, and in the middle of uptown is where all four quarters meet at the Pillar of the Unknown Mayor. Outward is the downtown and scattered islands of suburbs, and no one knows where it ends.

The Joneses live in downtown Sleepside. The light there even at noon is not very bright, but neither is it burning harsh as in Cokeside where it can fry your skull. Sleepside is tolerable. There are many good people in Sleepside and Snowside, and though confused, the general run is not vicious. Oliver grew up there and carries it in his bones and meat. No doubt the Night Metro driver smelled his origins and knew here was a young man crossing a border going uptown. No doubt Oliver was still alive because Miss Belle Parkhurst had protected him. That meant Miss Parkhurst had protected Momma, and perhaps lured her, as well.

The hallway was lighted by rows of candles held in gold eagle claws along each wall. At the end of the hall, Oliver stepped into a broad wood-paneled room set here and there with lush green ferns in brass spittoons. The Oriental carpet revealed a stylized garden in cream and black and red. Five empty black velvet-upholstered couches stood unoccupied, expectant, like a line of languorous women amongst the ferns. Along the walls, chairs covered by white sheets asserted their heavy wooden arms. Oliver stood, jaw open, not used to such luxury. He needed a long moment to take it all in.

Miss Belle Parkhurst was obviously a very rich woman, and not your ordinary whore. From what he had seen so far, she had power as well as money, power over cars and maybe over men and women. Maybe over Momma. "Momma?"

A tall, tenuous white-haired man in a cream-colored suit walked across the room, paying Oliver scant attention. He said nothing. Oliver watched him sit on a sheet-covered chair. He did not disturb the sheets, but sat through them. He leaned his head back reflectively, elevating a cigarette holder without a cigarette. He blew out clear air, or perhaps nothing at all, and then smiled at something just to Oliver's right. Oliver turned. They were alone. When he looked back, the man in the cream-colored suit was gone.

Oliver's arms tingled. He was in for more than he had bargained for, and he had bargained for a lot.

"This way," said a woman's deep voice, operatic, dignified, easy and friendly at once. He could not see her, but he squinted at the doorway, and she stepped between two fluted green onyx columns. He did not know at first that she was addressing him; there might be other gentlemen, or girls, equally as tenuous as the man in the cream-colored suit. But this small, imposing woman with upheld hands, dressed in gold and peach silk that clung to her smooth and silent, was watching only him with her large dark eyes. She smiled richly and warmly, but Oliver thought there was a hidden flaw in that smile, in her assurance. She was ill at ease from the instant their eyes met, though she might have been at ease before then, *thinking* of meeting him. She had had all things planned until that moment.

If he unnerved her slightly, this woman positively terrified him. She was beautiful and smooth-skinned, and he could smell the sweet roses and camellias and magnolia blossoms surrounding her like a crowd of familiar friends.

"This way," she repeated, gesturing through the doors.

"I'm looking for my momma. I'm supposed to meet Miss Belle Parkhurst."

"I'm Belle Parkhurst. You're Oliver Jones...aren't you?"

He nodded, face solemn, eyes wide. He nodded again and swallowed.

"I sent your momma on her way home. She'll be fine."

He looked back at the hallway. "She'll be on the Night Metro," he said.

"I sent her back in my car. Nothing will happen to her."

Oliver believed her. There was a long, silent moment. He realized he was twisting and wringing his hands before his crotch and he stopped this, embarrassed.

"Your momma's fine. Don't worry about her."

"All right," he said, drawing his shoulders up. "You wanted to talk to me?"

"Yes," she said. "And more."

His nostrils flared and he jerked his eyes hard right, his torso and then his hips and legs twisting that way as he broke into a scrambling rabbit-run for the hallway. The golden eagle claws on each side dropped their candles as he passed and reached out to hook him with their talons. The vast house around him seemed suddenly alert, and he knew even before one claw grabbed his collar that he did not have a chance.

He dangled helpless from the armpits of his jacket at the very end of the hall. In the far door appeared the whore, angry, fingers dripping small beads of fire onto the wooden floor. The floor smoked and sizzled.

"I've let your momma go," Belle Parkhurst said, voice deeper than a grave, face terrible and smoothly beautiful and very old, very experienced. "That was my agreement. You leave, and you break that agreement, and that means I take your sister, or I take back your momma."

She cocked an elegant, painted eyebrow at him and leaned her head to one side in query. He nodded as best he could with his chin jammed against the teeth of his jacket's zipper.

"Good. There's food waiting. I'd enjoy your company."

The dining room was small, no larger than his bedroom at home, occupied by two chairs and an intimate round table covered in white linen. A gold eagle claw candelabrum cast a warm light over the table top. Miss Parkhurst preceded Oliver, her long dress rustling softly at her heels. Other things rustled in the room as well; the floor might have been ankle-deep in windblown leaves by the sound, but it was spotless, a rich round red and cream Oriental rug centered beneath the table; and beneath that, smooth old oak flooring. Oliver looked up from his sneaker-clad feet. Miss Parkhurst waited expectantly a step back from her chair.

"Your momma teach you no manners?" she asked softly.

He approached the table reluctantly. There were empty gold plates and tableware on the linen now that had not been there before. Napkins seemed to drop from thin fog and folded themselves on the plates. Oliver stopped, his nostrils flaring.

"Don't you mind that," Miss Parkhurst said. "I live alone here. Good help is hard to find."

Oliver stepped behind the chair and lifted it by its maple headpiece, pulling it out for her. She sat and he helped her move closer to the table. Not once did he touch her; his skin crawled at the thought.

"The food here is very good," Miss Parkhurst said as he sat across from her.

"I'm not hungry," Oliver said.

She smiled warmly at him. It was a powerful thing, her smile. "I won't bite," she said. "Except supper. *That* I'll bite."

Oliver smelled wonderful spices and sweet vinegar. A napkin had been draped across his lap, and before him was a salad on a fine china plate. He was very hungry and he enjoyed salads, seeing fresh greens so seldom in Sleepside.

"That's it," Miss Parkhurst said soothingly, smiling as he ate. She lifted her fork in turn and speared a fold of olive-oiled butter lettuce, bringing it to her red lips.

The rest of the dinner proceeded in like fashion, but with no further conversation. She watched him frankly, appraising, and he avoided her eyes.

Down a corridor with tall windows set in an east wall, dawn gray and pink around their faint silhouettes on the west wall, Miss Parkhurst led Oliver to his room. "It's the quietest place in the mansion," she said.

"You're keeping me here," he said. "You're never going to let me go?"

"Please allow me to indulge myself. I'm not just alone. I'm lonely. Here, you can have anything you want... almost..."

A door at the corridor's far end opened by itself. Within, a fire burned brightly within a small fireplace, and a wide bed waited with covers turned down. Exquisitely detailed murals of forests and fields covered the walls; the ceiling was rich deep blue, flecked with gold and silver and jeweled stars. Books filled a case in one corner, and in another corner stood the most beautiful ebony grand piano he had ever seen. Miss Parkhurst did not approach the door too closely. There were no candles; within this room, all lamps were electric.

"This is your room. I won't come in," she said. "And after tonight, you don't ever come out after dark. We'll talk and see each other during the day, but never at night. The door isn't locked. I'll have to trust you."

"I can go anytime I want?"

She smiled. Even though she meant her smile to be nothing more than enigmatic, it shook him. She was deadly beautiful, the kind of woman his brothers dreamed about. Her smile said she might eat him alive, all of him that counted. Oliver could imagine his mother's reaction to Miss Belle Parkhurst.

He entered the room and swung the door shut, trembling. There were a dozen things he wanted to say; angry, frustrated, pleading things. He leaned against the door, swallowing them all back, keeping his hand from going to the gold and crystal knob.

Behind the door, her skirts rustled as she retired along the corridor. After a moment, he pushed off from the door and walked with an exaggerated swagger to the bookcase, mumbling. Miss Parkhurst would never have taken Oliver's sister Yolanda; that wasn't what she wanted. She wanted young boy flesh, he thought. She wanted to burn him down to his sneakers, smiling like that.

The books on the shelves were books he had heard about but had never found in the Sleepside library, books he wanted to read, that the librarians said only people from Sunside and the suburbs cared to read. His fingers lingered on the tops of their spines, tugging gently.

He decided to sleep instead. If she was going to pester him during the day, he didn't have much time. She'd be a late riser, he thought; a night person.

Then he realized: whatever she did at night, she had not done this night. This night had been set aside for him.

He shivered again, thinking of the food and napkins and the eagle claws. Was this room haunted, too? Would things keep watch over him?

Oliver lay back on the bed, still clothed. His mind clouded with thoughts of living sheets feeling up his bare skin. Tired, almost dead out.

The dreams that came were sweet and pleasant and she did not walk in them. This really was his time.

At eleven o'clock by the brass and gold and crystal clock on the bookcase, Oliver kicked his legs out, rubbed his face into the pillows and started up, back arched, smelling bacon and eggs and coffee. A covered tray waited on a polished brass cart beside the bed. A vase of roses on one corner of the cart scented the room. A folded piece of fine ivory paper leaned against the vase. Oliver sat on the edge of the bed and read the note, once again written in golden ink in a delicate hand.

I'm waiting for you in the gymnasium. Meet me after you've eaten. Got something to give to you.

He had no idea where the gymnasium was. When he had finished breakfast, he put on a plush robe, opened the heavy door to his room—both relieved and irritated that it did not open by itself—and looked down the corridor. A golden arc clung to the base of each tall window.

It was at least noon, Sunside time. She had given him plenty of time to rest.

A pair of new black jeans and a white silk shirt waited for him on the bed, which had been carefully made in the time it had taken him to glance down the hall. Cautiously, but less frightened now, he removed the robe, put on these clothes and the deerskin moccasins by the foot of the bed, and stood in the doorway, leaning as casually as he could manage against the frame.

A silk handkerchief hung in the air several yards away. It fluttered like a pigeon's ghost to attract his attention, then drifted slowly along the hall. He followed.

The house seemed to go on forever, empty and magnificent. Each public room had its own decor, filled with antique furniture, potted palms, plush couches and chairs, and love seats. Several times he thought he saw wisps of dinner jackets, top hats, eager, strained faces, in foyers, corridors, on staircases as he followed the handkerchief. The house smelled of perfume and dust, faint cigars, spilled wine, and old sweat.

He had climbed three flights of stairs before he stood at the tall ivory-white double door of the gymnasium. The handkerchief vanished with a flip. The doors opened.

Miss Parkhurst stood at the opposite end of a wide black tile dance floor, before a band riser covered with music stands and instruments. Oliver inspected the low half-circle stage with narrowed eyes. Would she demand he dance with her, while all the instruments played by themselves?

"Good morning," she said. She wore a green dress the color of fresh wet grass, high at the neck and down to her calves. Beneath the dress she wore white boots and white gloves, and a white feather curled around her black hair.

"Good morning," he replied softly, politely.

"Did you sleep well? Eat hearty?"

Oliver nodded, fear and shyness returning. What could she possibly want to give him? Herself? His face grew hot.

"It's a shame this house is empty during the day," she said. *And at night?* he thought. "I could fill this room with exercise equipment," she continued. "Weight benches, even a track around the outside." She smiled. The smile seemed less ferocious now, even wistful; younger.

He rubbed a fold of his shirt between two fingers. "I enjoyed the food, and your house is real fine, but I'd like to go home," he said.

She half turned and walked slowly from the stand. "You could have this house and all my wealth. I'd like you to have it."

"Why? I haven't done anything for you."

"Or to me, either," she said, facing him again. "You know how I've made all this money?"

"Yes, ma'am," he said after a moment's pause. "I'm not a fool."

"You've heard about me. That I'm a whore."

"Yes, ma'am. Mrs. Diamond Freeland says you are."

"And what is a whore?"

"You let men do it to you for money," Oliver said, feeling bolder, but with his face hot all the same.

Miss Parkhurst nodded. "I've got part of them all here with me," she said. "My bookkeeping. I know every name, every face. They keep me company now that business is slow."

"All of them?" Oliver asked.

Miss Parkhurst's faint smile was part pride, part sadness, her eyes distant and moist. "They gave me all the things I have here."

"I don't think it would be worth it," Oliver said.

"I'd be dead if I wasn't a whore," Miss Parkhurst said,

eyes suddenly sharp on him, flashing anger. "I'd have starved to death." She relaxed her clenched hands. "We got plenty of time to talk about my life, so let's hold it here for a while. I got something you need, if you're going to inherit this place."

"I don't want it, ma'am," Oliver said.

"If you don't take it, somebody who doesn't need it and deserves it a lot less will. I want you to have it. Please, be kind to me this once."

"Why me?" Oliver asked. He simply wanted out; this was completely off the planned track of his life. He was less afraid of Miss Parkhurst now, though her anger raised hairs on his neck; he felt he could be bolder and perhaps even demanding. There was a weakness in her: he was her weakness, and he wasn't above taking some advantage of that, considering how desperate his situation might be.

"You're kind," she said. "You care. And you've never had a woman, not all the way."

Oliver's face warmed again. "Please let me go," he said quietly, hoping it didn't sound as if he was pleading.

Miss Parkhurst folded her arms. "I can't," she said.

While Oliver spent his first day in Miss Parkhurst's mansion, across the city, beyond the borders of Sunside, Denver and Reggie Jones had returned home to find the apartment blanketed in gloom. Reggie, tall and gangly, long of neck and short of head, with a prominent nose, stood with back slumped in the front hall, mouth open in surprise. "He just took off and left you all here?" Reggie asked. Denver returned from the kitchen, shorter and stockier than his brother, dressed in black vinyl jacket and pants.

Yolanda's face was puffy from constant crying. She now enjoyed the tears she spilled, and had scheduled them at two-hour intervals, to her momma's sorrowful irritation. She herded the two babies into their momma's bedroom and closed a rickety gate behind them, then brushed her hands on the breast of her ragged blouse.

"You don't get it," she said, facing them and dropping her arms dramatically. "That whore took Momma, and Oliver traded himself for her."

"That whore," said Reggie, "is a rich old witch."

"Rich old bitch witch," Denver said, pleased with himself.

"That whore is opportunity knocking," Reggie continued, chewing reflectively. "I hear she lives alone."

"That's why she took Oliver," Yolanda said. The babies cooed and chirped behind the gate.

"Why him and not one of us?" Reggie asked.

Momma gently pushed the babies aside, swung open the gate, and marched down the hall, dressed in her best wool skirt and print blouse, wrapped in her overcoat against the gathering dark and cold outside. "Where you going?" Yolanda asked her as she brushed past.

"Time to talk to the police," she said, glowering at Reggie. Denver backed into the bedroom he shared with his brother, out of her way. He shook his head condescendingly, grinning: Momma at it again.

"Them dogheads?" Reggie said. "They got no say in Sunside."

Momma turned at the front door and glared at them. "How are you going to help your brother? He's the best of you all, you know, and you just stand here, flatfooted and jawboning yourselves."

"Momma's upset," Denver informed his brother solemnly.

"She should be," Reggie said sympathetically. "She was held prisoner by that witch bitch whore. We should go get Oliver and bring him home. We could pretend we was customers."

"She don't have customers anymore," Denver said. "She's too old. She's worn out." He glanced at his crotch and leaned his head to one side, glaring for emphasis. His glare faded into an amiable grin.

"How do you know?" Reggie asked.

"That's what I hear."

Momma snorted and pulled back the bars and bolts on the front door. Reggie calmly walked up behind her and stopped her. "Police don't do anybody any good, Momma," he said. "We'll go. We'll bring Oliver back."

Denver's face slowly fell at the thought. "We got to plan it out," he said. "We got to be careful."

"We'll be careful," Reggie said. "For Momma's sake."

With his hand blocking her exit, Momma snorted again, then let her shoulders droop and her face sag. She looked more and more like an old woman now, though she was only in her late thirties.

Yolanda stood aside to let her pass into the living room. "Poor Momma," she said, eyes welling up.

"What you going to do for your brother?" Reggie asked his sister pointedly as he in turn walked by her. She craned her neck and stuck out her chin resentfully. "Go trade places with him, work in *her* house?" he taunted.

"She's rich," Denver said to himself, cupping his chin in his hand. "We could make a whole lot of money, saving our brother."

"We start thinking about it now," Reggie mandated, falling into the chair that used to be their father's, leaning his head back against the lace covers Momma had made.

Momma, face ashen, stood by the couch staring at a family portrait hung on the wall in a cheap wooden frame. "He did it for me. I was so stupid, getting off there, letting her help me. Should of known," she murmured, clutching her wrist. Her face ashen, her ankle wobbled under her and she pirouetted, hands spread out like a dancer, and collapsed face down on the couch.

The gift, the thing that Oliver needed to inherit Miss Parkhurst's mansion, was a small gold box with three buttons, like a garage door opener. She finally presented it to him in the dining room as they finished dinner.

Miss Parkhurst was nice to talk to, something Oliver had not expected, but which he should have. Whores did more than lie with a man to keep him coming back and spending his money; that should have been obvious. The day had not been the agony he expected. He had even stopped asking her to let him go. Oliver thought it would be best to bide his time, and when something distracted her, make his escape. Until then, she was not treating him badly or expecting anything he could not freely give.

"It'll be dark soon," she said as the plates cleared themselves away. He was even getting used to the ghostly service. "I have to go soon, and you got to be in your room. Take this with you, and keep it there." She lifted a tray cover to reveal a white silk bag. Unstringing the bag, she removed the golden opener and shyly presented it to him. "This was given to me a long time ago. I don't need it now. But if you want to run this place, you got to have it. You can't lose it, or let anyone take it from you."

Oliver's hands went to the opener involuntarily. It seemed very desirable, as if there were something of Miss Parkhurst in it: warm, powerful, a little frightening. It fit his hand perfectly, familiar to his skin; he might have owned it forever.

He tightened his lips and returned it to her. "I'm sorry," he said. "It's not for me."

"You remember what I told you," she said. "If you don't take it, somebody else will, and it won't do anybody any good then. I want it to do some good now, when I'm done with it."

"Who gave it to you?" Oliver asked.

"A pimp, a long time ago. When I was a girl."

Oliver's eyes betrayed no judgment or disgust. She took a deep breath.

"He made you do it...?" Oliver asked.

"No. I was young, but already a whore. I had an old, kind pimp, at least he seemed old to me, I wasn't much more than a baby. He died, he was killed, so this new pimp came, and he was powerful. He had the magic. But he couldn't tame me. So he says..."

Miss Parkhurst raised her hands to her face. "He cut me up. I was almost dead. He says, 'You shame me, whore. You do this to me, make me lose control, you're the only one ever did this to me. So I curse you. You'll be the greatest whore ever was.' He gave me the opener then, and he put my face and body back together so I'd be pretty. Then he left town, and I was in charge. I've been here ever since, but all the girls have gone, it's been so long, died or left or I told them to go. I wanted this place closed, but I couldn't close it all at once."

Oliver nodded slowly, eyes wide.

"He gave me most of his magic, too. I didn't have any choice. One thing he didn't give me was a way out. Except..." This time, she was the one with the pleading expression.

Oliver raised an eyebrow.

"What I need has to be freely given. Now take this." She stood and thrust the opener into his hands. "Use it to find your way all around the house. But don't leave your room after dark."

She swept out of the dining room, leaving a scent of musk and flowers and something bittersweet. Oliver put the opener in his pocket and walked back to his room, finding his way without hesitation, without thought. He shut the door and went to the bookcase, sad and troubled and exultant all at once.

She had told him her secret. He could leave now if he wanted. She had given him the power to leave.

Sipping from a glass of sherry on the nightstand beside the bed, reading from a book of composers' lives, he decided to wait until morning.

Yet after a few hours, nothing could keep his mind away from Miss Parkhurst's prohibition—not the piano, the books, or the snacks delivered almost before he thought about them, appearing on the tray when he wasn't watching. Oliver sat with hands folded in the plush chair, blinking at the room's dark corners. He thought he had Miss Parkhurst pegged. She was an old woman tired of her life, a beautifully preserved old woman to be sure, very strong... But she was sweet on him, keeping him like some unused gigolo. Still, he couldn't help but admire her, and he couldn't help but want to be home, near Momma and Yolanda and the babies, keeping his brothers out of trouble—not that they appreciated his efforts.

The longer he sat, the angrier and more anxious he became. He felt sure something was wrong at home. Pacing around the room did nothing to calm him. He examined the opener time and again in the firelight, brow wrinkled, wondering what powers it gave him. She had said he could go anywhere in the house and know his way, just as he had found his room without her help.

He moaned, shaking his fists at the air. "She can't keep me here! She just *can't!*"

At midnight, he couldn't control himself any longer. He stood before the door. "Let me out, dammit!" he cried, and the door opened with a sad whisper. He ran down the corridor, scattering moonlight on the floor like dust, tears shining on his cheeks.

Through the sitting rooms, the long halls of empty bedrooms—now with their doors closed, shades of sound sifting from behind—through the vast deserted kitchen, with its rows of polished copper kettles and huge black coal cookstoves, through a courtyard surrounded by five stories of the mansion on all sides and open to the golden-starred night sky, past a tiled fountain guarded by three huge white porcelain lions, ears and empty eyes following him as he ran by, Oliver searched for Miss Parkhurst, to tell her he must leave.

For a moment, he caught his breath in an upstairs gallery. He saw faint lights under doors, heard more suggestive sounds. No time to pause, even with his heart pounding and his lungs burning. If he waited in one place long enough, he thought the ghosts might become real and make him join their revelry. This was Miss Parkhurst's past, hoary and indecent, more than he could bear contemplating. How could anyone have lived this kind of life, even if they were cursed?

Yet the temptation to stop, to listen, to give in and join in was almost stronger than he could resist. He kept losing track of what he was doing, what his ultimate goal was.

"Where are you?" he shouted, throwing open double doors to a game room, empty but for more startled ghosts, more of Miss Parkhurst's eternity of bookkeeping. Pale forms rose from the billiard tables, translucent breasts shining with an inner light, their pale lovers rolling slowly to one side, fat bellies prominent, ghost eyes black and startled. "Miss Parkhurst!"

Oliver brushed through hundreds of girls, no more substantial than curtains of raindrops. His new clothes became wet with their tears. *She* had presided over this eternity of sad lust. *She* had orchestrated the debaucheries, catered to what he felt inside him: the whims and deepest desires unspoken.

Thin antique laughter followed him.

He slid on a splash of sour-smelling champagne and came up abruptly against a heavy wooden door, a room he did not know. The golden opener told him nothing about what waited beyond.

"Open!" he shouted, but he was ignored. The door was not locked, but it resisted his entry as if it weighed tons. He pushed with both hands and then laid his shoulder on the paneling, bracing his sneakers against the thick wool pile of a champagne-soaked runner. The door swung inward with a deep iron and wood grumble, and Oliver stumbled past, saving himself at the last minute from falling on his face. Legs sprawled, down on both hands, he looked up from the wooden floor and saw where he was.

The room was narrow, but stretched on for what might have been miles, lined on one side with an endless row of plain double beds, and on the other with an endless row of freestanding cheval mirrors. An old man, the oldest he had ever seen, naked, white as talcum, rose stiffly from the bed, mumbling. Beneath him, red and warm as a pile of glowing coals, Miss Parkhurst lay with legs spread, incense of musk and sweat thick about her. She raised her head and shoulders, eyes fixed on Oliver's, and pulled a black peignoir over her nakedness. In the gloom of the room's extremities, other men, old and young, stood by their beds, smoking cigarettes or cigars or drinking champagne or whisky, all observing Oliver. Some grinned in speculation.

Miss Parkhurst's face wrinkled in agony like an old apple and she threw back her head to scream. The old man on the bed grabbed clumsily for a robe and his clothes.

Her shriek echoed from the ceiling and the walls, driving Oliver back through the door, down the halls and stairways. The wind of his flight chilled him to the bone in his tear-soaked clothing. Somehow he made his way through the sudden darkness and emptiness, and shut himself in his room, where the fire still burned warm and cheery yellow. Shivering uncontrollably, Oliver removed the wet new clothes and called for his own in a high-pitched, frantic voice. But the invisible servants did not deliver what he requested.

He fell into the bed and pulled the covers tight about him, eyes closed. He prayed that she would not come after him, not come into his room with her peignoir slipping aside, revealing her furnace body; he prayed her smell would not follow him the rest of his life.

The door to his room did not open. Outside, all was quiet. In time, as dawn fired the roofs and then the walls and finally the streets of Sunside, Oliver slept.

"You came out of your room last night," Miss Parkhurst said over the late breakfast. Oliver stopped chewing for a moment, glanced at her through bloodshot eyes, then shrugged.

"Did you see what you expected?"

Oliver didn't answer. Miss Parkhurst sighed like a young girl.

"It's my life. This is the way I've lived for a long time."

"None of my business," Oliver said, breaking a roll in half and buttering it.

"Do I disgust you?"

Again no reply. Miss Parkhurst stood in the middle of his silence and walked to the dining-room door. She looked over her shoulder at him, eyes moist. "You're not afraid of me now," she said. "You think you know what I am."

Oliver saw that his silence and uncaring attitude hurt her, and relished for a moment this power. When she remained standing in the doorway, he looked up with a purposefully harsh expression—copied from Reggie, sarcastic and angry at once—and saw tears flowing steadily down her cheeks. She seemed younger than ever now, not dangerous, just very sad. His expression faded. She turned away and closed the door behind her.

Oliver slammed half the roll into his plate of eggs and pushed his chair back from the table. "I'm not even full-grown!" he shouted at the door. "I'm not even a man! What do you want from me?" He stood up and kicked the chair away with his heel, then stuffed his hands in his pockets and paced around the small room. He felt bottled up, and yet she had said he could go anytime he wished.

Go where? Home?

He stared at the goldenware and the plates heaped with excellent food. Nothing like this at home. Home was a place he sometimes thought he'd have to fight to get away from; he couldn't protect Momma forever from the rest of the family, he couldn't be a breadwinner for five extra mouths for the rest of his life...

And if he stayed here, knowing what Miss Parkhurst did each night? Could he eat breakfast each morning, knowing how the food was earned, and all his clothes and books and the piano, too? He really would be a gigolo then.

Sunside. He was here, maybe he could live here, find work, get away from Sleepside for good.

The mere thought gave him a twinge. He sat down and buried his face in his hands, rubbing his eyes with the tips of his fingers, pulling at his lids to make a face, staring at himself reflected in the golden carafe, big-nosed, eyes monstrously bleared. He had to talk to Momma. Even talking to Yolanda might help.

But Miss Parkhurst was nowhere to be found. Oliver searched the mansion until dusk, then ate alone in the small dining room. He retired to his room as dark closed in, spreading through the halls like ink through water. To banish the night, and all that might be happening in it, Oliver played the piano loudly.

When he finally stumbled to his bed, he saw a single yellow rose on the pillow, delicate and sweet. He placed it by the lamp on the nightstand and pulled the covers over himself, clothes and all.

In the early hours of morning, he dreamed that Miss Parkhurst had fled the mansion, leaving it for him to tend to. The ghosts and old men crowded around, asking why he was so righteous. "She never had a Momma like you," said one decrepit dude dressed in black velvet night robes. "She's lived times you can't imagine. Now you just blew her right out of this house. Where will she go?"

Oliver came awake long enough to remember the dream, and then returned to a light, difficult sleep.

Mrs. Diamond Freeland scowled at Yolanda's hand-wringing and mumbling. "You can't help your momma acting that way," she said.

"I'm no doctor," Yolanda complained.

"No doctor's going to help her," Mrs. Freeland said, eyeing the door to Momma's bedroom.

Denver and Reggie lounged uneasily in the parlor.

"You two louts going to look for your brother?"

"We don't have to look for him," Denver said. "We know where he is. We got a plan to get him back."

"Then why don't you do it?" Mrs. Freeland asked.

"When the time's right," Reggie said decisively.

"Your Momma's pining for Oliver," Mrs. Freeland told them, not for the first time. "It's churning her insides thinking he's with that witch and what she might be doing to him."

Reggie tried unsuccessfully to hide a grin.

"What's funny?" Mrs. Freeland asked sternly.

"Nothing. Maybe our little brother needs some of what she's got."

Mrs. Freeland glared at them. "Yolanda," she said, rolling her eyes to the ceiling in disgust. "The babies. They dry?"

"No, ma'am," Yolanda said. She backed away from Mrs. Freeland's severe look. "I'll change them."

"Then you take them into your momma."

"Yes, ma'am."

The breakfast went as if nothing had happened. Miss Parkhurst sat across from him, eating and smiling. Oliver tried to be more polite, working his way around to asking a favor. When the breakfast was over, the time seemed right.

"I'd like to see how Momma's doing," he said.

Miss Parkhurst considered for a moment. "There'll be a TV in your room this evening," she said, folding her napkin and placing it beside her plate. "You can use it to see how everybody is."

That seemed fair enough. Until then, however, he'd be spending the entire day with Miss Parkhurst; it was time, he decided, to be civil. Then he might actually test his freedom.

"You say I can go," Oliver said, trying to sound friendly.

Miss Parkhurst nodded. "Anytime. I won't keep you."

"If I go, can I come back?"

She smiled ever so slightly. There was the young girl in that smile again, and she seemed very vulnerable. "The opener takes you anywhere across town."

"Nobody messes with me?"

"Nobody touches anyone I protect," Miss Parkhurst said.

Oliver absorbed that thoughtfully, steepling his hands below his chin. "You're pretty good to me," he said. "Even when I cross you, you don't hurt me. Why?"

"You're my last chance," Miss Parkhurst said, dark eyes on him. "I've lived a long time, and nobody like you's come along. I don't think there'll be another for even longer. I can't wait that long. I've lived this way so many years, I don't know another, but I don't want any more of it."

Oliver couldn't think of a better way to put his next question. "Do you like being a whore?"

Miss Parkhurst's face hardened. "It has its moments," she said stiffly.

Oliver screwed up his courage enough to say what was on his mind, but not to look at her while doing it. "You enjoy lying down with any man who has the money?"

"It's work. It's something I'm good at."

"Even ugly men?"

"Ugly men need their pleasures, too."

"Bad men? Letting them touch you when they've hurt people, maybe killed people?"

"What kind of work have you done?" she asked.

99

"Clerked a grocery store. Taught music."

"Did you wait on bad men in the grocery store?"

"If I did," Oliver said swiftly, "I didn't know about it."

"Neither did I," Miss Parkhurst said. Then, more quietly, "Most of the time."

"All those girls you've made whore for you..."

"You have some things to learn," she interrupted. "It's not the work that's so awful. It's what you have to be to do it. The way people expect you to be when you do it. Should be, in a good world, a whore's like a doctor or a saint, she doesn't mind getting her hands dirty any more than they do. She gives pleasure and smiles. But in the city, people won't let it happen that way. Here, a whore's always got some empty place inside her, a place you've filled with self-respect, maybe. A whore's got respect, but not for herself. She loses that whenever anybody looks at her. She can be worth a million dollars on the outside, but inside, she knows. That's what makes her a whore. That's the curse. It's beat into you sometimes, everybody taking advantage, like you're dirt. Pretty soon you think you're dirt, too, and who cares what happens to dirt? Pretty soon you're just sliding along, trying to keep from getting hurt or maybe dead, but who cares?"

"You're rich," Oliver said.

"Can't buy everything," Miss Parkhurst commented dryly.

"You've got magic."

"I've got magic because I'm here, and to stay here, I have to be a whore."

"Why can't you leave?"

She sighed, her fingers working nervously along the edge of the tablecloth.

"What stops you from just leaving?"

"If you're going to own this place," she said, and he

thought at first she was avoiding his question, "you've got to know all about it. All about me. We're the same, almost, this place and I. A whore's no more than what's in her purse, every pimp knows that. You know how many times I've been married?"

Oliver shook his head.

"Seventeen times. Sometimes they left me, once or twice they stayed. Never any good. But then, maybe I didn't deserve any better. Those who left me, they came back when they were old, asking me to save them from Darkside. I couldn't. But I kept them here anyway. Come on."

She stood and Oliver followed her down the halls, down the stairs, below the garage level, deep beneath the mansion's clutter-filled basement. The air was ageless, deep-earth cool, and smelled of old city rain. A few eternal clear light bulbs cast feeble yellow crescents in the dismal murk. They walked on boards over an old muddy patch, Miss Parkhurst lifting her skirts a few inches to clear the mire. Oliver saw her slim ankles and swallowed back the tightness in his throat.

Ahead, laid out in a row on moss-patched concrete biers, were fifteen black iron cylinders, each seven feet long and slightly flattened on top. They looked like big blockbuster bombs in storage. The first was wedged into a dark corner. Miss Parkhurst stood by its foot, running her hand along its rust-streaked surface.

"Two didn't come back. Maybe they were the best of the lot," she said. "I was no judge. I couldn't know. You judge men by what's inside you, and if you're hollow, they get lost in there, you can't know what you're seeing."

Oliver stepped closer to the last cylinder and saw a clear glass plate mounted at the head. Reluctant but fascinated, he wiped the dusty glass with two fingers and peered past a single cornered bubble. The coffin was filled with clear liquid. Afloat within, a face the color of green olives in a martini looked back at him, blind eyes murky, lips set in a loose line. The liquid and death had smoothed the face's wrinkles, but Oliver could tell nonetheless, this dude had been old, old.

"They all die," she said. "All but me. I keep them all, every john, every husband, no forgetting, no letting them go. We've always got this tie between us. That's the curse."

Oliver pulled back from the coffin, holding his breath, heart thumping with eager horror. Which was worse, this, or old men in the night? Old dead lusts laid to rest or lively ghosts? Wrapped in gloom at the far end of the line of bottle-coffins, Miss Parkhurst seemed for a moment to glow with the same furnace power he had felt when he first saw her.

"I miss some of these guys," she said, her voice so soft the power just vanished, a thing in his mind. "We had some good times together."

Oliver tried to imagine what Miss Parkhurst had lived through, the good times and otherwise. "You have any children?" he asked, his voice as thin as the buzz of a fly in a bottle. He jumped back as one of the coffins resonated with his shaky words.

Miss Parkhurst's shoulders shivered as well. "Lots," she said tightly. "All dead before they were born."

At first his shock was conventional, orchestrated by his Sundays in church. Then the colossal organic waste of effort came down on him like a pile of stones. All that motion, all that wanting, and nothing good from it, just these iron bottles and vivid lists of ghosts.

"What good is a whore's baby?" Miss Parkhurst asked. "Especially if the mother's going to stay a whore."

"Was your mother...?" It didn't seem right to use the word in connection with anyone's mother.

"She was, and her mother before her. I have no daddies, or lots of daddies."

Oliver remembered the old man chastising him in his dream. Before he could even sort out his words, wishing to give her some solace, some sign he wasn't completely unsympathetic, he said, "It can't be all bad, being a whore."

"Maybe not," she said. Miss Parkhurst hardly made a blot in the larger shadows. She might just fly away to dust if he turned his head.

"You said being a whore is being empty inside. Not everybody who's empty inside is a whore."

"Oh?" she replied, light as a cobweb. He was being pushed into an uncharacteristic posture, but Oliver was damned if he'd give in just yet, however much a fool he made of himself. His mixed feelings were betraying him.

"You've *lived*," he said. "You got memories nobody else has. You could write books. They'd make movies about you."

Her smile was a dull lamp in the shadows. "I've had important people visit me," she said. "Powerful men, even mayors. I had something they needed. Sometimes they opened up and talked about how hard it was not being little boys anymore. Sometimes, when we were relaxing, they'd cry on my shoulder, just like I was their momma. But then they'd go away and try to forget about me. If they remembered at all, they were scared of me, because of what I knew about them. Now, they know I'm getting weak," she said. "I don't give a damn about books or movies. I won't tell what I know, and besides, lots of those men are dead. If they aren't, they're waiting for me to die, so they can sleep easy."

"What do you mean, getting weak?"

"I got two days, maybe three, then I die a whore. My time is up. The curse is almost finished."

Oliver gaped. When he had first seen her, she had seemed as powerful as a diesel locomotive, as if she might live forever.

"And if I take over?"

"You get the mansion, the money."

"How much power?"

She didn't answer.

"You can't give me any power, can you?"

"No," faint as the breeze from her eyelashes.

"The opener won't be any good."

"No."

"You lied to me."

"I'll leave you all that's left."

"That's not why you made me come here. You took Momma—"

"She stole from me."

"My momma never stole anything!" Oliver shouted. The iron coffins buzzed.

"She took something after I had given her all my hospitality."

"What could she take from you? She was no thief."

"She took a sheet of music."

Oliver's face screwed up in sudden pain. He looked away, fists clenched. They had almost no money for his music. More often than not since his father died, he made up music, having no new scores to play. "Why'd you bring me here?" he croaked.

"I don't mind dying. But I don't want to die a whore."

Oliver turned back, angry again, this time for his momma as well as himself. He approached the insubstantial shadow. Miss Parkhurst shimmered like a curtain. "What do you want from me?"

"I need someone who loves me. Loves me for no reason."

For an instant, he saw standing before him a scrawny girl in a red shimmy, eyes wide. "How could that help you? Can that make you something else?"

"Just love," she said. "Just letting me forget all these" —she pointed to the coffins—"and all those," pointing up.

Oliver's body lost its charge of anger and accusation with an exhaled breath. "I can't love you," he said. "I don't even know what love is." Was this true? Upstairs, she had burned in his mind, and he *had* wanted her, though it upset him to remember how much. What *could* he feel for her? "Let's go back now. I have to look in on Momma."

Miss Parkhurst emerged from the shadows and walked past him silently, not even her skirts rustling. She gestured with a finger for him to follow.

She left him at the door to his room, saying, "I'll wait in the main parlor." Oliver saw a small television set on the nightstand by his bed and rushed to turn it on. The screen filled with static and unresolved images. He saw fragments of faces, patches of color and texture passing so quickly he couldn't make them out. The entire city might be on the screen at once, but he could not see any of it clearly. He twisted the channel knob and got more static. Then he saw the label past channel 13 on the dial: HOME, in small golden letters. He twisted the knob to that position and the screen cleared.

Momma lay in bed, legs drawn tightly up, hair mussed.

She didn't look good. Her hand, stretched out across the bed, trembled. Her breathing was hard and rough. In the background, Oliver heard Yolanda fussing with the babies, finally screaming at her older brothers in frustration.

105

Why don't you help with the babies? his sister demanded in a tinny, distant voice.

Momma told you, Denver replied.

She did not. She told us all. You could help.

Reggie laughed. *We got to make plans.*

Oliver pulled back from the TV. Momma was sick, and for all his brothers and sister and the babies could do, she might die. He could guess why she was sick, too; with worry for him. He had to go to her and tell her he was all right. A phone call wouldn't be enough.

Again, however, he was reluctant to leave the mansion and Miss Parkhurst. Something beyond her waning magic was at work here; he wanted to listen to her and to experience more of that fascinated horror. He wanted to watch her again, absorb her smooth, ancient beauty. In a way, she needed him as much as Momma did. Miss Parkhurst outraged everything in him that was lawful and orderly, but he finally had to admit, as he thought of going back to Momma, that he enjoyed the outrage.

He clutched the gold opener and ran from his room to the parlor. She waited for him there in a red velvet chair, hands gripping two lions at the end of the armrests. The lions' wooden faces grinned beneath her caresses. "I got to go," he said. "Momma's sick for missing me."

She nodded. "I'm not holding you," she said.

He stared at her. "I wish I could help you," he said.

She smiled hopefully, pitifully. "Then promise you'll come back."

Oliver wavered. How long would Momma need him?

What if he gave his promise and returned and Miss Parkhurst was already dead?

"I promise."

"Don't be too long," she said.

"Won't," he mumbled.

The limousine waited for him in the garage, white and beautiful, languid and sleek and fast all at once. No chauffeur waited for him this time. The door opened by itself and he climbed in; the door closed behind him, and he leaned back stiffly on the leather seats, gold opener in hand. "Take me home," he said. The glass partition and the windows all around darkened to an opaque smoky gold. He felt a sensation of smooth motion. *What would it be like to have this kind of power all the time?*

But the power wasn't hers to give.

Oliver arrived before the apartment building in a blizzard of swirling snow. Snow packed up over the curbs and coated the sidewalks a foot deep; Sleepside was heavy with winter. Oliver stepped from the limousine and climbed the icy steps, the cold hardly touching him even in his light clothing. He was surrounded by Miss Parkhurst's magic.

Denver was frying a pan of navy beans in the kitchen when Oliver burst through the door, the locks flinging themselves open before them. Oliver paused in the entrance to the kitchen. Denver stared at him, face slack, too surprised to speak.

"Where's Momma?"

Yolanda heard his voice in the living room and screamed.

Reggie met him in the hallway, arms open wide, smiling broadly. "Goddamn, little brother! You got away?"

"Where's Momma?"

"She's in her room. She's feeling low."

"She's sick," Oliver said, pushing past his brother. Yolanda stood before Momma's door as if to keep Oliver out. She sucked her lower lip between her teeth. She looked scared.

"Let me by, Yolanda," Oliver said. He almost pointed

the opener at her, and then pulled back, fearful of what might happen.

"You made Momma si-ick," Yolanda squeaked, but she stepped aside. Oliver pushed through the door to Momma's room. She sat up in bed, face drawn and thin, but her eyes danced with joy. "My boy!" She sighed. "My beautiful boy."

Oliver sat beside her and they hugged fiercely. "Please don't leave me again," Momma said, voice muffled by his shoulder. Oliver set the opener on her flimsy nightstand and cried against her neck.

The day after Oliver's return, Denver stood lank-legged by the window, hands in frayed pants pockets, staring at the snow with heavy-lidded eyes. "It's too cold to go anywhere now," he mused.

Reggie sat in their father's chair, face screwed in thought. "I listened to what he told Momma," he said. "That whore sent our little brother back here in a limo. A big white limo. See it out there?"

Denver peered down at the street. A white limousine waited at the curb, not even dusted by snow. A tiny vanishing curl of white rose from its tailpipe. "It's still there," he said.

"Did you see what he had when he came in?" Reggie asked. Denver shook his head. "A gold box. *She* must have given that to him. I bet whoever has that gold box can visit Miss Belle Parkhurst. Want to bet?"

Denver grinned and shook his head again.

"Wouldn't be too cold if we had that limo, would it?" Reggie asked.

Oliver brought his momma chicken soup and a half-rotten, carefully trimmed orange. He plumped her pillow for her, shushing her, telling her not to talk until she had eaten. She smiled weakly, beatific, and let him minister to her. When she had eaten, she lay back and closed her eyes, tears pooling in their hollows before slipping down her cheeks. "I was so afraid for you," she said. "I didn't know what she would do. She seemed so nice at first. I didn't see her. Just her voice, inviting me in over the security buzzer, letting me sit and rest my feet. I knew where I was...was it bad of me, to stay there, knowing?"

"You were tired, Momma," Oliver said. "Besides, Miss Parkhurst isn't that bad."

Momma looked at him dubiously. "I saw her piano. There was a shelf next to it with the most beautiful sheet music you ever saw, even big books of it. I looked at some. Oh, Oliver, I've never taken anything in my life..." She cried freely now, sapping what little strength the lunch had given her.

"Don't you worry, Momma. She used you. She *wanted* me to come." As an afterthought, he added, not sure why he lied, "Or Yolanda."

Momma absorbed that while her eyes examined his face in tiny, caressing glances. "You won't go back," she said, "will you?"

Oliver looked down at the sheets folded under her arms. "I promised. She'll die if I don't," he said.

"That woman is a liar," Momma stated unequivocally. "If she wants you, she'll do anything to get you."

"I don't think she's lying, Momma."

She looked away from him, a feverish anger flushing her cheeks. "Why did you promise her?"

"She's not that bad, Momma," he said again. He had thought that coming home would clear his mind, but Miss Parkhurst's face, her plea, stayed with him as if she were only a room away. The mansion seemed just a fading dream, unimportant; but Belle Parkhurst stuck. "She needs help. She wants to change."

Momma puffed out her cheeks and blew through her lips like a horse. She had often done that to his father, never before to him. "She'll always be a whore," she said.

Oliver's eyes narrowed. He saw a spitefulness and bitterness in Momma he hadn't noticed before. Not that spite was unwarranted; Miss Parkhurst had treated Momma roughly. Yet...

Denver stood in the doorway. "Reggie and I got to talk to Momma," he said. "About you." He jerked his thumb back over his shoulder. "Alone." Reggie stood grinning behind his brother. Oliver took the tray of dishes and sidled past them, going into the kitchen.

In the kitchen, he washed the last few days' plates methodically, letting the lukewarm water slide over his hands, eyes focused on the faucet's dull gleam. He had almost lost track of time when he heard the front door slam. Jerking his head up, he wiped the last plate and put it away, then went to Momma's room. She looked back at him guiltily. Something was wrong. He searched the room with his eyes, but nothing was out of place. Nothing that was normally present...

The opener.

His brothers had taken the gold opener.

"Momma!" he said.

"They're going to pay her a visit," she said, the bitterness plain now. "They don't like their momma mistreated."

It was getting dark and the snow was thick. He had hoped to return this evening. If Miss Parkhurst hadn't lied, she would be very weak by now, perhaps dead tomorrow. His lungs seemed to shrink within him, and he had a hard time taking a breath.

"I've got to go," he said. "She might *kill* them, Momma!"

But that wasn't what worried him. He put on his heavy coat, then his father's old cracked rubber boots with the snow tread soles. Yolanda came out of the room she shared with the babies. She didn't ask any questions, just watched him dress for the cold, her eyes dull.

"They got that gold box," she said as he flipped the last metal clasp on the boots. "Probably worth a lot."

Oliver hesitated in the hallway, then grabbed Yolanda's shoulders and shook her vigorously. "You take care of Momma, you hear?"

She shut her jaw with a clack and shoved free. Oliver was out the door before she could speak.

Day's last light filled the sky with a deep peachy glow tinged with cold gray. Snow fell golden above the buildings and smudgy brown within their shadow. The wind swirled around him mournfully, sending gust-fingers through his coat searching for any warmth that might be stolen. For a nauseating moment, all his resolve was sucked away by a vacuous pit of misery. The streets were empty; he briefly wondered what night this was, and then remembered it was the twenty-third of December, but too cold for whatever stray shoppers Sleepside might send out. *Why go? To save two worthless idiots?* Not that so much, although that would have been enough, since their loss would hurt Momma, and they *were* his brothers; not that so much as his promise. And something else.

He was afraid for Belle Parkhurst.

He buttoned his coat collar and leaned into the wind. He hadn't put on a hat. The heat flew from his scalp, and in a few moments he felt drained and exhausted. But he made it to the subway entrance and staggered down the steps, into the warmer heart of the city, where it was always sixty-four degrees.

Locked behind her thick glass and metal booth, wrinkled

eyes weary with night's wisdom, the fluorescent-lighted token seller took his money and dropped cat's head tokens into the steel tray with separate, distinct *chinks*. Oliver glanced at her face and saw the whore's printed there instead; this middle-aged woman did not spread her legs for money, but had sold her youth and life away sitting in this cavern. Whose emptiness was more profound?

"Be careful," she warned vacantly through the speaker grill. "Night Metro any minute now."

He dropped a token into the turnstile and pushed through, then stood shivering on the platform, waiting for the Sunside train. It seemed to take forever to arrive, and when it did, he was not particularly relieved. The driver's pit-eyes winked green, bull's head turning as the train slid to a halt beside the platform. The doors opened with an oiled groan, and Oliver stepped aboard, into the hard, cold, and unforgiving glare of the train's interior.

At first, Oliver thought the car was empty. He did not sit down, however. The hair on his neck and arm bristled. Hand gripping a stainless steel handle, he leaned into the train's acceleration and took a deep, half-hiccup breath.

He first consciously noticed the other passengers as their faces gleamed in silhouette against the passing dim lights of ghost stations. They sat almost invisible, crowding the car; they stood beside him, less substantial than a breath of air. They watched him intently, bearing no ill will for the moment, perhaps not yet aware that he was alive and they were not. They carried no overt signs of their wounds, but how they had come to be here was obvious to his animal instincts.

This train carried holiday suicides: men, women, teenagers, even a few children, delicate as expensive crystal in a shop window. Maybe the bull's head driver collected them, culling them out and caging them as they stumbled randomly aboard his train. Maybe he controlled them.

Oliver tried to sink away in his coat. He felt guilty, being alive and healthy, enveloped in strong emotions; they were so flimsy, with so little hold on this reality.

He muttered a prayer, stopping as they all turned toward him, showing glassy disapproval at this reverse blasphemy. Silently, he prayed again, but even that seemed to irritate his fellow passengers, and they squeaked among themselves in voices that only a dog or a bat might hear.

The stations passed one by one, mosaic symbols and names flashing in pools of light. When the Sunside station approached and the train slowed, Oliver moved quickly to the door. It opened with oily grace. He stepped onto the platform, turned, and bumped up against the tall, dark uniform of the bull's head driver. The air around him stank of grease and electricity and something sweeter, perhaps blood. He stood a bad foot and a half taller than Oliver, and in one outstretched, black-nailed, leathery hand he held his long silver shears, points spread wide, briefly suggesting Belle Parkhurst's horizontal position among the old men.

"You're in the wrong place, at the wrong time," the driver warned in a voice deeper than the train motors. "Down here, I can cut your cord." He closed the shears with a slick, singing whisper.

"I'm going to Miss Parkhurst's," Oliver said, voice quavering.

"Who?" the driver asked.

"I'm leaving now," Oliver said, backing away. The driver followed, slowly hunching over him. The shears sang open, angled toward his eyes. The crystal dead within the train passed through the open door and glided around them. Gluey waves of cold shivered the air.

"You're a bold little bastard," the driver said, voice managing to descend off any human scale and still be heard. The white tile walls vibrated. "All I have to do is cut your cord, right in front of your face"—he snicked the shears inches from Oliver's nose—"and you'll never find your way home."

The driver backed him up against a cold barrier of suicides. Oliver's fear could not shut out curiosity. Was the bull's head real, or was there a man under the horns and hide and bone? The eyes in their sunken orbits glowed ice-blue. The scissors crossed before Oliver's face again, even closer; mere hairs away from his nose.

"You're mine," the driver whispered, and the scissors closed on something tough and invisible. Oliver's head exploded with pain. He flailed back through the dead, dragging the driver after him by the pinch of the shears on that something unseen and very important. Roaring, the driver applied both hands to the shears' grips. Oliver felt as if his head were being ripped away. Suddenly he kicked out with all his strength between the driver's black-uniformed legs. His foot hit flesh and bone as unyielding as rock and his agony doubled. But the shears hung for a moment in air before Oliver's face, and the driver slowly curled over.

Oliver grabbed the shears, opened them, released whatever cord he had between himself and his past, his home, and pushed through the dead. The scissors reflected elongated gleams over the astonished, watery faces of the suicides. Suddenly, seeing a chance to escape, they spread out along the platform, some up the station's stairs, some to both sides. Oliver ran through them up the steps and stood on the warm evening sidewalk of Sunside. All he sensed from the station's entrance was a sour breath of oil and blood and a faint chill of fading hands as the dead evaporated in the balmy night air.

A quiet crowd had gathered at the front entrance to Miss Parkhurst's mansion. They stood vigil, waiting for something, their faces shining with a greedy sweat.

He did not see the limousine. His brothers must have arrived by now; they were inside, then.

Catching his breath as he ran, he skirted the old brownstone and looked for the entrance to the underground garage. On the south side, he found the ramp and descended to slam his hands against the corrugated metal door. Echoes replied. "It's me!" he shouted. "Let me in!"

A middle-aged man regarded him dispassionately from the higher ground of the sidewalk. "What do you want in there, young man?" he asked.

Oliver glared back over his shoulder. "None of your business," he said.

"Maybe it is, if you want in," the man said. "There's a way any man can get into that house. It never refuses gold."

Oliver pulled back from the door a moment, stunned. The man shrugged and walked on.

He still grasped the driver's shears. They weren't gold, they were silver, but they had to be worth something. "Let me in!" he said. Then, upping the ante, he dug in his pocket and produced the remaining cat's head token. "I'll pay!"

The door grumbled up. The garage's lights were off, but in the soft yellow glow of the streetlights, he saw an eagle's claw thrust out from the brick wall just within the door's frame, supporting a golden cup. Token in one hand, shears in another, Oliver's eyes narrowed. To pay Belle's mansion now was no honorable deed; he dropped the token into the cup, but kept the shears as he ran into the darkness.

A faint crack of light showed beneath the stairwell door. Around the door, the bones of ancient city dwellers glowed in their compacted stone, teeth and knuckles bright as fireflies. Oliver tried the door; it was locked. Inserting the point of the shears between the door and catchplate, he pried until the lock was sprung.

The quiet parlor was illuminated only by a few guttering candles clutched in drooping gold eagle's claws. The air was thick with the blunt smells of long-extinguished cigars and cigarettes. Oliver stopped for a moment, closing his eyes and listening. There was a room he had never seen in the time he had spent in Belle Parkhurst's house. She had never even shown him the door, but he knew it had to exist, and that was where she would be, alive or dead. Where his brothers were, he couldn't tell; for the moment he didn't care. He doubted they were in any mortal danger. Belle's power was as weak as the scattered candles.

Oliver crept along the dark halls, holding the gleaming shears before him as a warning to whatever might try to stop him. He climbed two more flights of stairs, and on the third floor, found an uncarpeted hallway, walls bare, that he had not seen before. The dry floorboards creaked beneath him. The air was cool and still. He could smell a ghost of Belle's rose perfume. At the end of the hall was a plain panel door with a tarnished brass knob.

This door was also unlocked. He sucked in a breath for courage and opened it.

This was Belle's room, and she was indeed in it. She hung suspended above her plain iron-frame bed in a weave of glowing threads. For a moment, he drew back, thinking she was a spider, but it immediately became clear she was more like a spider's prey. The threads reached to all corners of the room, transparent, binding her tightly, but to him as insubstantial as the air.

Belle turned to face him, weak, eyes clouded, skin like paper towels. "Why'd you wait so long?" she asked.

From across the mansion, he heard the echoes of Reggie's delighted laughter.

Oliver stepped forward. Only the blades of the shears plucked at the threads; he passed through unhindered. Arm straining at the silver instrument, he realized what the threads were; they were the cords binding Belle to the mansion, connecting her to all her customers. Belle had not one cord to her past, but thousands. Every place she had been touched, she was held by a strand. Thick twining ropes of the past shot from her lips and breasts and from between her legs; not even the toes of her feet were free.

Without thinking, Oliver lifted the driver's silver shears and began methodically snipping the cords. One by one, or in ropy clusters, he cut them away. With each meeting of the blades, they vanished. He did not ask himself which was her first cord, linking her to her childhood, to the few years she had lived before she became a whore; there was no time to waste worrying about such niceties.

"Your brothers are in my vault," she said. "They found my gold and jewels. I crawled here to get away."

"Don't talk," Oliver said between clenched teeth. The strands became tougher, more like wire the closer he came to her thin gray body. His arm muscles knotted and cold sweat soaked his clothes. She dropped inches closer to the bed.

"I never brought any men here," she said.

"Shh."

"This was my place, the only place I had."

There were hundreds of strands left now, instead of thousands. He worked for long minutes, watching her

117

grow more and more pale, watching her one-time furnace heat dull to less than a single candle, her eyes lose their feverish glitter. For a horrified moment, he thought cutting the cords might actually weaken her; but he hacked and swung at the cords, regardless. They were even tougher now, more resilient.

Far off in the mansion, Denver and Reggie laughed together, and there was a heavy clinking sound. The floor shuddered.

Dozens of cords remained. He had been working at them for an eternity, and now each cord took a concentrated effort, all the strength left in his arms and hands. He thought he might faint or throw up. Belle's eyes had closed. Her breathing was undetectable.

Five strands left. He cut through one, then another. As he applied the shears to the third, a tall man appeared on the opposite side of her bed, dressed in pale gray with a widebrimmed gray hat. His fingers were covered with gold rings. A gold eagle's claw pinned his white silk tie.

"I was her friend," the man said. "She came to me and she cheated me."

Oliver held back his shears, eyes stinging with rage. "Who are you?" he demanded, nearly doubled over by his exertion. He stared up at the gray man through beads of sweat on his eyebrows.

"That other old man, he hardly worked her at all. I put her to work right here, but she cheated me."

"You're her *pimp*," Oliver spat out the word.

The gray man grinned.

"Cut that cord, and she's nothing."

"She's nothing now. Your curse is over and she's dying."

"She shouldn't have messed with me," the pimp said. "I was a strong man, lots of connections. What do you want with an old drained-out whore, boy?"

Oliver didn't answer. He struggled to cut the third cord but it writhed like a snake between the shears.

"She would have been a whore even without me," the pimp said. "She was a whore from the day she was born."

"That's a lie," Oliver said.

"Why do you want to get at her? She give you a pox and you want to finish her off?"

Oliver's lips curled and he flung his head back, not looking as he brought the shears together with all his remaining strength, boosted by a killing anger. The third cord parted and the shears snapped, one blade singing across the room and sticking in the wall with a spray of plaster chips. The gray man vanished like a double-blown puff of cigarette smoke, leaving a scent of onions and stale beer.

Belle hung awkwardly by two cords now. Swinging the single blade like a knife, he parted them swiftly and fell over her, lying across her, feeling her cool body for the first time. She could not arouse lust now. She might be dead.

"Miss Parkhurst," he said. He examined her face, almost as white as the bed sheets, high cheekbones pressing through waxy flesh. "I don't want anything from you," Oliver said. "I just want you to be all right." He lowered his lips to hers, kissed her lightly, dripping sweat on her closed eyes.

Far away, Denver and Reggie cackled with glee.

The house grew quiet. All the ghosts, all accounts received, had fled, had been freed.

The single candle in the room guttered out, and they lay in the dark alone. Oliver fell against his will into an exhausted slumber.

Cool, rose-scented fingers lightly touched his forehead.

He opened his eyes and saw a girl in a white nightgown leaning over him, barely his age. Her eyes were very big and her lips bowed into a smile beneath high, full cheekbones. "Where are we?" she asked. "How long we been here?"

Late morning sun filled the small, dusty room with warmth. He glanced around the bed, looking for Belle, and then turned back to the girl. She vaguely resembled the chauffeur who had brought him to the mansion that first night, though younger, her face more bland and simple.

"You don't remember?" he asked.

"Honey," the girl said sweetly, hands on hips, "I don't remember much of anything. Except that you kissed me. You want to kiss me again?"

Momma did not approve of the strange young woman he brought home, and wanted to know where Reggie and Denver were. Oliver did not have the heart to tell her. They lay cold as ice in a room filled with mounds of cat's head subway tokens, bound by the pimp's magic. They had dressed themselves in white, with broad white hats; dressed themselves as pimps. But the mansion was empty, stripped during that night of all its valuables by the greedy crowds.

They were pimps in a whorehouse without whores. As the young girl observed, with a tantalizing touch of wisdom beyond her apparent years, there was nothing much lower than that.

"Where'd you find that girl? She's hiding something, Oliver. You mark my words."

Oliver ignored his mother's misgivings, having enough of his own. The girl agreed she needed a different name now, and chose Lorelei, a name she said "Just sings right."

He saved money, lacking brothers to borrow and never repay, and soon rented a cheap studio on the sixth floor of the same building. The girl came to him sweetly in his bed, her mind no more full—for the most part—than that of any young girl. In his way, he loved her—and feared her, though less and less as days passed.

She played the piano almost as well as he, and they planned to give lessons. They had brought a trunk full of old sheet music and books with them from the mansion. The crowds had left them at least that much.

Momma did not visit for two weeks after they moved in. But visit she did, and eventually the girl won her over.

"She's got a good hand in the kitchen," Momma said. "You do right by her, now."

Yolanda made friends with the girl quickly and easily, and Oliver saw more substance in his younger sister than he had before. Lorelei helped Yolanda with the babies. She seemed a natural.

Sometimes, at night, he examined her while she slept, wondering if there still weren't stories, and perhaps skills, hidden behind her sweet, peaceful face. Had she forgotten everything?

In time, they were married.

And they lived—

Well, enough.

They lived.

Dead Run

There aren't many hitchhikers on the road to Hell.

I noticed this dude four miles away. He stood where the road is straight and level, crossing what looks like desert except it has empty towns and motels and shacks. I had been on the road for six hours and the folks in the cattle trailers behind me had been quiet for some time—resigned, I guess—so my nerves had settled a bit and I decided to see what the dude was up to. Maybe he was one of the employees. That would be interesting, I thought. Truth to tell, once the wailing settles down, I get bored.

The dude stood on the right side of the road, thumb out. I piano-keyed down the gears and the air brakes hissed and squealed at the tap of my foot. The semi slowed and the big diesel made that gut-deep dinosaur-belch of shuddered-downness. I leaned across the cab as everything came to a halt and swung the door open.

"Where you heading?" I asked.

He laughed and shook his head, then spit on the soft shoulder. "I don't know," he said. "Hell, maybe." He was thin and tanned with long greasy black hair and bluejeans and a vest. His straw hat was dirty and full of holes, but the feathers around the crown were bright and new, pheasant if I was any judge. A worn gold fob hung out of his vest. He wore old Frye boots with the toes turned up and soles thinner than my retreads. He looked a lot like me when I had hitchhiked out of Fresno, broke and unemployed, looking for work.

"Can I take you there?" I asked.

"Sure. Why not?" He climbed in and slammed the door shut, took out a kerchief and mopped his forehead, then blew his long nose and stared at me with bloodshot eyes. "What you hauling?" he asked.

"Souls," I said. "Whole shitload of them."

"What kind?" He was young, not more than twenty-five. He tried to sound easy and natural but I could hear the nerves.

"Human kind," I said. "Got some Hare Krishnas this time. Don't look that close anymore."

I coaxed the truck along, wondering if the engine was as bad as it sounded. When we were up to speed—eighty, eighty-five, no smokies on *this* road—he asked, "How long you been hauling?"

"Two years."

"Good pay?"

"I get by."

"Good benefits?"

"Union, like everyone else."

"That's what they told me in that little dump about two miles back. Perks and benefits."

"People live there?" I asked. I didn't think anything lived along the road. Anything human.

He bobbled his head. "Real down folks. They say Teamsters bosses get carried in limousines, when their time comes."

"Don't really matter how you get there or how long it takes. Forever is a slow bitch to pull."

"Getting there's all the fun?" he asked, trying for a grin. I gave him a shallow one.

"What're you doing out here?" I asked a few minutes later. "You aren't dead, are you?" I'd never heard of dead folks running loose or looking quite as vital as he did but I couldn't imagine anyone else being on the road. Dead folks—and drivers.

"No," he said. He was quiet for a bit. Then, slowly, as

if it embarrassed him, he said, "I'm here to find my woman."

"No shit?" Not much surprised me but this was a new twist. "There ain't no going back, for the dead, you know."

"Sherill's her name, spelled like sheriff but with two L's."

"Got a cigarette?" I asked. I didn't smoke but I could use them later. He handed me the last three in a crush-proof pack, not just one but all. He bobbled his head some more, peering through the clean windshield.

No bugs on this road. No flat rabbits on the road, snakes, nothing.

"Haven't heard of her," I said. "But then, I don't get to converse with everyone I haul. There are lots of trucks, lots of drivers."

"I heard about benefits," he said. "Perks and benefits. Back in that town." He had a crazy sad look.

I tightened my jaw and stared straight ahead.

"You know," he said, "They talk in that town. They tell about how they use old trains for Chinese, and in Russia there's a tramline. In Mexico it's old buses, always at night—"

"Listen. I don't use all the benefits," I said. "Some do but I don't."

"I got you," he said, nodding that exaggerated goddamn young bobble, his whole neck and shoulders moving, it's all right everything's cool.

"How you gonna find her?" I asked.

"I don't know. Hitch the road, ask the drivers."

"How'd you get in?"

He didn't answer for a moment. "I'm coming here when I die. That's pretty sure. It's not so hard for folks like me to get in beforehand. And...my daddy was a driver. He told me the route. By the way, my name's Bill."

"Mine's John," I said.

"Pleased to meet you."

We didn't say much for a while. He stared out the right window and I watched the desert and faraway shacks go by. Soon the mountains loomed up—space seems compressed on the road, especially out of the desert—and I sped up for the approach.

They made some noise in the back. Lost, creepy sounds, like tired old sirens in a factory.

"What'll you do when you get off work?" Bill asked.

"Go home and sleep."

"That's the way it was with Daddy, until just before the end. Look, I didn't mean to make you mad. I'd just heard about the perks and I thought..." He swallowed, his Adam's apple bobbing. "You might be able to help. I don't know how I'll ever find Sherill. Maybe back in the annex..."

"Nobody in their right minds goes into the yards by choice," I said. "You'd have to look at everybody that's died in the last four months. They're way backed up."

Bill took that like a blow across the face and I was sorry I'd said it. "She's only been gone a week," he said.

"Well," I said.

"My mom died two years ago, just before Daddy."

"The High Road," I said.

"What?"

"Hope they both got the High Road."

"Mom, maybe. Yeah. She did. But not Daddy. He knew." Bill hawked and spit out the window. "Sherill, she's here—but she don't belong."

I couldn't help but smirk.

"No, man, I mean it, I belong but not her. She was in this car wreck couple of months back. Got messed up. I sold her crystal and heroin at first and then fell in love with her and by the time she landed in the hospital, from the wreck—she was the only one who lived, man, shouldn't that tell you something?—but she was, you know, hooked on about four different things."

My arms stiffened on the wheel.

"I tried to tell her when I visited, no more dope, it wouldn't be good, but she begged. What could I do? I loved her." He looked down at his worn boots and bobbled sadly. "She begged me, man. I brought her stuff. She took it all when they weren't looking. I mean, she just took it *all*. They pumped her but her insides were mush. I didn't hear about her dying until two days ago. That really burned, man. I was the only one who loved her and they didn't even like *inform* me. I had to go up to her room and find the empty bed. *Jesus.* I hung out at Daddy's union hall. Someone talked to someone else and I found the name on a list. *Sherill.* They'd put her down the Low Road."

I hadn't known it was that easy to find out; but then, I'd never traveled with junkies. Dope can loosen a lot of lips.

"I don't do those perks," I said. "Folks in back got enough trouble. I think the union went too far there."

"Bet they thought you'd get lonely, need company," Bill said quietly, looking at me. "It don't hurt the women back there, does it? Maybe give them another chance to, you know, think things over. Give 'em relief for a couple of hours, a break from the mash—"

"A couple of hours don't mean nothing in relation to eternity," I said, too loud. "I'm not so sure I won't be joining them someday, and if that's the way it is I want it smooth, nobody pulling me out of a trailer and,—and putting me back in."

"Yeah," he said. "Got you. I know where you're at. But

she might be back there right now, and all you'd have to—"

"Bad enough I'm driving this fucking rig in the first place." I wanted to change the subject.

Bill stopped bobbling and squinted. "How'd that happen?"

"Couple of accidents. I hot-rodded with an old fart in a Triumph. Nearly ran down some joggers. My premiums went up to where I couldn't afford payments and finally they took my truck away."

"You coulda gone without insurance."

"Not me," I said. "Anyway, word got out. No companies would hire me. I went to the union to see if they could help. They told me I was a dead-ender, either get out of trucking or..." I shrugged. "This. I couldn't leave trucking. It's bad out there, getting work. Couldn't see myself driving a hack in some big city."

"No way, man," Bill said, giving me his whole-body rumba again. He cackled sympathetically.

"They gave me an advance, enough for a down payment on my rig." The truck was grinding a bit but maintaining. Over the mountains, through a really impressive pass like from an old engraving, and down in a rugged rocky valley, the City waited. I'd deliver my cargo, grab my slip, and run the rig (with Bill) back to Baker. Let him out someplace in the real. Park the truck in the yard next to my cottage. Go in, flop down, suck back a few beers, and get some sleep.

Start all over again Monday, two loads a week.

Hell, I never even got into Pahrump any more. I used to be a regular, but after driving the Low Road, the women at the Lizard Ranch all looked like prisoners, too dumb to notice their iron bars. I saw too much of hell in the those air-conditioned trailers.

"I don't think I'd better go on," Bill said. "I'll hitch with some other rig, ask around."

"I'd feel better if you rode with me back out of here. Want my advice?" Bad habit, giving advice.

"No," Bill said. "Thanks anyway. I can't go home. Sherill don't belong here." He took a deep breath. "I'll try to work up a trade with some bosses. I stay, in exchange, and she gets the High Road. That's the way the game works down here, isn't it?"

I didn't say otherwise. I couldn't be sure he wasn't right. He'd made it this far. At the top of the pass I pulled the rig over and let him out. He waved, I waved, and we went our different ways.

Poor rotten doping sonofabitch, I thought. I'd screwed up my life half a dozen different ways—three wives, liquor, three years at Tehachapi—but I'd never done dope. I felt self-righteous just listening to the dude. I was glad to be rid of him, truth be told.

As I geared the truck down for the decline, the noise in the trailers got irritating again. They could smell what was coming, I guess, like pigs stepping up to the man with the knife.

The City looks a lot like a dry country full of big white cathedrals. Casting against type. High wall around the perimeter, stretching right and left as far as my eye can see, like a pair of endless highways turned on their sides.

No compass. No magnetic fields. No sense of direction but down.

No horizon.

I pulled into the disembarkation terminal and backed the first trailer up to the holding pen. Employees let down the gates and used their big, ugly prods to offload my herd. These people do not respond to bodily pain. The prod gets them where we all hurt when we're dead.

After the first trailer was empty, employees unhooked it, pulled it away by hand or claw, strong as horses, and I backed in the second.

I got down out of the cab and an employee came up to me, a big fellow with red eyes and brand new coveralls. "Poke any good ones?" he asked. His breath was like the bad end of a bean and garlic dinner. I shook my head, took out the crush-proof box, and held my cigarette up for a light. He pressed his fingernail against the tip. The tip flared and settled down to a steady glow. He regarded it with pure lust. There's no in-between for employees. Lust or nothing.

"Listen," I said.

"I'm all ears," he said, and suddenly, he was. I jumped back and he laughed joylessly. "You're new," he said, and eyed my cigarette again.

"You had anyone named Sherill through here?"

"Who's asking?" he grumbled. He started a slow dance. He had to move around, otherwise his shoes melted the asphalt and got stuck. He lifted one foot, then the other, twisting a little.

"Just curious. I heard you guys know all the names."

"So?" He stopped his dance. His shoes made the tar stink.

"So," I said, with just as much sense, and held out the cigarette.

"Like Cherry with an L?"

"No. Sherill, like sheriff but with two L's."

"Couple of Cheryls. No Sherills," he said. "Sorry."

I handed him the cigarette, then pulled another out of the pack. He snapped it away between two thick, horny nails.

"Thanks," I said.

He popped both of them into his mouth and chewed, bliss rushing over his wrinkled face. Smoke shot out of his nose and he swallowed.

"Think nothing of it," he said, and walked on.

The road back is shorter than the road in. Don't ask how. I'd have thought it was the other way around but barriers are what's important not distance. Maybe we all get our chances so the road to Hell is long. But once we're there, there's no returning. You have to save on the budget somewhere.

I took the empties back to Baker. Didn't see Bill. Eight hours later I was in bed, beer in hand, paycheck on the bureau, my eyes wide open.

Shit, I thought. Now my conscience was working. I could have sworn I was past that. But then I didn't use the perks. I wouldn't drive without insurance.

I wasn't really cut out for the life.

There are no normal days and nights on the road to Hell. No matter how long you drive, it's always the same time when you arrive as when you left, but it's not necessarily the same time from trip to trip.

The next trip it was cool dusk and the road didn't pass through desert and small, empty towns. Instead, it crossed a bleak flatland of skeletal trees, all the same uniform gray as if cut from paper. When I pulled over to catch a nap—never sleeping more than two hours at a stretch—the shouts of the damned in the trailers bothered me even more than usual. Silly things they said, like:

"You can take us back, mister! You really can!"

"Can he?"

"Shit no, mofuck pig."

"You can let us out! We can't hurt you!"

That was true enough. Drivers were alive and the dead could never hurt the living. But I'd heard what happened when you let them out. There were about ninety of them in back and in any load there was always one would make you want to use your perks.

I scratched my itches in the narrow bunk, looking at the Sierra Club calendar hanging just below the fan. The Devil's Postpile. The load became quieter as the voices gave up, one after the other. There was one last shout—some obscenity—then silence.

It was then I decided I'd let them out and see if Sherill was there, or if anyone knew her. They mingled in the annex, got their last socializing before the City. Someone might know. Then if I saw Bill again—

What? What could I do to help him? He had screwed Sherill up royally, but then she'd had a hand in it too, and that was what Hell was all about. Poor stupid sons of bitches.

I swung out of the cab, tucking in my shirt and pulling my straw hat down on my crown. "Hey!" I said, walking alongside the trailers. Faces peered at me from the two inches between each white slat. "I'm going to let you out. Just for a while. I need some information."

"Ask!" someone screamed. "Just ask, goddammit!"

"You know you can't run away. You can't hurt me. You're all dead. Understand?"

"We know," said another voice, quieter.

"Maybe we can help."

"I'm going to open the gates one trailer at a time." I went to the rear trailer first, took out my keys and undid the Yale padlock. Then I swung the gates open, standing back a little like there was some kind of infected wound about to drain.

They were all naked but they weren't dirty. I'd seen them in the annex yards and at the City; I knew they weren't like concentration camp prisoners. The dead can't really be unhealthy. Each just had some sort of air about him telling why he was in Hell; nothing specific but subliminal.

Like three black dudes in the rear trailer, first to step out. Why they were going to Hell was all over their faces. They weren't in the least sorry for the lives they'd led. They wanted to keep on doing what had brought them here in the first place—scavenging, hurting, hurting me in particular.

"Stupid ass mofuck," one of them said, staring at me beneath thin, expressive eyebrows. He nodded and swung his fists, trying to pound the slats from the outside, but the blows hardly made them vibrate.

An old woman crawled down, hair white and neatly coiffed. I couldn't be certain what she had done but she made me uneasy. She might have been the worst in the load. And lots of others, young, old, mostly old. Quiet for the most part.

They looked me over, some defiant, most just bewildered.

"I need to know if there's anyone here named Sherill," I said, "who happens to know a fellow named Bill."

"That's my name," said a woman hidden in the crowd.

"Let me see her." I waved my hand at them. The black dudes came forward. A funny look got in their eyes and they backed away. The others parted and a young woman walked out. "How do you spell your name?" I asked.

She got a panicked expression. She spelled it, hesitating, hoping she'd make the grade. I felt horrible already. She was a Cheryl.

"Not who I'm looking for," I said.

"Don't be hasty," she said, real soft. She wasn't trying hard to be seductive but she was succeeding. She was very pretty with medium-sized breasts, hips like a teenager's, legs not terrific but nice. Her black hair was clipped short and her eyes were almost Asian. I figured maybe she was Lebanese or some other kind of Middle Eastern.

I tried to ignore her. "You can walk around a bit," I told them. "I'm letting out the first trailer now." I opened the side gates on that one and the people came down. They didn't smell, didn't look hungry, they just all looked pale. I wondered if the torment had begun already, but if so, I decided, it wasn't the physical kind.

One thing I'd learned in my two years was that all the Sunday school and horror movie crap about Hell was dead wrong.

"Woman named Sherill," I repeated. No one stepped forward. Then I felt someone close to me and I turned. It was the Cheryl woman. She smiled. "I'd like to sit up front for a while," she said.

"So would we all, sister," said the white-haired old woman. The black dudes stood off separate, talking low.

I swallowed, looking at her. Other drivers said they were real insubstantial except at one activity. That was the perk. And it was said the hottest ones always ended up in Hell.

"No," I said. I motioned for them to get back into the trailers. Whatever she was on the Low Road for, it wouldn't affect her performance in the sack, that was obvious.

It had been a dumb idea all around. They went back and I returned to the cab, lighting up a cigarette and thinking what had made me do it.

I shook my head and started her up. Thinking on a dead run was no good. "No," I said, "goddamn," I said, "good."

Cheryl's face stayed with me.

Cheryl's body stayed with me longer than the face.

Something always comes up in life to lure a man onto the Low Road, not driving but riding in the back. We all have some weakness. I wondered what reason God had to give us each that little flaw, like a chip in crystal, you press the chip hard enough everything splits up crazy.

At least now I knew one thing. My flaw wasn't sex, not this way. What most struck me about Cheryl was wonder. She was so pretty; how'd she end up on the Low Road?

For that matter, what had Bill's Sherill done?

I returned hauling empties and found myself this time outside a small town called Shoshone. I pulled my truck into the cafe parking lot. The weather was cold and I left the engine running. It was about eleven in the morning and the cafe was half full. I took a seat at the counter next to an old man with maybe four teeth in his head, attacking French toast with downright solemn dignity. I ordered eggs and hashbrowns and juice, ate quickly, and went back to my truck.

Bill stood next to the cab. Next to him was an enormous young woman with a face like a bulldog. She was wrapped in a filthy piece of plaid fabric that might have been snatched from a trash dump somewhere. "Hey," Bill said. "Remember me?"

"Sure."

"I saw you pulling up. I thought you'd like to know... This is Sherill. I got her out of there." The woman stared at me with all the expression of a brick. "It's all screwy. Like a power failure or something. We just walked out on the road and nobody stopped us."

Sherill could have hid any number of weirdnesses beneath her formidable looks and gone unnoticed by ordinary folks. But I didn't have any trouble picking out the biggest thing wrong with her: she was dead. Bill had brought her out of Hell. I looked around to make sure I was in the World. I was. He wasn't lying. Something serious had happened on the Low Road.

"Trouble?" I asked.

"Lots." He grinned at me. "Pan-demon-ium." His grin broadened.

"That can't happen," I said. Sherill trembled, hearing my voice.

"He's a *driver,* Bill," she said. "He's the one takes us there. We should git out of here." She had that soul-branded air and the look of a pig that's just escaped slaughter, seeing the butcher again. She took a few steps backward. Gluttony, I thought. Gluttony and buried lust and a real ugly way of seeing life, inner eye pulled all out of shape by her bulk.

Bill hadn't had much to do with her ending up on the Low Road.

"Tell me more," I said.

"There's folks running all over down there, holing up in them towns, devils chasing them—"

"Employees," I corrected.

"Yeah. Every which way."

Sherill tugged on his arm. "We got to go, Bill."

"We got to go," he echoed. "Hey, man, thanks. I found her!" He nodded his whole-body nod and they were off down the street, Sherill's plaid wrap dragging in the dirt.

I drove back to Baker, wondering if the trouble was responsible for my being rerouted through Shoshone. I parked in front of my little house and sat inside with a beer while it got dark, checking my calendar for the next day's run and feeling very cold. I can take so much supernatural in its place, but now things were spilling over, smudging the clean-drawn line between my work and the World. Next day I was scheduled to be at the annex and take another load.

Nobody called that evening. If there was trouble on the Low Road, surely the union would let me know, I thought.

I drove to the annex early in the morning. The crossover from the World to the Low Road was normal; I followed the route and the sky muddied from blue to solder-color and I was on the first leg to the annex. I backed the rear trailer up to the yard's gate and unhitched it, then placed the forward trailer at a ramp, all the while keeping my ears tuned to pick up interesting conversation.

The employees who work the annex look human. I took my invoice from a red-faced old guy with eyes like billiard balls and looked at him like I was in the know but could use some updating. He spit smoking saliva on the pavement, returned my look slantwise and said nothing. Maybe it was all settled. I hitched up both full trailers and pulled out.

I didn't even mention Sherill and Bill. Like in most jobs keeping one's mouth shut is good policy. That and don't volunteer.

It was the desert again this time, only now the towns and tumbledown houses looked bomb-blasted, like something big had come through, flushing out game with a howitzer.

Eyes on the road. Push that rig.

Four hours in, I came to a roadblock. Nobody on it, no employees, just big carved-lava barricades cutting across all lanes and beyond them a yellow smoke which, the driver's unwritten instructions advised, meant absolutely no entry.

I got out. The load was making noises. I suddenly hated them. Nothing beautiful there—just naked Hell-bounders shouting and screaming and threatening like it wasn't already over for them. They'd had their chance and crapped out and now they were still bullshitting the World.

Least they could do was go with dignity and spare me their misery.

That's probably what the engineers on the trains to Auschwitz thought. Yeah, yeah, except I was the fellow who might be hauling those engineers to their just deserts.

Crap, I just couldn't be one way or the other about the whole thing. I could feel mad and guilty and I could think Jesus, probably I'll be complaining just as much when my time comes. Jesus H. Twentieth Century Man Christ.

I stood by the truck, waiting for instructions or some indication what I was supposed to do. The load became quieter after a while but I heard noises off the road, screams mostly and far away.

"There isn't anything," I said to myself, lighting up one of Bill's cigarettes even though I don't smoke and dragging deep, *"anything* worth this shit." I vowed I would quit after this run.

I heard something come up behind the trailers and I edged closer to the cab steps. High wisps of smoke obscured things at first but a dark shape three or four yards high plunged through and stood with one hand on the top slats of the rear trailer. It was covered with naked people, crawling all over, biting and scratching and shouting obscenities. It made little grunting noises, fell to its knees, then stood again and lurched off the road. Some of the people hanging on saw me and shouted for me to come help.

"Help us get this sonofabitch down!"

"Hey, you! We've almost got 'im! "

"He's a driver—"

"Fuck 'im, then."

I'd never seen an employee so big before, nor in so much trouble. The load began to wail like banshees. I threw down my cigarette and ran after it.

Workers will tell you. Camaraderie extends even to those on the job you don't like. If they're in trouble it's part of the mystique to help out. Besides, the unwritten instructions were very clear on such things and I've never knowingly broken a job rule—not since getting my rig back—and couldn't see starting now.

Through the smoke and across great ridges of lava, I ran until I spotted the employee about ten yards ahead. It had shaken off the naked people and was standing with one in each hand. Its shoulders smoked and scales stood out at all angles. They'd really done a job on the bastard. Ten or twelve of the dead were picking themselves off the lava, unscraped, unbruised. They saw me.

The employee saw me.

Everyone came at me. I turned and ran for the truck, stumbling, falling, bruising and scraping myself everywhere. My hair stood on end. People grabbed me, pleading for me to haul them out, old, young, all fawning and screeching like whipped dogs.

Then the employee swung me up out of reach. Its hand was cold and hard like iron tongs kept in a freezer. It grunted and ran toward my truck, opening the door wide and throwing me roughly inside. It made clear with huge, wild gestures that I'd better turn around and go back, that waiting was no good and there was no way through.

I started the engine and turned the rig around. I rolled up my window and hoped the dead weren't substantial enough to scratch paint or tear up slats.

All rules were off now. What about the ones in my load? All the while I was doing these things my head was full of questions, like how could souls fight back and wasn't there some inflexible order in Hell that kept such things from happening? That was what had been implied when I hired on. Safest job around.

I headed back down the road. My load screamed like no load I'd ever had before. I was afraid they might get loose but they didn't. I got near the annex and they were quiet again, too quiet for me to hear over the diesel.

The yards were deserted. The long, white-painted cement platforms and whitewashed wood-slat loading ramps were unattended. No souls in the pens.

The sky was an indefinite gray. An out-of-focus yellow sun gleamed faintly off the stark white employee's lounge. I stopped the truck and swung down to investigate.

There was no wind, only silence. The air was frosty without being particularly cold. What I wanted to do most was unload and get out of there, go back to Baker or Barstow or Shoshone.

I hoped that was still possible. Maybe all exits had been closed. Maybe the overseers had closed them to keep any more souls from getting out.

I tried the gate latches and found I could open them. I did so and returned to the truck, swinging the rear trailer around until it was flush with the ramp. Nobody made a sound. "Go on back," I said. "Go on back. You've got more time here. Don't ask me how."

"Hello, John." That was behind me. I turned and saw an older man without any clothes on. I didn't recognize him at first. His eyes finally clued me in.

"Mr. Martin?" My high school history teacher. I hadn't seen him in maybe twenty years. He didn't look much older, but then I'd never seen him naked. He was dead, but he wasn't like the others. He didn't have that look that told me why he was here.

"This is not the sort of job I'd expect one of my students

to take," Martin said. He laughed the smooth laugh he was famous for, the laugh that seemed to take everything he said in class and put it in perspective.

"You're not the first person I'd expect to find here," I responded.

"The cat's away, John. The mice are in charge now. I'm going to try to leave."

"How long you been here?" I asked.

"I died a month ago, I think," Martin said, never one to mince words.

"You can't leave," I said. Doing my job even with Mr. Martin. I felt the ice creep up my throat.

"Still the screwball team player," Martin said, "even when the team doesn't give a damn what you do."

I wanted to explain but he walked away toward the annex and the road out. Looking back over his shoulder, he said, "Get smart, John. Things aren't what they seem. Never have been."

"Look!" I shouted after him. "I'm going to quit, honest, but this load is my responsibility." I thought I saw him shake his head as he rounded the corner of the annex.

The dead in my load had pried loose some of the ramp slats and were jumping off the rear trailer. Those in the forward trailer were screaming and carrying on, shaking the whole rig.

Responsibility, shit, I thought. As the dead followed after Mr. Martin, I unhitched both trailers. Then I got in the cab and swung away from the annex, onto the incoming road. "I'm going to quit," I said. "Sure as anything, I'm going to quit."

The road out seemed awfully long. I didn't see any of the dead, surprisingly, but then maybe they'd been shunted away. I was taking a route I'd never been on before and I had no way of knowing if it would put me where I wanted to be. But I hung in there for two hours, running the truck dead-out on the flats.

The air was getting grayer like somebody turning down the contrast on a TV set. I switched on the high-beams but they didn't help. By now I was shaking in the cab and saying to myself, Nobody deserves this. Nobody deserves going to Hell no matter what they did. I was scared. It was getting colder.

Three hours and I saw the annex and yards ahead of me again. The road had looped back. I swore and slowed the rig to a crawl. The loading docks had been set on fire. Dead were wandering around with no idea what to do or where to go. I sped up and drove over the few that were on the road. They'd come up and the truck's bumper would hit them and I wouldn't feel a thing, like they weren't there. I'd see them in the rearview mirror, getting up after being knocked over. Just knocked over. Then I was away from the loading docks and there was no doubt about it this time.

I was heading straight for Hell.

The disembarkation terminal was on fire, too. But beyond it the City was bright and white and untouched. For the first time I drove past the terminal and took the road into the City.

It was either that or stay on the flats with everything screwy. Inside, I thought maybe they'd have things under control.

The truck roared through the gate between two white pillars maybe seventy or eighty feet thick and as tall as the Washington Monument. I didn't see anybody, employees or the dead. Once I was through the pillars— and it came as a shock—

There was no City, no walls, just the road winding along and countryside in all directions, even behind.

The countryside was covered with shacks, houses, little clusters and big clusters. Everything was tight-packed, people working together on one hill, people sitting on their porches, walking along paths, turning to stare at me as the rig barreled on through. No employees—no monsters. No flames. No bloody lakes or rivers.

This must be the outside part, I thought. Deeper inside it would get worse.

I kept on driving. The dog part of me was saying let's go look for authority and ask some questions and get out. But the monkey was saying let's just go look and find out what's going on, what Hell is all about.

Another hour of driving through that calm, crowded landscape and the truck ran out of fuel. I coasted to the side and stepped down from the cab, very nervous.

Again I lit up a cigarette and leaned against the fender, shaking a little. But the shaking was running down and a tight kind of calm was replacing it.

The landscape was still condensed, crowded, but nobody looked tortured. No screaming, no eternal agony. Trees and shrubs and grass hills and thousands and thousands of little houses.

It took about ten minutes for the inhabitants to get around to investigating me. Two men came over to my truck and nodded cordially. Both were middle-aged and healthy-looking. They didn't look dead. I nodded back.

"We were betting whether you're one of the drivers or not," said the first, a black-haired fellow. He wore a simple handwoven shirt and pants. "I think you are. That so?"

"I am."

"You're lost, then."

I agreed. "Maybe you can tell me where I am?"

"Hell," said the second man, younger by a few years and just wearing shorts. The way he said it was just like you might say you came from Los Angeles or Long Beach. Nothing big, nothing dramatic.

"We've heard rumors there's been problems outside," a woman said, coming up to join us. She was about sixty and skinny. She looked like she should be twitchy and nervous but she acted rock-steady. They were all rock-steady.

"There's some kind of strike," I said. "I don't know what it is, but I'm looking for an employee to tell me."

"They don't usually come this far in," the first man said. "We run things here. Or rather, nobody tells us what to do."

"You're alive?" the woman asked, a curious hunger in her voice. Others came around to join us, a whole crowd. They didn't try to touch. They stood their ground and stared and talked.

"Look," said an old black fellow. "You ever read about the Ancient Mariner?"

I said I had in school.

"Had to tell everybody what he did," the black fellow said. The woman beside him nodded. "We're all Ancient Mariners here. But there's nobody to tell it to. Would you like to know?" The way he asked was pitiful. "We're sorry. We just want everybody to know how sorry we are."

"I can't take you back," I said. "I don't know how to get there myself."

"We can't go back," the woman said. "That's not our place."

More people were coming and I was nervous again. I stood my ground trying to seem calm and the dead gathered around me, eager.

"I never thought of anybody but myself," one said. Another interrupted with, "Man, I fucked my whole life away, I hated everybody and everything. I was burned out—"

"I thought I was the greatest. I could pass judgment on everybody—"

"I was the stupidest goddamn woman you ever saw. I was a sow, a pig. I farrowed kids and let them run wild, without no guidance. I was stupid and cruel, too. I used to hurt things—"

"Never cared for anyone. Nobody ever cared for me. I was left to rot in the middle of a city and I wasn't good enough not to rot."

"Everything I did was a lie after I was about twelve years old—"

"Listen to me, mister, because it hurts, it hurts so bad—"

I backed up against my truck. They were lining up now, organized, not like any mob. I had a crazy thought they were behaving better than any people on Earth, but these were the damned.

I didn't hear or see anybody famous. An ex-cop told me about what he did to people in jails. A Jesus-freak told me that knowing Jesus in your heart wasn't enough. "Because I should have made it, man, I should have made it."

"A time came and I was just broken by it all, broke myself really. Just kept stepping on myself and making all the wrong decisions—"

They confessed to me, and I began to cry. Their faces were so clear and so pure, yet here they were, confessing, and except maybe for specific things—like the fellow who had killed Ukrainians after the Second World War in Russian camps—they didn't sound any worse than the crazy sons of bitches I called friends who spent their lives in trucks or bars or whorehouses.

They were all recent. I got the impression the deeper

into Hell you went, the older the damned became, which made sense; Hell just got bigger, each crop of damned got bigger, with more room on the outer circles.

"We wasted it," someone said. "You know what my greatest sin was? I was dull. Dull and cruel. I never saw beauty. I saw only dirt. I loved the dirt and the clean just passed me by."

Pretty soon my tears were uncontrollable. I kneeled down beside the truck, hiding my head, but they kept on coming and confessing. Hundreds must have passed, talking quietly, gesturing with their hands.

Then they stopped. Someone had come and told them to back away, that they were too much for me. I took my face out of my hands and a very young-seeming fellow stood looking down on me. "You all right?" he asked.

I nodded, but my insides were like broken glass. With every confession I had seen myself, and with every tale of sin I had felt an answering echo.

"Someday, I'm going to be here. Someone's going to drive me in a cattle car to Hell," I mumbled. The young fellow helped me to my feet and cleared a way around my truck.

"Yeah, but not now," he said. "You don't belong here yet." He opened the door to my cab and I got back inside.

"I don't have any fuel," I said.

He smiled that sad smile they all had and stood on the step, up close to my ear. "You'll be taken out of here soon anyway. One of the employees is bound to get around to you." He seemed a lot more sophisticated than the others. I looked at him maybe a little queerly, like there was some explaining in order.

"Yeah, I know all that stuff," he said. "I was a driver once. Then I got promoted. What are they all doing back there?" He gestured up the road. "They're really messing things up now, ain't they?"

"I don't know," I said, wiping my eyes and cheeks with my sleeve.

"You go back, and you tell them that all this revolt on the outer circles, it's what I expected. Tell them Charlie's here and that I warned them. Word's getting around. There's bound to be discontent."

"Word?"

"About who's in charge. Just tell them Charlie knows and I warned them. I know something else, and you shouldn't tell anybody about this..." He whispered an incredible fact into my ear then, something that shook me deeper than what I had already been through.

I closed my eyes. Some shadow passed over. The young fellow and everybody else seemed to recede. I felt rather than saw my truck being picked up like a toy.

Then I suppose I was asleep for a time.

In the cab in the parking lot of a truck stop in Bakersfield, I jerked awake, pulled my cap out of my eyes and looked around. It was about noon. There was a union hall in Bakersfield. I checked and my truck was full of diesel, so I started her up and drove to the union hall.

I knocked on the door of the office. I went in and recognized the fat old dude who had given me the job in the first place. I was tired and I smelled bad but I wanted to get it all done with now.

He recognized me but didn't know my name until I told him. "I can't work the run anymore," I said. The shakes were on me again. "I'm not the one for it. I don't feel right driving them when I know I'm going to be there myself, like as not."

"Okay," he said, slow and careful, sizing me up with a knowing eye. "But you're out. You're busted then. No more driving, no more work for us, no more work for any union we support. It'll be lonely."

"I'll take that kind of lonely any day," I said.

"Okay." That was that. I headed for the door and stopped with my hand on the knob.

"One more thing," I said. "I met Charlie. He says to tell you word's getting around about who's in charge, and that's why there's so much trouble in the outer circles."

The old dude's knowing eye went sort of glassy. "You're the fellow got into the City?"

I nodded.

He got up from his seat real fast, jowls quivering and belly doing a silly dance beneath his work blues. He flicked one hand at me, come 'ere. "Don't go. Just you wait a minute. Outside in the office."

I waited and heard him talking on the phone. He came out smiling and put his hand on my shoulder. "Listen, John, I'm not sure we should let you quit. I didn't know you were the one who'd gone inside. Word is, you stuck around and tried to help when everybody else ran. The company appreciates that. You've been with us a long time, reliable driver, maybe we should give you some incentive to stay. I'm sending you to Vegas to talk with a company man..."

The way he said it, I knew there wasn't much choice and I better not fight it. You work union long enough and you know when you keep your mouth shut and go along.

They put me up in a motel and fed me and by late morning I was on my way to Vegas, arriving about two in the afternoon. I was in a black union car with a silent driver and air conditioning and some *Newsweeks* to keep me company.

The limo dropped me off in front of a four-floor office building, glass and stucco, with lots of divorce lawyers and a dentist and small companies with anonymous names. White plastic letters on a ribbed felt background in a glass case. There was no name on the office number I had been told to go to, but I went up and knocked anyway.

I don't know what I expected. A district supervisor opened the door and asked me a few questions and I said what I'd said before. I was adamant. He looked worried. "Look," he said. "It won't be good for you now if you quit."

I asked him what he meant by that but he just looked unhappy and said he was going to send me to somebody higher up.

That was in Denver, nearer my God to thee. The same black car took me there and Saturday morning, bright and early, I stood in front of a very large corporate building with no sign out front and a bank on the bottom floor. I went past the bank and up to the very top.

A secretary met me, pretty but her hair done up very tight and her jaw grimly square. She didn't like me. She let me into the next office, though.

I swear I'd seen the fellow before, but maybe it was just a passing resemblance. He wore a narrow tie and a tasteful but conservative gray suit. His shirt was pastel blue and there was a big Rembrandt Bible on his desk, sitting on the glass top next to an alabaster pen holder. He shook my hand firmly and perched on the edge of the desk.

"First, let me congratulate you on your bravery. We've had some reports from the...uh...field, and we're hearing nothing but good about you." He smiled like that fellow on TV who's always asking the audience to give him some help. Then his face got sincere and serious. I honestly believe he was sincere; he was also well trained in dealing with not-very-bright people. "I hear you have a report for me. From Charles Frick."

"He said his name was Charlie." I told him the story. "What I'm curious about, what did he mean, this thing about who's in charge?"

"Charlie was in Organization until last year. He died in a car accident. I'm shocked to hear he got the Low Road." He didn't look shocked. "Maybe I'm shocked but not surprised. To tell the truth, he was a bit of a troublemaker." He smiled brightly again and his eyes got large and there was a little too much animation in his face. He had on these MacArthur wire-rimmed glasses too big for his eyes.

"What did he mean?"

"John, I'm proud of all our drivers. You don't know how proud we all are of you folks down there doing the dirty work."

"What did Charlie mean?"

"The abortionists and pornographers, the hustlers and muggers and murderers. Atheists and heathens and idol-worshippers. Surely there must be some satisfaction in keeping the land clean. Sort of a giant sanitation squad, you people keep the scum away from the good folks. The plain good folks. Now we know that driving's maybe the hardest job we have in the company, and that not everyone can stay on the Low Road indefinitely. Still, we'd like you to stay on. Not as a driver—unless you really wish to continue. For the satisfaction of a tough job. No, if you want to move up—and you've earned it by now, surely—we have a place for you here. A place where you'll be comfortable and—"

"I've already said I want out. You're acting like I'm hot stuff and I'm just shit. You know that, I know that. What is going on?"

His face hardened on me. "It isn't easy up here, either,

buster." The "buster" bit tickled me. I laughed and got up
from the chair. I'd been in enough offices and this fancy
one just made me queasy. When I stood, he held up his
hand and pursed his lips as he nodded. "Sorry. There's
incentive, there's certainly a reason why you should want
to work here. If you're so convinced you're on your way
to the Low Road, you can work it off here, you know."

"How can you say that?"

Bright smile. "Charlie told you something. He told you
about who's in charge here."

Now I could smell something terribly wrong, like with
the union boss. I mumbled, "He said that's why there's
trouble."

"It comes every now and then. We put it down gentle.
I tell you where we really need good people, compassion-
ate people. We need them to help with the choosing."

"Choosing?"

"Surely you don't think the Boss does all the choosing
directly?"

I couldn't think of a thing to say.

"Listen, the Boss...let me tell you. A long time ago, the
Boss decided to create a new kind of worker, one with
more decision-making ability. Some of the supervisors
disagreed, especially when the Boss said the workers would
be around for a long, long time—that they'd be indestructible. Sort of like nuclear fuel, you know. Human souls.
The waste builds up after a time, those who turn out bad,
turn out to be chronically unemployable. They don't go
along with the scheme, or get out of line. Can't get along
with their fellow workers. You know the type. What do
you do with them? Can't just let them go away—they're
indestructible, and that ain't no joke, so—"

"Chronically unemployable?"

"You're a union man. Think of what it must feel like to be out of *work...forever.* Damned. Nobody will hire you."

I knew the feeling, both the way he meant it and the way it had happened to me.

"The Boss feels the project half succeeded, so He doesn't dump it completely. But He doesn't want to be bothered with all the pluses and minuses, the bookkeeping."

"You're in charge," I said, my blood cooling.

And I knew where I had seen him before.

On television.

God's right-hand man.

And human. Flesh-and-blood.

We ran Hell.

He nodded. "Now, that's not the sort of thing we'd like to get around."

"You're in charge, and you let the drivers take their perks on the loads, you let—" I stopped, instinct telling me I would soon be on a rugged trail with no turnaround.

"I'll tell you the truth, John. I have only been in charge here for a year, and my predecessor let things get out of hand. He wasn't a religious man, John, and he thought this was a job like any other, where you could compromise now and then. I know that isn't so. There's no compromise here, and we'll straighten out those inequities and bad decisions very soon. You'll help us, I hope. You may know more about the problems than we do."

"How do you...how do you qualify for a job like this?" I asked. "And who offered it to you?"

"Not the Boss, if that's what you're getting at, John. It's been kind of traditional. You may have heard about me. I'm the one, when there was all this talk about after-death experiences and everyone was seeing bright light and beauty, I'm the one who wondered why no one was seeing the other side. I found people who had almost died and had seen Hell, and I turned their lives around. The management in the company decided a fellow with my ability could do good work here. And so I'm here. And I'll tell you, it isn't easy. I sometimes wish we had a little more help from the Boss, a little more guidance, but we don't, and somebody has to do it. Somebody has to clean out the stables, John." Again the smile.

I put on my mask. "Of course," I said. I hoped a gradual increase in piety would pass his sharp-eyed muster.

"And you can see how this all makes you much more valuable to the organization."

I let light dawn slowly.

"We'd hate to lose you now, John. Not when there's security, so much security, working for us. I mean, here we learn the real ins and outs of salvation."

I let him talk at me until he looked at his watch, and all the time I nodded and considered and tried to think of the best ploy. Then I eased myself into a turnabout. I did some confessing until his discomfort was stretched too far—I was keeping him from an important appointment—and made my concluding statement.

"I just wouldn't feel right up here," I said. "I've driven all my life. I'd just want to keep on, working where I'm best suited."

"Keep your present job?" he said, tapping his shoe on the side of the desk.

"Lord, yes," I said, grateful as could be.

Then I asked him for his autograph. He smiled real big and gave it to me, God's right-hand man, who had prayed with presidents.

The next time out, I thought about the incredible thing that Charlie Frick had told me. Halfway to Hell, on the part of the run that he had once driven, I pulled the truck onto the gravel shoulder and walked back, hands in pockets, squinting at the faces. Young and old. Mostly old, or in their teens or twenties. Some were clearly bad news... But I was looking more closely this time, trying to discriminate. And sure enough, I saw a few that didn't seem to belong.

The dead hung by the slats, sticking their arms through, beseeching. I ignored as much of that as I could. "You," I said, pointing to a pale, thin fellow with a listless expression. "Why are you here?"

They wouldn't lie to me. I'd learned that inside the City. The dead don't lie.

"I kill people," the man said in a high whisper. "I kill children."

That confirmed my theory. I had *known* there was something wrong with him. I pointed to an old woman, plump and white-haired, lacking any of the signs. "You. Why are you going to Hell?"

She shook her head. "I don't know," she said. "Because I'm bad, I suppose."

"What did you do that was bad?"

"I don't know!" she said, flinging her hands up. "I really don't know. I was a librarian. When all those horrible people tried to take books out of my library, I fought them. I tried to reason with them... They wanted to remove Salinger and Twain and Baum..."

I picked out another young man. "What about you?"

"I didn't think it was possible," he said. "I didn't believe that God hated me, too."

"What did you do?" These people *didn't need to confess.*

"I loved God. I loved Jesus. But, dear Lord, I couldn't help it. I'm gay. I never had a choice. God wouldn't send me here just for being gay, would he?"

I spoke to a few more, until I was sure I had found all

I had in this load. "You, you, you and you, out," I said, swinging open the rear gate. I closed the gate after them and led them away from the truck. Then I told them what Charlie Frick had told me, what he had learned on the road and in the big offices.

"Nobody's really sure where it goes," I said. "But it doesn't go to Hell, and it doesn't go back to Earth."

"Where, then?" the old woman asked plaintively. The hope in her eyes made me want to cry, because I just wasn't sure.

"Maybe it's the High Road," I said. "At least it's a chance. You light out across this stretch, go back of that hill, and I think there's some sort of trail. It's not easy to find, but if you look carefully, it's there. Follow it."

The young man who was gay took my hand. I felt like pulling away, because I've never been fond of homos. But he held on and he said, "Thank you. You must be taking a big risk."

"Yes, thank you," the librarian said. "Why are you doing it?"

I had hoped they wouldn't ask. "When I was a kid, one of my Sunday schoolteachers told me about Jesus going down to Hell during the three days before he rose up again. She told me Jesus went to Hell to bring out those who didn't belong. I'm certainly no Jesus, I'm not even much of a Christian, but that's what I'm doing. She called it Harrowing Hell." I shook my head. "Never mind. Just go," I said. I watched them walk across the gray flats and around the hill, then I got back into my truck and took the rest into the annex. Nobody noticed. I suppose the records just aren't that important to the employees.

None of the folks I've let loose have ever come back.

I'm staying on the road. I'm talking to people here and there, being cautious. When it looks like things are getting chancy, I'll take my rig back down to the City. And then I'm not sure what I'll do.

I don't want to let everybody loose. But I want to know who's ending up on the Low Road who shouldn't be. People unpopular with God's right-hand man.

My message is simple.

The crazy folks are running the asylum. We've corrupted Hell.

If I get caught, I'll be riding in back. And if you're reading this, chances are you'll be there, too.

Until then, I'm doing my bit. How about you?

The Visitation

The Trinity arrived under a blossoming almond tree in Rebecca Sandia's backyard in the early hours of Easter morning. She watched it appear as she sipped tea on her back porch. Because of the peace radiating from the three images—a lion, a lamb, and a dove—she did not feel alarm or even much concern. She was not an overtly religious person, but she experienced considerable relief at having a major question—the existence of a God—answered in the affirmative. The Trinity approached her table on hooves, paws, and wings; and this, she knew, expressed the ultimate assurance and humility of God—that He should not require her to approach Him.

"Good morning," she said. The lamb nuzzled her leg affectionately. "An especially significant morning for you, is it not?" The lamb bleated and spun its tail. "I am so pleased you have chosen me, though I wonder why."

The lion spoke with a voice like a typhoon confined in a barrel:

"Once each year on this date we reveal the Craft of Godhead to a selected human. Seldom are the humans chosen from My formal houses of worship, for I have found them almost universally unable to comprehend the Mystery. They have preconceived ideas and cannot remove the blinds from their eyes."

Rebecca Sandia felt a brief *frisson* then, but the dove rubbed its breast feathers against her hand where it lay on the table. "I have never been a strong believer," she said, "though I have always had hopes."

"That is why you were chosen," the dove sang, its voice as dulcet as a summer's evening breeze. The lamb cavorted about the grass; and Rebecca's heart was filled with gladness watching it, for she remembered it had gone through hard times not long ago.

"I have asked only one thing of My creations," the lion said, "that once a year I find some individual capable of understanding the Mystery. Each year I have chosen the most likely individual and appeared to speak and enthuse. And each year I have chosen correctly and found understanding and allowed the world to continue. And so it will be until My creation is fulfilled."

"But I am a scientist," Rebecca said, concerned by the lion's words. "I am enchanted by the creation more than the God. I am buried in the world and not the spirit."

"I have spun the world out of My spirit," the dove sang. "Each particle is as one of my feathers; each event, a note in my song."

"Then I am joyful," Rebecca said, "for that I understand. I have often thought of you as a scientist, performing experiments."

"Then you do not understand," the lion said. "For I seek not to comprehend My creation but to know MySelf."

"Then is it wrong for me to be a scientist?" Rebecca asked. "Should I be a priest or a theologian, to help You understand YourSelf?"

"No, for I have made your kind as so many mirrors, that you may see each other; and there are no finer mirrors than scientists, who are so hard and bright. Priests and theologians, as I have said, shroud their brightness with mists for their own comfort and sense of well-being."

"Then I am still concerned," Rebecca said, "for I would like the world to be ultimately kind and nurturing. Though as a scientist I see that it is not, that it is cruel and harsh and demanding."

"What is pain?" the lion asked, lifting one paw to show

a triangle marked by thorns. "It is transitory, and suffering is the moisture of My breath."

"I don't understand," Rebecca said, shivering.

"Among My names are disease and disaster, and My hand lies on every pockmark and blotch and boil, and My limbs move beneath every hurricane and earthquake. Yet you still seek to love Me. Do you not comprehend?"

"No," Rebecca said, her face pale, for the world's particles seemed to lose some of their stability at that moment. "How can it be that You love us?"

"If I had made all things comfortable and sweet, then you would not be driven to examine Me and know My motives. You would dance and sing and withdraw into your pleasures."

"Then I understand," Rebecca said. "For it is the work of a scientist to know the world and control it, and we are often driven by the urge to prevent misery. Through our knowledge we see You more clearly."

"I see MySelves more clearly through you."

"Then I can love You and cherish You, knowing that ultimately You are concerned for us."

The world swayed; and Rebecca was sore afraid, for the peace of the lamb had faded, and the lion glowed red as coals. "Whom are you closest to," the lion asked, its voice deeper than thunder, "your enemies or your lovers? Whom do you scrutinize more thoroughly?"

Rebecca thought of her enemies and her lovers, and she was not sure.

"In front of your enemies you are always watchful, and with your lovers you may relax and close your eyes."

"Then I understand," Rebecca said. "For this might be a kind of war; and after the war is over, we may come together, former enemies, and celebrate the peace."

The sky became black as ink. The blossoms of the

almond tree fell, and she saw, within the branches, that the almonds would be bitter this year

"In peace the former enemies would close their eyes," the lion said, "and sleep together peacefully."

"Then we must be enemies forever?"

"For I am a zealous God. I am zealous of your eyes and your ears, which I gave you that you might avoid the agonies I visit upon you. I am zealous of your mind, which I made wary and facile, that you might always be thinking and planning ways to improve upon this world."

"Then I understand," Rebecca said fearfully, her voice breaking, "that all our lives we must fight against you...but when we die?"

The lamb scampered about the yard, but the lion reached out with a paw and laid the lamb out on the grass with its back broken. "*This* is the Mystery," the lion roared, consuming the lamb, leaving only a splash of blood steaming on the ground.

Rebecca leaped from her chair, horrified, and held out her hands to fend off the prowling beast. "I understand!" she screamed "You are a selfish God, and Your creation is a toy You can mangle at will! You do not love; you do not care; you are cold and cruel."

The lion sat to lick its chops. "And?" it asked menacingly.

Rebecca's face flushed. She felt a sudden anger. "I am better than You," she said quietly, "for I can love and feel compassion. How wrong we have been to send our prayers to You!"

"And?" the lion asked with a growl.

"There is much we can teach You!" she said. "For You do not know how to love or respect Your creation, or YourSelf! You are a wild beast, and it is our job to tame You and train You."

"Such dangerous knowledge," the lion said. The dove landed among the hairs of its mane. "Catch Me if you can," the dove sang. For an instant the Trinity shed its symbolic forms and revealed Its true Self, a thing beyond ugliness or beauty, a vast cyclic thing of no humanity whatsoever, dark and horribly young—and that truth reduced Rebecca to hysterics.

Then the Trinity vanished, and the world continued for another year.

But Rebecca was never the same again, for she had understood, and by her grace we have lived this added time.

Through Road No Whither

The long black Mercedes rumbled out of the fog on the road south from Dijon, moisture running in cold trickles across its windshield. Horst von Ranke carefully read the maps spread on his lap, eyeglasses perched low on his nose, while Waffen Schutzstaffel Oberleutnant Albert Fischer drove. "Thirty-five kilometers," Von Ranke said under his breath. "No more."

"We are lost," Fischer said. "We've already come thirty-six."

"Not quite that many. We should be there any minute now."

Fischer nodded and then shook his head. His high cheekbones and long, sharp nose only accentuated the black uniform with silver death's heads on the high, tight collar. Von Ranke wore a broad-striped gray suit; he was an undersecretary in the Propaganda Ministry. They might have been brothers, yet one had grown up in Czechoslovakia, the other in the Ruhr; one was the son of a brewer, the other of a coal-miner. They had met and become close friends in Paris, two years before, and were now sightseeing on a three-day pass in the countryside.

"Wait," Von Ranke said, peering through the drops on the side window. "Stop."

Fischer braked the car and looked in the direction of Von Ranke's long finger. Near the roadside, beyond a copse of young trees, was a low, thatch-roofed house with dirty gray walls, almost hidden by the fog.

"Looks empty," Von Ranke said.

"It is occupied; look at the smoke," Fischer said. "Perhaps somebody can tell us where we are."

They pulled the car over and got out, Von Ranke leading

the way across a mud path littered with wet straw. The hut looked even dirtier close-up. Smoke curled in a darker brown-gray twist from a hole in the peak of the thatch. Fischer nodded at his friend and they cautiously approached. Over the crude wooden door, letters wobbled unevenly in some alphabet neither knew, and between them they spoke nine languages. "Could that be Rom?" Fischer asked, frowning. "It does look familiar—like Slavic Rom."

"Gypsies? Romany don't live in huts like this, and besides, I thought they were rounded up long ago."

"That's what it looks like," Von Ranke repeated. "Still, maybe we can share some language, if only French."

He knocked on the door. After a long pause, he knocked again, and the door opened before his knuckles made the final rap. A woman too old to be alive stuck her long, wood-colored nose through the crack and peered at them with one good eye. The other was wrapped in a sunken caul of flesh. The hand that gripped the door edge was filthy, its nails long and black. Her toothless mouth cracked into a wrinkled grin. "Good evening," she said in perfect, even elegant, German. "What can I do for you?"

"We need to know if we are on the road to Dôle," Von Ranke said, controlling his revulsion.

"Then you're asking the wrong guide," the old woman said. Her hand withdrew and the door started to close. Fischer kicked out and pushed her back. The door swung open and began to lean on worn-out leather hinges.

"You do not treat us with the proper respect," he said. "What do you mean, 'the wrong guide'? What kind of guide are you?"

"*So strong,*" the old woman crooned, wrapping her hands in front of her withered chest and backing into the gloom. She wore ageless gray rags. Tattered knit sleeves extended to her wrists.

"Answer me!" Fischer said, advancing despite the strong odor of urine and decay in the hut.

"The maps I know are not for this land," she sang, doddering before a cold and empty hearth.

"She's crazy," Von Ranke said. "Let the local authorities take care of her. Let's be off." But a wild look was in Fischer's eyes. So much filth, so much disarray, and impudence as well; these things made him angry.

"What maps *do* you know, crazy woman?" he demanded.

"Maps in time," the old woman said. She let her hands fall to her sides and lowered her head as if, in admitting her specialty, she were suddenly humble.

"Then tell us where we are," Fischer sneered.

"Come," Von Ranke said, but he knew it was too late. There would be an end, but it would be on his friend's terms, and it might not be pleasant.

"On a through road no whither," the old woman said.

"What?" Fischer towered over her. She stared up as if at some prodigal son, her gums shining spittle.

"If you wish a reading, sit," she said, indicating a low table and three dilapidated cane and leather chairs. Fischer glanced at her, then at the table.

"Very well," he said, suddenly and falsely obsequious. Another game, Von Ranke realized. Cat and mouse.

Fischer pulled out a chair for his friend and sat across from the old woman. "Put your hands on the table, palms down, both of them, both of you," she said. They did so. She lay her ear to the table as if listening, eyes going to the beams of light sneaking through the thatch. "Arrogance," she said. Fischer did not react.

"A road going into fire and death," she said. "Your cities

in flame, your women and children shriveling to black dolls in the heat of their burning homes. The camps are found and you stand accused of hideous crimes. Many are tried and hung. Your nation is disgraced, your cause abhorred." Now a peculiar gleam appeared in her eye. "Only psychotics will believe in you, the lowest of the low. Your nation will be divided between your enemies. All will be lost."

Fischer's smile did not waver. He pulled a coin from his pocket and threw it down before the woman, then pushed the chair back and stood. "Your maps are as crooked as your chin, you filthy old hag," he said. "Let's go."

"I've been suggesting that," Von Ranke said. Fischer made no move to leave. Von Ranke tugged on his arm but the SS Oberleutnant shrugged free of his friend's grip.

"Gypsies are few, now, hag," he said. "Soon to be fewer by one." Von Ranke managed to urge him just outside the door. The woman followed and shaded her eye against the misty light.

"I am no gypsy," she said. "You do not even recognize the words?" She pointed at the letters above the door.

Fischer squinted, and the light of recognition dawned in his eyes. "Yes," he said. "Yes, I do, now. A dead language."

"What are they?" Von Ranke asked, uneasy.

"Hebrew, I think," Fischer said. "She is a Jewess."

"No!" the woman cackled. "I am no Jew."

Von Ranke thought the woman looked younger now, or at least stronger, and his unease deepened.

"I do not care what you are," Fischer said quietly. "I only wish we were in my father's time." He took a step toward her. She did not retreat. Her face became almost youthfully bland, and her bad eye seemed to fill in. "Then, there would be no regulations, no rules—I could take this pistol"—he tapped his holster—"and apply it to your filthy Kike head, and perhaps kill the last Jew in Europe." He unstrapped the holster. The woman straightened in the dark hut, as if drawing strength from Fischer's abusive tongue. Von Ranke feared for his friend. Rashness could get them in trouble.

"This is not our fathers' time," he reminded Fischer.

Fischer paused, pistol in hand, his finger curling around the trigger. "Filthy, smelly old woman." She did not look nearly as old as when they had entered the hut, perhaps not old at all, and certainly not bent and crippled. "You have had a very narrow escape this afternoon."

"You have no idea who I am," the woman half sang, half moaned.

"*Scheisse,*" Fischer spat. "Now we will go to report you and your hovel."

"I am the scourge," she breathed. Her breath smelled like burning stone even three strides away. She backed into the hut but her voice did not diminish. "I am the visible hand, the pillar of cloud by day and the pillar of fire by night."

Fischer laughed. "You're right," he said to Von Ranke. "She isn't worth our trouble." He turned and stamped out the door. Von Ranke followed with one last glance over his shoulder into the gloom, the decay. *No one has lived in this hut for years,* he thought. Her shadow was gray and indefinite before the ancient stone hearth, behind the leaning, dust-covered table.

In the car, Von Ranke sighed. "You *do* tend to arrogance, you know that?"

Fischer grinned and shook his head. "You drive, old friend. *I'll* look at the maps." Von Ranke ramped up the Mercedes' turbine until its whine was high and steady and its exhaust cut a swirling hole in the fog. "No wonder we're lost," Fischer said. He shook out the Pan-Deutschland map peevishly. "This is five years old—1979."

"We'll find our way," Von Ranke said.

From the door of the hut, the old woman watched, head bobbing. "I am not a Jew," she said, "but I loved them, too, oh, yes. I loved all my children."

She raised her hand as the long black car roared into the fog. "I will bring you to justice, wherever and whenever you live, and all your children, and their children's children," she said. She dropped a twist of smoke from her elbow to the dirt floor and waggled her finger. The smoke danced and drew black figures in the dirt. "Into the time of your fathers." The fog grew thinner. She brought her arm down, and forty years melted away with the mist.

High above, a deeper growl descended on the road. A wide-winged shadow passed over the hut, wings flashing stars, black and white invasion stripes, and cannon fire.

"Hungry bird," the shapeless figure said. "Time to feed."

Petra

"'God is dead, God is dead'... Perdition! When God dies, you'll know it."

—Confessions of St. Argentine

I'm an ugly son of stone and flesh, there's no denying it. I don't remember my mother. It's possible she abandoned me shortly after my birth. More than likely she is dead. My father—ugly beaked, half-winged thing, if he resembles his son—I have never seen.

Why should such an unfortunate aspire to be a historian? I think I can trace the moment my choice was made. It's among my earliest memories, and it must have happened about thirty years ago, though I'm sure I lived many years before that—years now lost to me. I was squatting behind thick, dusty curtains in a vestibule, listening to a priest instructing other novitiates, all of pure flesh, about Mortdieu. His words are still vivid.

"As near as I can discover," he said, "Mortdieu occurred about seventy-seven years ago. Learned ones deny that magic was set loose on the world, but few deny that God, as such, had died."

Indeed. That's putting it mildly. All the hinges of our once-great universe fell apart, the axis tilted, cosmic doors swung shut, and the rules of existence lost their foundations. The priest continued in measured, awed tones to describe that time.

"I have heard wise men speak of the slow decline. Where human thought was strong, reality's sudden quaking was reduced to a tremor. Where thought was weak, reality disappeared completely, swallowed by chaos. Every delusion became as real as solid matter." His voice trembled with emotion. "Blinding pain, blood catching fire in our veins, bones snapping and flesh powdering. Steel flowing like liquid. Amber raining from the sky. Crowds gathering in streets that no longer followed any maps, if the maps themselves had not altered. They knew not what to do. Their weak minds could not grab hold..."

Most humans, I take it, were entirely too irrational to begin with. Whole nations vanished or were turned into incomprehensible whirlpools of misery and depravity. It is said that certain universities, libraries, and museums survived, but to this day we have little contact with them.

I think often of those poor victims of the early days of Mortdieu. They had known a world of some stability; we have adapted since. They were shocked by cities turning into forests, by their nightmares taking shape before their eyes. Prodigal crows perched atop trees that had once been buildings, pigs ran through the streets on their hind legs...and so on. (The priest did not encourage contemplation of the oddities. "Excitement," he said, "breeds even more monsters.")

Our Cathedral survived. Rationality in this neighborhood, however, had weakened some centuries before Mortdieu, replaced only by a kind of rote. The Cathedral suffered. Survivors—clergy and staff, worshipers seeking sanctuary—had wretched visions, dreamed wretched dreams. They saw the stone ornaments of the Cathedral come alive. With someone to see and believe, in a universe lacking any other foundation, my ancestors shook off stone and became flesh. Centuries of stone celibacy weighed upon them. Forty-nine nuns who had sought shelter in the Cathedral were discovered and were not entirely loath, so the coarser versions of the tale go. Mortdieu had had a surprising aphrodisiacal effect on the faithful and conjugation took place.

No definite gestation period has been established, for at that time the great stone wheel had not been set twisting back and forth to count the hours. Nor had anyone been given the chair of Kronos to watch over the wheel and provide a baseline for everyday activities.

But flesh did not reject stone, and there came into being the sons and daughters of flesh and stone, including me. Those who had fornicated with the inhuman figures were cast out to raise or reject their monstrous young in the highest hidden recesses. Those who had accepted the embraces of the stone saints and other human figures were less abused but still banished to the upper reaches. A wooden scaffolding was erected, dividing the great nave into two levels. A canvas drop cloth was fastened over the scaffold to prevent offal raining down, and on the second level of the Cathedral the more human offspring of stone and flesh set about creating a new life.

I have long tried to find out how some semblance of order came to the world. Legend has it that it was the archexistentialist Jansard crucifier of the beloved St. Argentine—who, realizing and repenting his error, discovered that mind and thought could calm the foaming sea of reality.

The priest finished his all-too-sketchy lecture by touching on this point briefly: "With the passing of God's watchful gaze, humanity had to reach out and grab hold the unraveling fabric of the world. Those left alive—those who had the wits to keep their bodies from falling apart—became the only cohesive force in the chaos."

I had picked up enough language to understand what he said; my memory was good—still is—and I was curious enough to want to know more.

Creeping along stone walls behind the curtains, I listened to other priests and nuns intoning scripture to gaggles of flesh children. That was on the ground floor, and I was in great danger; the people of pure flesh looking on my kind as abominations. But it was worth it.

I was able to steal a Psalter and learned to read. I stole other books; they defined my world by allowing me to compare it with others. At first I couldn't believe the others had ever existed; only the Cathedral was real. I still have my doubts. I can look out a tiny round window on one side of my room and see the great forest and river that surround the Cathedral, but I can see nothing else. So my experience with other worlds is far from direct.

No matter. I read a great deal, but I'm no scholar. What concerns me is recent history—the final focus of that germinal hour listening to the priest. From the metaphysical to the acutely personal.

I am small—barely three English feet in height—but I can run quickly through most of the hidden passageways. This lets me observe without attracting attention. I may be the only historian in this whole structure. Others who claim the role disregard what's before their eyes, in search of ultimate truths, or at least Big Pictures. So if you prefer history where the historian is not involved, look to the others. Objective as I try to be, I do have my favorite subjects.

In the time when my history begins, the children of stone and flesh were still searching for the Stone Christ. Those of us born of the union of the stone saints and gargoyles with the bereaved nuns thought our salvation lay in the great stone celibate, who came to life as all the other statues had.

Of smaller import were the secret assignations between the bishop's daughter and a young man of stone and flesh. Such assignations were forbidden even between those of pure flesh; and as these two lovers were unmarried, their compound sin intrigued me.

Her name was Constantia, and she was fourteen, slender

of limb, brown of hair, mature of bosom. Her eyes carried the stupid sort of divine life common in girls that age. His name was Corvus, and he was fifteen. I don't recall his precise features, but he was handsome enough and dexterous: he could climb through the scaffolding almost as quickly as I. I first spied them talking when I made one of my frequent raids on the repository to steal another book. They were in shadow, but my eyes are keen. They spoke softly, hesitantly. My heart ached to see them and to think of their tragedy, for I knew right away that Corvus was not pure flesh and that Constantia was the daughter of the bishop himself. I envisioned the old tyrant meting out the usual punishment to Corvus for such breaches of level and morality—castration. But in their talk was a sweetness that almost masked the closed-in stench of the lower nave.

"Have you ever kissed a man before?"

"Yes."

"Who?"

"My brother." She laughed.

"And?" His voice was sharper; he might kill her brother, he seemed to say.

"A friend named Jules."

"Where is he?"

"Oh, he vanished on a wood-gathering expedition."

"Oh." And he kissed her again.

I'm a historian, not a voyeur, so I discreetly hide the flowering of their passion. If Corvus had had any sense, he would have reveled in his conquest and never returned. But he was snared and continued to see her despite the risk. This was loyalty, love, faithfulness, and it was rare. It fascinated me.

*   *   *

I have just been taking in sun, a nice day, and looking out over the buttresses.

The Cathedral is like a low-bellied lizard, the nave its belly, the buttresses its legs. There are little houses at the base of each buttress, where rainspouters with dragon faces used to lean out over the trees (or city or whatever was down below once). Now people live there. It wasn't always that way—the sun was once forbidden. Corvus and Constantia from childhood were denied its light, and so even in their youthful prime they were pale and dirty with the smoke of candles and tallow lamps. The most sun anyone received in those days was obtained on wood-gathering expeditions.

After spying on one of the clandestine meetings of the young lovers, I mused in a dark corner for an hour, then went to see the copper giant Apostle Thomas. He was the only human form to live so high in the Cathedral. He carried a ruler on which was engraved his real name—he had been modeled after the Cathedral's restorer in times past, the architect Viollet-le-Duc. He knew the Cathedral better than anyone, and I admired him greatly. Most of the monsters left him alone—out of fear, if nothing else. He was huge, black as night, but flaked with pale green, his face creased in eternal thought. He was sitting in his usual wooden compartment near the base of the spire, not twenty feet from where I write now, thinking about times none of the rest of us ever knew: of joy and past love, some say; others say of the burden that rested on him now that the Cathedral was the center of this chaotic world.

It was the giant who selected me from the ugly hordes when he saw me with a Psalter. He encouraged me in my efforts to read. "Your eyes are bright," he told me. "You move as if your brain were quick, and you keep yourself dry and clean. You aren't hollow like the rainspouters—you have substance. For all our sakes, put it to use and learn the ways of the Cathedral."

And so I did.

He looked up as I came in. I sat on a box near his feet and said, "A daughter of flesh is seeing a son of stone and flesh."

He shrugged his massive shoulders. "So it shall be, in time."

"Is it not a sin?"

"It is something so monstrous it is past sin and become necessity," he said. "It will happen more as time passes."

"They're in love, I think, or will be."

He nodded. "I—and One Other—were the only ones to abstain from fornication on the night of Mortdieu," he said. "I am—except for the Other—alone fit to judge."

I waited for him to judge, but he sighed and patted me on the shoulder. "And I never judge, do I, ugly friend?"

"Never," I said.

"So leave me alone to be sad." He winked. "And more power to them."

The bishop of the Cathedral was an old, old man. It was said he hadn't been bishop before the Mortdieu, but a wanderer who came in during the chaos, before the forest had replaced the city. He had set himself up as titular head of this section of God's former domain by saying it had been willed to him.

He was short, stout, with huge hairy arms like the clamps of a vise. He had once killed a spouter with a single squeeze of his fist, and spouters are tough things, since they have no guts like you (I suppose) and I. The hair surrounding his bald pate was white, thick, and unruly, and his eyebrows leaned over his nose with marvelous flexibility. He rutted like a pig, ate hugely, and shat liquidly (I know all). A man for this time, if ever there was one.

It was his decree that all those not pure of flesh be banned and that those not of human form be killed on sight.

When I returned from the giant's chamber, I saw that the lower nave was in an uproar. They had seen someone clambering about in the scaffold, and troops had been sent to shoot him down. Of course it was Corvus. I was a quicker climber than he and knew the beams better, so when he found himself trapped in an apparent cul-de-sac, it was I who gestured from the shadows and pointed to a hole large enough for him to escape through. He took it without a breath of thanks, but etiquette has never been important to me. I entered the stone wall through a nook a spare hand's width across and wormed my way to the bottom to see what else was happening. Excitement was rare.

A rumor was passing that the figure had been seen with a young girl, but the crowds didn't know who the girl was. The men and women who mingled in the smoky light, between the rows of open-roofed hovels, chattered gaily. Castrations and executions were among the few joys for us then; I relished them too, but I had a stake in the potential victims now and I worried.

My worry and my interest got the better of me. I slid through an unrepaired gap and fell to one side of the alley between the outer wall and the hovels. A group of dirty adolescents spotted me. "There he is!" they screeched. "He didn't get away!"

The bishop's masked troops can travel freely on all levels. I was almost cornered by them, and when I tried one escape route, they waited at a crucial spot in the stairs—which I had to cross to complete the next leg—and

I was forced back. I prided myself in knowing the Cathedral top to bottom, but as I scrambled madly, I came upon a tunnel I had never noticed before. It led deep into a broad stone foundation wall. I was safe for the moment but afraid that they might find my caches of food and poison my casks of rainwater. Still, there was nothing I could do until they had gone, so I decided to spend the anxious hours exploring the tunnel.

The Cathedral is a constant surprise; I realize now I didn't know half of what it offered. There are always new ways to get from here to there (some, I suspect, created while no one is looking), and sometimes even new theres to be discovered. While troops snuffled about the hole above, near the stairs—where only a child of two or three could have entered—I followed a flight of crude steps deep into the stone. Water and slime made the passage slippery and difficult. For a moment I was in darkness deeper than any I had experienced before—a gloom more profound than mere lack of light could explain. Then below I saw a faint yellow gleam. More cautious, I slowed and progressed silently. Behind a rusting, scabrous metal gate, I set foot into a lighted room. There was the smell of crumbling stone, a tang of mineral water, slime—and the stench of a dead spouter. The beast lay on the floor of the narrow chamber, several months gone but still fragrant.

I have mentioned that spouters are very hard to kill—and this one had been murdered. Three candles stood freshly placed in nooks around the chamber, flickering in a faint draft from above. Despite my fears, I walked across the stone floor, took a candle, and peered into the next section of tunnel.

It sloped down for several dozen feet, ending at another metal gate. It was here that I detected an odor I had never before encountered—the smell of the purest of stones, as

of rare jade or virgin marble. Such a feeling of lightheaded-
ness passed over me that I almost laughed, but I was too
cautious for that. I pushed aside the gate and was greeted
by a rush of the coldest, sweetest air, like a draft from the
tomb of a saint whose body does not corrupt but rather,
draws corruption away and expels it miraculously into
the nether pits. My beak dropped open. The candlelight
fell across the darkness onto a figure I at first thought to
be an infant. But I quickly disagreed with myself. The
figure was several ages at once. As I blinked, it became a
man of about thirty, well formed, with a high forehead
and elegant hands, pale as ice. His eyes stared at the wall
behind me. I bowed down on scaled knee and touched my
forehead as best I could to the cold stone, shivering to my
vestigial wing-tips. "Forgive me, Joy of Man's Desiring,"
I said. "Forgive me." I had stumbled upon the hiding place
of the Stone Christ.

"You are forgiven," He said wearily. "You had to come
sooner or later. Better now than later, when..." His voice
trailed away and He shook His head. He was very thin,
wrapped in a gray robe that still bore the scars of centuries
of weathering. "Why did you come?"

"To escape the bishop's troops," I said.

He nodded. "Yes. The bishop. How long have I been
here?"

"Since before I was born, Lord. Sixty or seventy years."
He was thin, almost ethereal, this figure I had imagined
as a husky carpenter. I lowered my voice and beseeched,
"What may I do for you, Lord?"

"Go away," He said.

"I could not live with such a secret," I said. "You are
salvation. You can overthrow the bishop and bring all the
levels together."

"I am not a general or a soldier. Please go away and tell no—"

I felt a breath behind me, then the whisper of a weapon. I leaped aside, and my hackles rose as a stone sword came down and shattered on the floor beside me. The Christ raised His hand. Still in shock, I stared at a beast much like myself. It stared back, face black with rage, stayed by the power of His hand. I should have been more wary—something had to have killed the spouter and kept the candles fresh.

"But, Lord," the beast rumbled, "he will tell all."

"No," the Christ said. "He'll tell nobody." He looked half at me, half through me, and said, "Go, go."

Up the tunnels, into the orange dark of the Cathedral, crying, I crawled and slithered. I could not even go to the giant. I had been silenced as effectively as if my throat had been cut.

The next morning I watched from a shadowy corner of the scaffold as a crowd gathered around a lone man in a dirty sackcloth robe. I had seen him before—his name was Psalo, and he was left alone as an example of the bishop's largess. It was a token gesture; most of the people regarded him as barely half-sane.

Yet this time I listened and, in my confusion, found his words striking responsive chords in me. He was exhorting the bishop and his forces to allow light into the Cathedral again by dropping the canvas tarps that covered the windows. He had talked about this before, and the bishop had responded with his usual statement—that with the light would come more chaos, for the human mind was now a pesthole of delusions. Any stimulus would drive away whatever security the inhabitants of the Cathedral had.

* * *

At this time it gave me no pleasure to watch the love of Constantia and Corvus grow. They were becoming more careless. Their talk grew bolder:

"We shall announce a marriage," Corvus said.

"They will never allow it. They'll...cut you."

"I'm nimble. They'll never catch me. The church needs leaders, brave revolutionaries. If no one breaks with tradition, everyone will suffer."

"I fear for your life—and mine. My father would push me from the flock like a diseased lamb."

"Your father is no shepherd."

"He is my father," Constantia said, eyes wide, mouth drawn tight.

I sat with beak in paws, eyes half-lidded, able to mimic each statement before it was uttered. Undying love...hope for a bleak future...shite and onions! I had read it all before, in a cache of romance novels in the trash of a dead nun. As soon as I made the connection and realized the timeless banality—and the futility—of what I was seeing, and when I compared their prattle with the infinite sadness of the Stone Christ, I went from innocent to cynic. The transition dizzied me, leaving little backwaters of noble emotion, but the future seemed clear. Corvus would be caught and executed; if it hadn't been for me, he would already have been gelded, if not killed. Constantia would weep, poison herself; the singers would sing of it (those selfsame warble-throats who cheered the death of her lover); perhaps I would write of it (I was planning this chronicle even then), and afterward, perhaps, I would follow them both, having succumbed to the sin of boredom.

With night, things become less certain. It is easy to stare at a dark wall and let dreams become manifest. At one time, I've deduced from books, dreams could not take shape beyond sleep or brief fantasy. All too often I've had to fight things generated in my dreams, flowing from the walls, suddenly independent and hungry. People often die in the night, devoured by their own nightmares.

That evening, falling to sleep with visions of the Stone Christ in my head, I dreamed of holy men, angels, and saints. I came awake abruptly, by training, and saw that one had stayed behind. The others I saw flitting outside the round window, where they whispered and made plans for flying off to heaven. The wraith that had lingered made a dark, vague shape in one corner. His breath came new to him, raw and harsh. "I am Peter," he said, "also called Simon. I am the Rock of the Church, and popes are told that they are heir to my task."

"I'm rock, too," I said. "At least, part of me is."

"So be it, then. You are heir to my task. Go forth and be Pope. Do not revere the Stone Christ, for a Christ is only as good as He does, and if He does nothing, there is no salvation in Him."

The shadow reached out to pat my head. I saw his eyes grow wide as he made out my form. He muttered some formula for banishing devils and oozed out the window to join his fellows.

I imagined that if such a thing were actually brought before the council, it would be decided under the law that the command of a dream saint is not binding. I did not care. The wraith had given me better orders than any I'd had since the giant told me to read and learn.

But to be Pope, one must have a hierarchy of servants to carry out one's plans. The biggest of rocks does not move by itself. So it was that, swollen with power, I decided to appear in the upper nave and announce myself to the people.

*　　*　　*

It took a great deal of courage to show myself in broad daylight, without my cloak, and to walk across the scaffold's surface, on the second level, through crowds of vendors setting up the market for the day. Some saw me and reacted with typical bigotry. They kicked and cursed at me. My beak was swift and discouraged them.

I clambered to the top of a prominent stall and stood in the murky glow of a small lamp, rising to my full height and clearing my throat, making ready to give my commands. Under a hail of rotten pomegranates and limp vegetables, I told the throng who I was. I boldly told them about my vision. I tried to make myself speak clearly, starting over from the beginning several times, but the deluge of opprobrium was too thick. Jeweled with beads of offal, I jumped down and fled to a tunnel entrance too small for most men. Some boys followed, ready to do me real harm, and one lost his finger while trying to slice me with a fragment of colored glass.

I recognized, almost too late, that the tactic of open revelation was worthless. There are levels of fear and bigotry, and I was at the very bottom.

My next strategy was to find some way to disrupt the Cathedral from top to bottom. Even bigots, when reduced to a mob, could be swayed by the presence of one obviously ordained and capable. I spent two days skulking through the walls. There had to be a basic flaw in so fragile a structure as the church, and, while I wasn't contemplating total destruction, I wanted something spectacular, unavoidable.

While I cogitated, hanging from the bottom of the second scaffold, above the community of pure flesh, the bishop's deep gravelly voice roared over the noise of the crowd. I opened my eyes and looked down. The masked troops were holding a bowed figure, and the bishop was intoning over its head, "Know all who hear me now, this young bastard of flesh and stone—"

Corvus, I told myself. Finally caught. I shut one eye, but the other refused to close out the scene.

"—has violated all we hold sacred and shall atone for his crimes on this spot, tomorrow at this time. Kronos! Mark the wheel's progress." The elected Kronos, a spindly old man with dirty gray hair down to his buttocks, took a piece of charcoal and marked an X on the huge bulkhead chart, behind which the wheel groaned and sighed in its circuit.

The crowd was enthusiastic. I saw Psalo pushing through the people.

"What crime?" he called out. "Name the crime!"

"Violation of the lower level!" the head of the masked troops declared.

"That merits a whipping and an escort upstairs," Psalo said. "I detect a more sinister crime here. What is it?"

The bishop looked Psalo down coldly. "He tried to rape my daughter, Constantia."

Psalo could say nothing to that. The penalty was castration and death. All the pure humans accepted such laws. There was no other recourse.

I mused, watching Corvus being led to the dungeons. The future that I desired at that moment startled me with its clarity. I wanted that part of my heritage that had been denied to me—to be at peace with myself, to be surrounded by those who accepted me, by those no better than I. In time that would happen, as the giant had said. But would I ever see it? What Corvus, in his own lusty way, was trying to do was equalize the levels, to bring stone into flesh until no one could define the divisions.

Well, my plans beyond that point were very hazy. They were less plans than glowing feelings, imaginings of happiness and children playing in the forest and fields beyond the island as the world knit itself under the gaze of God's heir. My children, playing in the forest. A touch of truth came to me at this moment. I had wished to be Corvus when he tupped Constantia.

So I had two tasks, then, that could be merged if I was clever. I had to distract the bishop and his troops, and I had to rescue Corvus, fellow revolutionary.

I spent that night in feverish misery in my room. At dawn I went to the giant and asked his advice. He looked me over coldly and said, "We waste our time if we try to knock sense into their heads. But we have no better calling than to waste our time, do we?"

"What shall I do?"

"Enlighten them."

I stomped my claw on the floor. "They are bricks! Try enlightening bricks!"

He smiled his sad, narrow smile. "Enlighten them," he said.

I left the giant's chamber in a rage. I did not have access to the great wheel's board of time, so I couldn't know exactly when the execution would take place. But I guessed—from memories of a grumbling stomach—that it would be in the early afternoon. I traveled from one end of the nave to the other and, likewise, the transept. I nearly exhausted myself.

Then, traversing an empty aisle, I picked up a piece of colored glass and examined it, puzzled. Many of the boys on all levels carried these shards with them, and the girls used them as jewelry—against the wishes of their elders, who held that bright objects bred more beasts in the mind. Where did they get them?

In one of the books I had perused years before, I had seen brightly colored pictures of the Cathedral windows. "Enlighten them," the giant had said.

Psalo's request to let light into the Cathedral came to mind.

Along the peak of the nave, in a tunnel running its length, I found the ties that held the pulleys of the canvases over the windows. The best windows, I decided, would be the huge ones of the north and south transepts. I made a diagram in the dust, trying to decide what season it was and from which direction the sunlight would come—pure theory to me, but at this moment I was in a fever of brilliance. All the windows had to be clear. I could not decide which was best.

I was ready by early afternoon, just after sext prayers in the upper nave. I had cut the major ropes and weakened the clamps by prying them from the walls with a pick stolen from the bishop's armory. I walked along a high ledge, took an almost vertical shaft through the wall to the lower floor, and waited.

Constantia watched from a wooden balcony, the bishop's special box for executions. She had a terrified, fascinated look on her face. Corvus was on the dais across the nave, right in the center of the cross of the transept. Torches illumined him and his executioners, three men and an old woman.

I knew the procedure. The old woman would castrate him first, then the men would remove his head. He was dressed in the condemned red robe to hide any blood. Blood excitement among the impressionable was the last thing the bishop wanted. Troops waited around the dais to purify the area with scented water.

I didn't have much time. It would take minutes for the system of ropes and pulleys to clear and the canvases to fall. I went to my station and severed the remaining ties. Then, as the Cathedral filled with a hollow creaking sound, I followed the shaft back to my viewing post.

In three minutes the canvases were drooping. I saw Corvus look up, his eyes glazed. The bishop was with his daughter in the box. He pulled her back into the shadows. In another two minutes the canvases fell onto the upper scaffold with a hideous crash. Their weight was too great for the ends of the structure, and it collapsed, allowing the canvas to cascade to the floor many yards below. At first the illumination was dim and bluish, filtered perhaps by a passing cloud. Then, from one end of the Cathedral to the other, a burst of light threw my smoky world into clarity. The glory of thousands of pieces of colored glass, hidden for decades and hardly touched by childish vandals, fell upon upper and lower levels at once. A cry from the crowds nearly wrenched me from my post. I slid quickly to the lower level and hid, afraid of what I had done. This was more than simple sunlight. Like the blossoming of two flowers, one brighter than the other, the transept windows astounded all who beheld them.

Eyes accustomed to orangey dark, to smoke and haze and shadow, cannot stare into such glory without drastic effect. I shielded my own face and tried to find a convenient exit.

But the population was increasing. As the light brightened and more faces rose to be locked, phototropic, the splendor unhinged some people. From their minds poured contents too wondrous to be accurately cataloged. The monsters thus released were not violent, however, and most of the visions were not monstrous.

The upper and lower nave shimmered with reflected glories, with dream figures and children clothed in baubles of light. Saints and prodigies dominated. A thousand newly created youngsters squatted on the bright floor and began to tell of marvels, of cities in the East, and times as they had once been. Clowns dressed in fire entertained from the tops of the market stalls. Animals unknown to the Cathedral cavorted between the dwellings, giving friendly advice. Abstract things, glowing balls in nets of gold and ribbons of silk, sang and floated around the upper reaches. The Cathedral became a great vessel of all the bright dreams known to its citizens.

Slowly, from the lower nave, people of pure flesh climbed to the scaffold and walked the upper nave to see what they couldn't from below. From my hideaway I watched the masked troops of the bishop carrying his litter up narrow stairs. Constantia walked behind, stumbling, her eyes shut in the new brightness.

All tried to cover their eyes, but none for long succeeded.

I wept. Almost blind with tears, I made my way still higher and looked down on the roiling crowds. I saw Corvus, his hands still wrapped in restraining ropes, being led by the old woman.

Constantia saw him, too, and they regarded each other like strangers, then joined hands as best they could. She borrowed a knife from one of her father's soldiers and cut his ropes away. Around them the brightest dreams of all began to swirl, pure white and blood-red and sea-green, coalescing into visions of all the children they would innocently have.

I gave them a few hours to regain their senses—and to regain my own. Then I stood on the bishop's abandoned podium and shouted over the heads of those on the lowest level.

"The time has come!" I cried. "We must all unite now; we must unite—"

At first they ignored me. I was quite eloquent, but their excitement was still too great. So I waited some more, began to speak again, and was shouted down. Bits of fruit and vegetables arced up. "Freak!" they screamed, and drove me away.

I crept along the stone stairs, found the narrow crack, and hid in it, burying my beak in my paws, wondering what had gone wrong. It took a surprisingly long time for me to realize that, in my case, it was less the stigma of stone than the ugliness of my shape that doomed my quest for leadership.

I had, however, paved the way for the Stone Christ. He will surely be able to take His place now, I told myself. So I maneuvered along the crevice until I came to the hidden chamber and the yellow glow. All was quiet within. I met first the stone monster, who looked me over suspiciously with glazed gray eyes. "You're back," he said. Overcome by his wit, I leered, nodded, and asked that I be presented to the Christ.

"He's sleeping."

"Important tidings," I said.

"What?"

"I bring glad tidings."

"Then let me hear them."

"His ears only."

Out of the gloomy corner came the Christ, looking much older now. "What is it?" He asked.

"I have prepared the way for You," I said. "Simon called Peter told me I was the heir to his legacy, that I should go before You—"

The Stone Christ shook His head. "You believe I am the fount from which all blessings flow?"

I nodded, uncertain.

"What have you done out there?"

"Let in the light," I said.

He shook His head. "You seem a wise enough creature. You know about Mortdieu."

"Yes."

"Then you should know that I barely have enough power to keep myself together, to heal myself, much less to minister to those out there." He gestured beyond the walls. "My own source has gone away," He said mournfully. "I'm operating on reserves, and those none too vast."

"He wants you to go away and stop bothering us," the monster explained.

"They have their light out there," the Christ said. "They'll play with that for a while, get tired of it, go back to what they had before. Is there any place for you in that?"

I thought for a moment, then shook my head. "No place," I said. "I'm too ugly."

"You are too ugly, and I am too famous," He said. "I'd have to come from their midst, anonymous, and that is clearly impossible. No, leave them alone for a while. They'll make me over again, perhaps, or better still, forget about me. About us. We don't have any place there."

I was stunned. I sat down hard on the stone floor, and the Christ patted me on my head as He walked by. "Go back to your hiding place; live as well as you can," He said. "Our time is over."

I turned to go. When I reached the crevice, I heard His voice behind, saying, "Do you play bridge? If you do, find another. We need four to a table."

I clambered up the crack, through the walls, and along the arches over the revelry. Not only was I not going to be Pope—after an appointment by Saint Peter himself!—but I couldn't convince someone much more qualified than I to assume the leadership.

It is the sign of the eternal student, I suppose, that when his wits fail him, he returns to the teacher.

I returned to the copper giant. He was lost in meditation. About his feet were scattered scraps of paper with detailed drawings of parts of the Cathedral. I waited patiently until he saw me. He turned, chin in hand, and looked me over.

"Why so sad?"

I shook my head. Only he could read my features and recognize my moods.

"Did you take my advice below? I heard a commotion."

"Mea maxima culpa," I said.

"And...?"

I hesitantly made my report, concluding with the refusal of the Stone Christ. The giant listened closely without interrupting. When I was done, he stood, towering over me, and pointed with his ruler through an open portal.

"Do you see that out there?" he asked. The ruler swept over the forests beyond the island, to the far green horizon. I replied that I did and waited for him to continue. He seemed to be lost in thought again.

"Once there was a city where trees now grow," he said. "Artists came by the thousands, and whores, and philosophers, and academics. And when God died, all the academics and whores and artists couldn't hold the fabric of the world together. How do you expect us to succeed now?"

Us? "Expectations should not determine whether one acts or not," I said. "Should they?"

The giant laughed and tapped my head with the ruler. "Maybe we've been given a sign, and we just have to learn how to interpret it correctly."

I leered to show I was puzzled.

"Maybe Mortdieu is really a sign that we have been

weaned. We must forage for ourselves, remake the world without help. What do you think of that?"

I was too tired to judge the merits of what he was saying, but I had never known the giant to be wrong before. "Okay. I grant that. So?"

"The Stone Christ tells us His charge is running down. If God weans us from the old ways, we can't expect His Son to replace the nipple, can we?"

"No..."

He hunkered next to me, his face bright. "I wondered who would really stand forth. It's obvious He won't. So, little one, who's the next choice?"

"Me?" I asked, meekly. The giant looked me over almost pityingly.

"No," he said after a time. "I am the next. We're *weaned!*" He did a little dance, startling my beak up out of my paws. I blinked. He grabbed my vestigial wing-tips and pulled me upright. "Stand straight. Tell me more."

"About what?"

"Tell me all that's going on below, and whatever else you know."

"I'm trying to figure out what you're saying," I protested, trembling a bit.

"Dense as stone!" Grinning, he bent over me. Then the grin went away, and he tried to look stern. "It's a grave responsibility. We must remake the world ourselves now. We must coordinate our thoughts, our dreams. Chaos won't do. What an opportunity, to be the architect of an entire universe!" He waved the ruler at the ceiling. "To build the very skies! The last world was a training ground, full of harsh rules and strictures. Now we've been told we're ready to leave that behind, move on to something more mature. Did I teach you any of the rules of architecture? I mean, the aesthetics. The need for harmony, interaction, utility, beauty?"

"Some," I said.

"Good. I don't think making the universe anew will require any better rules. No doubt we'll need to experiment, and perhaps one or more of our great spires will topple. But now we work for ourselves, to our own glory, and to the greater glory of the God who made us! No, ugly friend?"

Like many histories, mine must begin with the small, the tightly focused, and expand into the large. But unlike most historians, I don't have the luxury of time. Indeed, my story isn't even concluded yet.

Soon the legions of Viollet-le-Duc will begin their campaigns. Most have been schooled pretty thoroughly. Kidnapped from below, brought up in the heights, taught as I was. We'll begin returning them, one by one.

I teach off and on, write off and on, observe all the time.

The next step will be the biggest. I haven't any idea how we're going to do it.

But, as the giant puts it, "Long ago the roof fell in. Now we must push it up again, strengthen it, repair the beams." At this point he smiles to the pupils. "Not just repair them. Replace them! Now we are the beams. Flesh and stone become something much stronger."

Ah, but then some dolt will raise a hand and inquire, "What if our arms get tired holding up the sky?"

Our task, I think, will never end.

THE WAY OF ALL GHOSTS

A Myth from Thistledown

For William Hope Hodgson

And now, a long venture back to the Borderlands of SF...

The following novella pushes the boundaries between science fiction and fantasy. I think it still comes out on the side of science fiction—and it is part of my *Thistledown* sequence, *Eon, Eternity,* and *Legacy.* But the fantasy elements and underpinnings will be apparent to any sophisticated reader of fantasy, and so, I include it here.

William Hope Hodgson wrote a number of extraordinary novels and stories in his short career. My favorite is *The House on the Borderland,* an authentic visionary masterpiece that just tips the scales into fantasy. While it borrows some mood and timescale from H.G. Wells's *The Time Machine*, it also points toward authors as diverse as Arthur Machen and George MacDonald, and presages H.P. Lovecraft.

Hodgson's magnum opus, *The Night Land,* published in 1912, is less successful, but still brilliant. Today, *The Night Land* is a difficult book to read—Hodgson affected an oddly stilted, mock-antiquated style (perhaps hoping to replicate the success of William Morris) that doesn't really work for contemporary readers. But more important is the incredible atmosphere of his most fabulous creation, the Night Land itself.

Hodgson died in 1918 at Ypres, ending a very short and very influential career.

Check out *The Night Land* and William Hope Hodgson's many shorter works, currently being reprinted in hardback by Nightshade Books.

We lost something very special at Ypres.

Introduction

Once upon a very long extension, not precisely time nor any space we know, there existed an endless hollow thread of adventure and commerce called the Way, introduced in *Eon* (Bluejay/Tor, 1985). The Way, an artificial universe fifty kilometers in diameter and infinitely long, was created by the human inhabitants of an asteroid starship called *Thistledown*. They had become bored with their seemingly endless journey between the stars; the Way, with its potential of openings to other times and other universes, made reaching their destination unnecessary.

That the Way was destroyed (in *Eternity*, Warner, 1988) is known; that it never ends in any human space or time is less obvious.

Even before its creators completed their project, the Way was discovered and invaded by the nonhuman Jarts, who sought to announce themselves to Deity, what they called Descendant Mind, by absorbing and understanding everything, everywhere. The Jarts nearly destroyed the Way's creators, but were held at bay for a time, and for a price.

Yet there were stranger encounters. The plexus of universes is beyond the mind of any individual, human or Jart.

One traveler experienced more of this adventure than any other. His name was Olmy Ap Sennen. In his centuries of life, he lived to see himself become a living myth, be forgotten, rediscovered, and made myth again. So many stories have been told of Olmy that history and myth intertwine.

This is an early story. Olmy has experienced only one re-incarnation (*Legacy*, Tor, 1995). In fee for his memories, he has been rewarded with a longing to return to death everlasting.

1

"Probabilities fluctuated wildly, but always passed through zero, and gate openers, their equipment, and all associated personnel within a few hundred meters of the gate, were swallowed by a null that can only be described in terms of mathematics. It became difficult to remember that they had ever existed; records of their histories were corrupted or altered, even though they lay millions of kilometers from the incident. We had tapped into the geometric blood of the gods. But we knew we had to continue. We were compelled."

—Testimony of Master Gate Opener Ry Ornis, Secret Hearings Conducted by the Infinite Hexamon Nexus, "On the Advisability of Opening Gates into Chaos and Order"

The ghost of his last lover found Olmy Ap Sennen in the oldest columbarium of Alexandria, within the second chamber of the *Thistledown*.

Olmy stood in the middle of the hall, surrounded by stacked tiers of hundreds of small golden spheres. The spheres were urns, most of them containing only a sample of ashes. They rose to the glassed-in ceiling, held within columns of gentle yellow suspension fields. He reached out to touch a blank silver plate at the base of one column. The names of the dead appeared as if suddenly engraved, one after another.

He removed his hand when the names reached *Ilmo, Paul Yan*. This is where the soldiers from his childhood neighborhood were honored; in this column, five names, all familiar to him from days in school, all killed in a single skirmish with the Jarts near 3 ex 9, three billion kilometers down the Way. All had been obliterated without trace. These urns were empty.

He did not know the details. He did not need to. These dead had served *Thistledown* as faithfully as Olmy, but they would never return.

Olmy had spent seventy-three years stranded on the planet Lamarckia, in the service of the Hexamon, cut off from the *Thistledown* and the Way that stretched beyond the asteroid's seventh chamber. On Lamarckia, he had raised children, loved and buried wives...lived a long and memorable life in primitive conditions on an extraordinary world. His rescue and return to the Way, converted within days from an old and dying man to a fresh-bodied youth, had been a shock worse than the return of any real and ancient ghost.

Axis City, slung on the singularity that occupied the geodesic center of the Way, had been completed during those tumultuous years before Olmy's rescue and resurrection. It had moved four hundred thousand kilometers "north," down the Way, far from the seventh chamber cap. Within the Geshel precincts of Axis City, the mental patterns of many who died were now transferred to City Memory, a technological afterlife not very different from the ancient dream of heaven. Using similar technology, temporary partial personalities could be created to help an individual multi-task. These were sometimes called ghosts. Olmy had heard of partials, sent to do the bidding of their originals, with most of their mental faculties duplicated, but limited power to make decisions. He had never actually met one, however.

The ghost appeared just to his right and announced its nature by flickering slightly, growing translucent, then briefly turning into a negative. This display lasted only a few seconds. After, the simulacrum seemed perfectly solid and real. Olmy jumped, disoriented, then surveyed the ghost's features. He shook his head and smiled wryly.

"It will give my original joy to find you well," the partial said. "You seem lost, Ser Olmy."

Olmy did not quite know what form of speech to use with the partial. Should he address it with respect due to the original, a corprep and a woman of influence... The last woman he had tried to be in love with... Or as he might address a servant?

"I come here often. Old acquaintances."

The image looked concerned. "Poor Olmy. Still don't belong anywhere?"

Olmy ignored this. He looked for the ghost's source. It was projected from a small fist-sized flier hovering several meters away.

"I'm here on behalf of my original, corporeal representative Neya Taur Rinn. You realize... I am not her?"

"I'm not ignorant," Olmy said sharply, finding himself once more at a disadvantage with this woman.

The ghost fixed her gaze on him. The image, of course, was not actually doing the seeing. "The presiding minister of the Way, Yanosh Ap Kesler, instructed me to find you. My original was reluctant. I hope you understand."

Olmy folded his hands behind his back as the partial picted a series of ID symbols: Office of the Presiding Minister, Hexamon Nexus Office of Way Defense, Office of Way Maintenance. Quite a stack of bureaucracies, Olmy thought, Way Maintenance currently being perhaps the most powerful and arrogant of them all.

"What does Yanosh want with me?" he asked bluntly.

The ghost lifted her hands and pointed her index finger into her palm, tapping with each point. "You supported him in his bid to become presiding minister of the Seventh

Chamber and the Way. You've become a symbol for the advance of Geshel interests."

"Against my will," Olmy said. Yanosh, a fervent progressive and Geshel, had sent Olmy to Lamarckia—and had also brought him back and arranged for his new body. Olmy for his own part had never known quite which camp he belonged to: conservative Naderites, grimly opposed to the extraordinary advances of the last century; or the enthusiastically progressive Geshels.

Neya Taur Rinn's people were Geshels of an ancient radical faction, among the first to move into Axis City. The partial continued. "Ser Kesler has won re-election as presiding minister of the Way and now also serves as mayor of three precincts in Axis City."

"I'm aware of that."

"Of course. The presiding minister extends his greetings and hopes you are agreeable."

"I am very agreeable," Olmy said mildly. "I stay out of politics and disagree with nobody. I can't pay back Yanosh for all he has done—but then, I have rendered him due service as well." He did not like being baited—and could not understand why Yanosh would send Neya to fetch him. The presiding minister knew enough about Olmy's private life—probably too much. "Yanosh knows I've put myself on permanent leave." Olmy could not restrain himself. "Pardon me for boldness, but I'm curious. How do you feel? Do you actually *think* you are Neya Taur Rinn?"

The partial smiled. "I am a high-level partial given subordinate authority by my original," it said. *She* said... Olmy decided he would not cut such fine distinctions.

"Yes, but what does it *feel* like?" he asked.

"At least you're still alive enough to be curious," the partial said.

"Your original regarded my curiosity as a kind of perversity," Olmy said.

"A morbid curiosity," the partial returned, clearly uncomfortable. "I couldn't stand maintaining a relationship with a man who wanted to be *dead*."

"You rode my fame until I bored you," Olmy rejoined, then regretted the words. He used old training to damp his sharper emotions.

"To answer your question, I *feel* everything my original would feel. And my original would hate to see you here. What do *you* feel like, Ser Olmy?" The ghost's arm swung out to take in the urns, the columbarium. "Coming here, walking among the dead, that's pretty melodramatic."

That a ghost could remember their time together, could carry tales of this meeting to her original, to a woman he had admired with all that he had left of his heart, both irritated and intrigued him. "You were attracted to me because of my history."

"I was attracted to you because of your strength," she said. "It hurt me that you were so intent on living in your memories."

"I clung to you."

"And to nobody else..."

"I don't come here often," Olmy said. He shook his hands out by his side and stepped back. "All my finest memories are on a world I can never go back to. Real loves...real life. Not like *Thistledown* now." He squinted at the image. The image's focus was precise; still, there was something false about it, a glossiness, a prim neatness unlike Neya. "You didn't help."

The partial's expression softened. "I don't take the blame entirely, but your distress doesn't please me. My original."

"I didn't say I was in distress. I feel a curious peace in

fact. Why did Yanosh send you? Why did you agree to come?"

The ghost reached out to him. Her hand passed through his arm. She apologized for this breach of etiquette. "For your sake, to get you involved, and for the sake of my original, please, at least speak to our staff. The presiding minister needs you to join an expedition." She seemed to consider for a moment, then screw up her courage. "There's trouble at the Redoubt."

Olmy felt a sting of shock at the mention of that name. The conversation had suddenly become more than a little risky. He shook his head vigorously. "I do not acknowledge even knowing of such a place," he said.

"You know more than I do," the partial said. "I've been assured that it's real. Way Defense tells the Office of Way Maintenance that it now threatens us all."

"I'm not comfortable holding this conversation in a public place," Olmy protested.

This seemed to embolden the partial, and she projected her image closer. "This area is quiet and clean. No one listens."

Olmy stared up at the high glass ceiling.

"We are not being observed," the partial insisted. "The Nexus and Way Defense are concerned that the Jarts are closing in on that sector of the Way. I am told that if they occupy it, gain control of the Redoubt, *Thistledown* might as well be ground to dust and the Way set on fire like a piece of string. That scares my original. It scares *me* as I am now. Does it bother you in the least, Olmy?"

Olmy looked along the rows of urns... Centuries of *Thistledown* history, lost memory, now turned to pinches of ash, or less.

"Yanosh says he's positive you can help," the partial

said with a strong lilt of emotion. "It's a way to rejoin the living and make a new place for yourself."

"Why should that matter to you? To your original?" Olmy asked.

"Because my original still regards you as a hero. I still hope to emulate your service to the Hexamon."

Olmy smiled wryly. "Better to find a living model," he said. "I don't belong out there. I'm rusted over."

"That is not true," the partial said. "You have been given a new body. You are youthful and strong, and very experienced..." She seemed about to say more, but hesitated, rippled again, and faded abruptly. Her voice faded as well, and he heard only "Yanosh says he's never lost faith in you—"

The floor of the columbarium trembled. The solidity of *Thistledown* seemed to be threatened; a quake through the asteroid material, an impact from outside...or something occurring within the Way. Olmy reached out to brace himself against a pillar. The golden spheres vibrated in their suspensions, jangling like hundreds of small bells.

From far away, sirens began to wail.

The partial reappeared. "I have lost contact with my original," it said, its features blandly stiff. "Something has broken my link with City Memory."

Olmy watched Neya's image with fascination as yet untouched by any visceral response.

"I do not know when or if there will be a recovery," she said. "There's a failure on Axis City." Suddenly the image appeared puzzled, then stricken. She held out her phantom arms. "My original..." As if she were made of solid flesh, her face crinkled with fear. "She's died. I've *died*. Oh my God, Olmy!"

Olmy tried to understand what this might mean, under

the radical new rules of life and death for Geshels such as Neya. "What's happened? What can we do?"

The image flickered wildly. "My body is *gone*. There's been a complete system failure. I don't have any legal existence."

"What about the whole-life records? Connect with them." Olmy walked around the unsteady image, as if he might capture it, stop it from fading.

"I kept putting it off... So stupid! I haven't put myself in City Memory yet."

He tried to touch her and of course could not. He could not believe what she was saying, yet the sirens still wailed, and another small shudder rang through the asteroid.

"I have no place to go. Olmy, please! Don't let me just *stop!*" The ghost of Neya Taur Rinn drew herself up, tried to compose herself. "I have only a few seconds before..."

Olmy felt a sudden and intense attraction to the shimmering image. He wanted to know what actual death, final death, could possibly feel like. He reached out again, as if to embrace her.

She shook her head. The flickering increased. "It feels so strange—losing—"

Before she could finish, the image vanished completely. Olmy's arms hung around silent and empty air.

The sirens continued to wail, audible throughout Alexandria. He slowly dropped his arms, all too aware of being alone. The projector flew in a small circle, emitting small *wheep*ing sounds. Without instructions from its source, it could not decide what to do.

For a moment, he shivered and his neck hair pricked—a sense of almost religious awe he had not experienced since his time on Lamarckia.

Olmy had started walking toward the end of the hall before he consciously knew what to do. He turned right to exit through the large steel doors and looked up through the thin clouds enwrapping the second chamber, through the glow of the flux tube to the axis borehole on the southern cap. His eyes were warm and wet. He wiped them with the back of his hand and his breath hitched.

Emergency beacons had switched on around the flux tube, forming a bright ring two thirds of the way up the cap.

His shivering continued, and it angered him. He had died once already, yet this new body was afraid of dying, and its wash of emotions had taken charge of his senses.

Deeper still and even more disturbing was a scrap of the old loyalty...To his people, to the vessel that bore them between the stars, that served as the open chalice of the infinite Way. A loyalty to the woman who had found him too painful to be with. "Neya!" he moaned. Perhaps she had been wrong. A partial might not have access to all information; perhaps things weren't as bad as they seemed.

But he knew that they were. He had never felt *Thistledown* shake so.

Olmy hurried to the rail terminal three city squares away, accompanied by throngs of curious and alarmed citizens. Barricades had been set across the entrances to the northern cap elevators; all inter-chamber travel was temporarily restricted. No news was available.

Olmy showed the ID marks on his wrist to a cap guard, who scanned them quickly and transmitted them to her commanders. She let him pass, and he entered the elevator and rode swiftly to the borehole.

Within the workrooms surrounding the borehole waited an arrowhead-shaped official transport, as the presiding minister's office had requested. None of the soldiers or guards he questioned knew what had happened. There were still no official pronouncements on any of the citizen nets. Olmy rode the transport, accompanied by five other officials, through the vacuum above the atmospheres of the next four chambers, threading the boreholes of each of the massive concave walls that separated them. None of the chambers showed any sign of damage.

In the southern cap borehole of the sixth chamber, Olmy transferred from the transport to a tuberider, designed to run along the singularity that formed the core of the Way. On this most unusual railway, he sped at many thousands of miles per hour toward the Axis City at 4 ex 5—four hundred thousand kilometers north of *Thistledown*.

A few minutes from Axis City, the tuberider slowed and the forward viewing port darkened. There was heavy radiation in the vicinity, the pilot reported. Something had come down the Way at relativistic velocity and struck the northern precincts of Axis City.

Olmy had little trouble guessing the source.

2

A day passed before Olmy could see the presiding minister. Emergency repairs on Axis City had rendered only one precinct, Central City, habitable; the rest, including Axis Prime and Axis Nader, were being evacuated. Axis Prime had taken the brunt of the impact. Tens of thousands had lost their lives, both Geshels and Naderites. Naderites by and large did not participate in the practice of storing their body patterns and recent memories as insurance against such a calamity.

Some Geshels would receive their second incarnation—many thousands more would not. City Memory itself had been damaged. Even had Neya taken the time to make her whole-life record, store her patterns, she might still have died.

The last functioning precinct, Central City, now contained the combined offices of Presiding Minister of the Way and the Axis City government, and it was here that Yanosh met with Olmy.

"Her name was Deirdre Enoch," the presiding minister said, floating over the transparent external wall of the new office. His body was wrapped below the chest in a shining blue medical support suit; the impact had broken both of his legs and caused severe internal injuries. For the time being, the presiding minister was a functioning cyborg, until new organs could be grown and placed. "She opened a gate illegally at three ex nine, fifty years ago. Just beyond the point where we last repulsed the Jarts. She was helped by a master gate opener who deliberately disobeyed Nexus and guild orders. We learned about the breach six months after she had smuggled eighty of her colleagues—or maybe a hundred and twenty, we aren't sure how many—into a small research center—and just days after the gate was opened. There was nothing we could do to stop it."

Olmy gripped a rail that ran around the perimeter of the office, watching Kesler without expression. The irony was too obvious. "I've only heard rumors. Way Maintenance—"

Kesler was hit by a wave of pain, quickly damped by the suit. He continued, his face drawn. "Damn Way Maintenance. Damn the in-fighting and politics." He forced a smile. "Last time it was a Naderite renegade on Lamarckia."

Olmy nodded.

"This time—Geshel. Even worse—a member of the Openers Guild. I never imagined running this damned starship would ever be so complicated. Makes me almost understand why you long for Lamarckia."

"It wasn't any easier there," Olmy said.

"Yes—but there were fewer people." Yanosh rotated his support suit and crossed the chamber. "We don't know precisely what happened. Something disturbed the immediate geometry around the gate. The conflicts between Way physics and the universe Enoch accessed were too great. The gate became a lesion, impossible to close. By that time, most of Enoch's scientists had retreated to the main station, a protective pyramid—what she called the Redoubt."

"She tapped into chaos?" Olmy asked. Some universes accessed through the Way were empty voids, dead, useless but relatively harmless; others were virulent, filled with a bubbling stew of unstable "constants" that reduced the reality of any observer or instrumentality. Only two such

gates had ever been opened in the Way; the single fortu-
nate aspect of these disasters had been that the gates
themselves had quickly closed and could not be reopened.

"Not chaos," Kesler said, swallowing and bowing his
head at more discomfort. "This damn suit...could be doing
a better job."

"You should be resting," Olmy said.

"No time. The Opener's Guild tells me Enoch was looking for a domain of enhanced structure, hyper-order. What
she found was more dangerous than any chaos. Her gate
may have opened into a universe of endless fecundity.
Not just order: Creativity. Every universe is in a sense a
plexus, its parts connected by information links; but
Enoch's universe contained no limits to the propagation
of information. No finite speed of light, no separation
between anything analogous to the Bell continuum...and
other physicality."

Olmy frowned, trying to make sense of this. "My
knowledge of Way physics is shaky..."

"Ask your beloved Konrad Korzenoswki," Kesler
snapped.

Olmy did not react to this provocation.

Kesler apologized under his breath. He floated slowly
back across the chamber, his face a mask of pain, a
pathetic parody of restlessness. "We lost three expeditions
trying to save her people and close the gate. The last was
six months ago. Something like life-forms had grown up
around the main station, fueled by the lesion. They've
became *huge*, unimaginably bizarre. No one can make
sense of them. What was left of our last expedition managed to build a barrier about a thousand kilometers south
of the lesion. We thought that would give us the luxury
of a few years to decide what to do next. But that barrier
has been destroyed. We've not been able to get close

enough since to discover what's happened. We have defenses in that sector, key defenses that keep the flaw from being used against us." He looked down through the transparent floor at the segment of the Way twenty-four kilometers below.

"The Jarts were able to send a relativistic projectile along the flaw, hardly more than a gram of rest mass. We couldn't stop it. It struck Axis City at twelve hundred hours yesterday."

Olmy had been told the details of the attack: A pellet less than a millimeter in diameter, traveling very close to the speed of light. Only the safety and control mechanisms of the sixth chamber machinery had kept the entire Axis City from disintegrating. The original of Neya Taur Rinn had been conducting business on behalf of her boss, Yanosh, in Axis Prime while her partial had visited Olmy.

"We're moving the city south as fast as we can and still keep up the evacuation," Kesler said. "The Jarts are drawing close to the lesion now. We're not sure what they can do with it. Maybe nothing—but we can't afford to take the chance."

Olmy shook his head in puzzlement. "You've just told me nothing can be done. Why call me here when we're helpless?"

"I didn't say *nothing* could be done," Kesler responded, eyes glittering. "Some of our gate openers think they can build a cirque, a ring gate, and seal off the lesion."

"That would cut us off from the rest of the Way," Olmy said.

"Worse. In a few days or weeks it would destroy the Way completely, seal us off in *Thistledown* forever. Until now, we've never been that desperate." He smiled, lips twisted by pain. "Frankly, you were not my choice. I'm no longer sure that you can be relied upon, and this matter is far too complicated to allow anyone to act alone."

Neya had not told him the truth, then. "Who chose me?" Olmy asked.

"A gate opener. You made an impression on him when he escorted you down the Way some decades ago. He was the one who opened the gate to Lamarckia."

"Frederik Ry Ornis?"

Kesler nodded. "From what I'm told, he's become the most powerful opener in the guild. A senior master."

Olmy took a deep breath. "I'm not what I appear to be, Yanosh. I'm an old man who's seen women and his friends die. I miss my sons. You should have left me on Lamarckia."

Kesler closed his eyes. The blue jacket around his lower body adjusted slightly, and his face tightened. "The Olmy I knew would never have turned down a chance like this."

"I've seen too many things already," Olmy said.

Yanosh moved forward. "We both have. This...is beyond me," he said quietly. "The lesion... The gate openers tell me it's the strangest place in creation. All the boundaries of physics have collapsed. Time and causality have new meanings. Heaven and hell have married. Only those in the Redoubt have seen all that's happened there—if they still exist in any way we can understand. They haven't communicated with us since the lesion formed."

Olmy listened intently, something slowly stirring to life, a small speck of ember glowing brighter.

"It may be over, Olmy," Yanosh said. "The whole grand experiment may be at an end. We're ready to close off the Way, pinch it, seal the lesion within its own small bubble...dispose of it."

"Tell me more," Olmy said, folding his arms.

"Three citizens escaped from the Redoubt, from Enoch's

small colony, before the lesion became too large. One died, his mind scrambled beyond retrieval. The second has been confined for study, as best we're able. What afflicts him—or *it*—is something we can never cure. The third survived relatively unharmed. She's become... unconventional, more than a little obsessed by the mystical, but I'm told she's still rational. If you accept, she will accompany you." Yanosh's tone indicated he was not going to allow Olmy to decline. "We have two other volunteers, both apprentice gate openers, both failed by the guild. All have been chosen by Frederik Ry Ornis. He will explain why."

Olmy shook his head. "A mystic, failed openers... What would I do with such a team?"

Yanosh smiled grimly. "Kill them if it goes wrong. And kill yourself. If you can't close off the Way, and if the lesion remains, you will not be allowed to come back. The third expedition I sent never even reached the Redoubt. But they were absorbed by the lesion." Another grimace of pain. "Do you believe in ghosts, Olmy?"

"What kind?"

"Real ghosts?"

"No," Olmy said.

"I think I do. Some members of our rescue expeditions came back. Several versions of them. We *think* we destroyed them."

"Versions?"

"Copies of some sort. They were sent back—echoed—along their own world-lines in a way no one understands. They returned to their loved ones, their relatives, their friends. If more return, everything we call real could be in jeopardy. It's been very difficult keeping this secret."

Olmy raised an eyebrow skeptically. He wondered if Yanosh was himself still rational. "I've served my time. More than my time. Why should I go active?"

"Damn it, Olmy, if not for love of *Thistledown*—if you're beyond that, then because you *want to die*," Kesler grunted, his face betraying quiet disgust behind the pain, "You've wanted to die since I brought you back from Lamarckia. This time, if you make it to the Redoubt, you're likely to have your wish granted.

"Think of it as a gift from me to you, or to what you once were."

3

"If you were enhanced, this would go a lot faster," Jarr Flynch said, pointing to Olmy's head. Frederik Ry Ornis smiled. The three of them walked side by side down a long, empty hall, approaching a secure room deep in the old Thistledown Defense Tactical College building in Alexandria.

Ry Ornis had aged not at all physically. In appearance he was still the same long-limbed, mantis-like figure, but his gawkiness had been replaced by an eerie grace, and his youthful, eccentric volubility by a wry spareness of language.

Olmy dismissed Flynch's comment with a wave of his hand. "I've gone through the important files," he said. "I think I know them well enough. I have questions about the choice of people to go with me. The apprentice gate openers... They've been rejected by the guild. Why?"

Flynch smiled. "They're flamboyant."

Olmy glanced at the master opener. "Ry Ornis was as flamboyant as they come."

"The guild has changed," Ry Ornis said. "It demands more now."

Flynch agreed. "In the time since I've been a teacher in the guild, that's certainly true. They tolerate very little...creativity. The defection of Enoch's pupils scared them. The lesion terrified all of us. Rasp and Karn are young, innovative. Nobody denies they're brilliant, but they've refused to settle in and play their roles. So...the guild denied them final certification."

"Why choose them for this job?" Olmy asked.

"Ry Ornis did the choosing," Flynch said.

"We've discussed this," Ry Ornis said.

"Not to my satisfaction. When do I meet them?"

"No meeting has been authorized with Rasp and Karn until you're on the flawship. They're still in emergency conditioning." Flynch glanced at Ry Ornis. "The training has been a little rough on them."

Olmy felt less and less sure that he wanted anything to do with the guild, or with Ry Ornis's chosen openers. "The files only tell half a story," he said. "Deirdre Enoch never became an opener—she never even tried to qualify. She was just a teacher. How could she become so important to the guild?"

Flynch shook his head. "Like me, she was never qualified to be an opener, but also like me, as a teacher, she was considered one of the best. She became a leader to some apprentice openers. Philosopher."

"Prophet," Ry Ornis said softly.

"Training for the guild is grueling," Flynch continued. "Some say it's become torture. The mathematical conditioning alone is enough to produce a drop-out rate of over ninety per cent. Deirdre Enoch worked as a counselor in mental balance, compensation, and she was good... In the last twenty years, she worked with many who went on to become very powerful in Way Maintenance. She kept up her contacts. She convinced a lot of her students—"

"That human nature is corrupt," Olmy ventured sourly.

Flynch shook his head. "That the laws of our universe are inadequate. Incomplete. That there is a way to become better human beings, and of course, better openers. Disorder, competition, and death corrupt us, she thought."

"She knew high-level theory, speculations circulated privately among master openers," Ry Ornis said. "She heard about domains where the rules were very different."

"She heard about a gate into complete order?"

"It had been discussed, on a theoretical basis. None had ever been attempted. No limits have been found to the variety of domains—of universes. She speculated that a well-tuned gate could access almost any domain a good opener could conceive of."

Olmy scowled. "She expected order to balance out competition and death? Order versus disorder, a fight to the finish?"

Ry Ornis made a small noise, and Flynch nodded. "There's a reason none of this is in the files," Flynch said. "No opener will talk about it, or admit they knew anybody involved in making the decision. It's been very embarrassing to the guild. I'm impressed that you know what questions to ask. But it's better that you ask Ry Ornis—"

Olmy focused on Flynch. "You say you and Enoch occupied similar positions. I'd rather ask you."

Flynch gestured for them to turn to the left. The lights came on before them, and at the end of a much shorter hall, a door stood open. "Deirdre Enoch read extensively in the old religious texts. As did her followers. I believe they lost themselves in a dream," he said. "They thought that anyone who bathed in a stream of pure order, as it were—in a domain of unbridled creation without destruction—would be enhanced. Armored. Annealed. That's my opinion...what they might have been thinking. She might have told them such things."

"A fountain of youth?" Olmy ventured, still scowling.

"Openers don't much care about temporal immortality," Ry Ornis said. "When we open a gate—we glimpse eternity. A hundred gates, a hundred different eternities. Coming back is just an interlude between forevers. Those who listened to Enoch thought they would end up more skilled, more brilliant. Less corrupted by competitive evolution."

He smiled, a remarkably unpleasant expression on his skeletal face. "Free of original sin."

Olmy's scowl faded. He glanced at Flynch, who had turned away from Ry Ornis. Something between them, a coolness. "All right. I can see that."

"Really?" Flynch shook his head dubiously.

Perhaps the master opener could tell even more. But it did not seem wise at this point to push the matter.

A bell chimed and they entered the conference room.

Already seated within was the only surviving and whole escapee from the Redoubt: Gena Plass. As a radical Geshel, she had designed her own body and appearance decades ago, opting for a solid frame, close to her natural physique. Her face she had tuned to show strength as well as classic beauty, but she had allowed it to age, and the experience of her time with the expedition, the trauma at the lesion, had not been erased. Olmy noted that she carried a small book with her, an antique printed on paper—a Bible.

Flynch made introductions. Plass looked proud and more than a little confused. They sat around the table.

"Let's start with what we know," Flynch said. He ordered up visual records made by the retreating flawship that had carried Plass.

Olmy looked at the images hovering over the table: the great pipeline of the Way, sheets of field fluorescing brilliantly as they were breached, debris caught in whirling clouds along the circumference, the flaw itself, running along the center of the Way like a wire heated to blinding blue-white.

Plass did not look. Olmy watched her reaction closely. For a moment, something seemed to swirl around her, a wisp of shadow, smoothly transparent, like a small slice of twilight. The others did not see or ignored what they saw, but Plass's eyes locked on Olmy's and her lips tightened.

"I'm pleased you've both agreed to come," Ry Ornis said as the images came to an end.

Plass looked at the opener, and then back at Olmy. She studied Olmy's face closely. "I can't stay here. That's why I'm going back. I don't belong in *Thistledown*."

"Ser Plass is haunted," Flynch said. "Ser Olmy has been told about some of these visitors."

"My husband," she said, swallowing. "Just my husband, so far. Nobody else."

"Is he still there?" Olmy asked. "In the Redoubt?"

Bitterly, she said, "They haven't told you much that's useful, have they? As if they want us to fail."

"He's dead?"

"He's not in the Redoubt and I don't know if you could call it death," Plass said. "May I tell you what this really means? What we've actually done?" She stared around the table, eyes wide.

Ry Ornis lifted his hand tolerantly.

"I have diaries from before the launch of *Thistledown*, from my family," she said. "As far back as my ancestors can remember, my family was special... They had access to the world of the spiritual. They all saw ghosts. The old-fashioned kind, not the ones we use now for servants. Some described the ghosts in their journals." She reached up and pinched her lower lip, released it, pinched it again. "I think they all saw the ghost of my husband. I recognize that now. Everyone on my world-line, back to before I was born, haunted by the same figure. My husband. Now I see him, too."

"I have a hard time visualizing this sort of ghost," Olmy said.

Plass looked up at the ceiling and clutched her Bible.

"Whatever it is that we tapped into—a domain of pure order, something else clever—it's *suffused* into the Way, into the *Thistledown*. It's like a caterpillar crawling up our lives, grabbing hold of events and...crawling, spreading backward, maybe even forward in time. They try to keep us quiet. I cooperate...but my husband tells me things when he returns. Do the others hear...reports? Messages from the Redoubt?"

Ry Ornis shook his head, but Olmy doubted this meant simple denial.

"What happened when the gate became a lesion?" Olmy asked.

Plass grew pale. "My husband was at the gate with Enoch's master opener, Tom Issa Danna."

"One of our finest," Ry Ornis said.

"Enoch's gate into order was the second they had opened. The first was a well to an established supply world where we could bring up raw materials."

"Standard practice for all far-flung stations," Flynch said.

"I wasn't there when they opened the second gate," Plass continued, her eyes darting between Flynch and Olmy. She seemed to have little sympathy for either. "I was at a support facility about a kilometer from the gate, and two kilometers from the Redoubt. There was already an atmospheric envelope and a cushion of sand and soil around the site. My husband and I had started a quick-growth garden. An orchard. We heard they had opened the second gate. My husband was with Issa Danna. Ser Enoch came by on a tractor and said it was a complete success. We were celebrating, a small group of researchers, opening bottles of champagne. We got reports of something going wrong two hours later. We came out of our bungalows—a scout from the main flawship was just landing. Enoch had returned to the new gate to join Issa Danna. My husband must have been right there with them."

"What did you see?"

"Nothing at first. We watched them on the monitors inside the bungalows. Issa Danna and his assistants were working, talking, laughing. Issa Danna was so confident. He radiated his genius. The second gate looked normal—a well, a cupola. But in a little while, a few hours, we saw that the people around the new gate sounded drunk. All of them. Something had come out of the gate, something intoxicating. They spoke about a shadow."

She looked up at Olmy, and Olmy realized that before this experience, she must have been a very lovely woman. Some of that beauty still shone through.

"We saw that some kind of veil covered the gate. Then the assistant openers in the bungalows, students of Issa Danna, said that the gate was out of control. They were feeling it in their clavicles, slaved to the master's clavicle."

Clavicles were devices used by gate-openers to create the portals that gave access to other times, other universes, "outside" the Way. Typically, they were shaped like bicycle handlebars attached to a small sphere.

"How many openers were there?" Olmy asked.

"Two masters and seven apprentices," Plass said.

Olmy turned to Ry Ornis. He held up his hand, urging patience.

"A small truck came out of the gate site. Its tires wobbled and all the people clinging to it were shouting and laughing. Then everyone around the truck—the bungalows were almost empty now—began to shout, and an assistant grabbed me—I was the closest to her—and said we had to get onto the scout and return to the flawship. She—her name was Jara—said she had never felt anything like this. She said they must have made a mistake and opened a gate into chaos. I had never heard about such a thing—but she seemed to think if we didn't leave now, we'd all die. Four people. Two men and me and Jara. We were the only ones who made it into the scout ship. Shadows covered everything around us. Everybody was drunk, laughing, screaming."

Plass stopped and took several breaths to calm herself. "We flew up to the flawship. The rest is on the record. The Redoubt was the last thing I saw, surrounded by something like ink in water, swirling. A storm."

Flynch started to speak, but Plass cut him off. "Two of the others on the flawship, the men, were afflicted. They came out of the veil around the truck and Jara helped them get into the scout. As for Jara... Nobody remembers her but me."

Flynch waited a moment, then said, "There were only three people aboard the scout when it reached the flaw-ship. You, and the figure we haven't identified. There was no other man, and there has never been an assistant opener named Jara."

"They were real."

"It doesn't matter," Ry Ornis said impatiently. "Issa Danna knew better than to open a gate into chaos. He knew the signs and never would have completed the opening. But—in the linkage, the slaving, qualities can be reversed if the opener loses control."

"A gate into order—but the slaved clavicles behaving as if they were associated with chaos?" Olmy asked, trying to grasp the complexities.

Ry Ornis seemed reluctant to go into more detail. "They no longer exist in our world-line," he said. "Ser Plass remembers that one hundred and twenty people accompanied Enoch and Issa Danna. She remembers two master

GREG BEAR

openers and seven assistants. Here on *Thistledown*, we have records, life-histories, of only eighty, with one master and two assistants."

"I survived. You remember me," Plass said, her expression desperate.

"You're in our records. You survived," Ry Ornis confirmed. "We don't know why or how."

"What about the other survivor?" Olmy said.

"We don't know who he or she was," Ry Ornis said.

"Show him the other," Plass said. "Show him Number 2, show him what happens when you survive, but you *don't return.*"

"That's next," Ry Ornis said. "If you're ready, Ser Olmy."

"I may never be *ready*, Ser Ry Ornis," Olmy said.

4

The flawship cradled in the borehole dock was sleek and new and very fast. Olmy tracted along the flank of the ship, resisting the urge to run his fingers along the featureless reflecting surface.

He was still pondering the meeting with the figure called Number 2.

Around the ship's dock, the bore hole between the sixth and seventh chamber glowed with a violet haze, a cup-shaped field erected to receive the southernmost extensors of Axis City, gripping the remaining precincts during their evacuation and repair. Olmy swiveled to face the axis and the flaw's blunt conclusion and watch the workers and robots guiding power grids and huge steel beams to act as buffers.

The dock manager, a small man with boyish features and no hair, his scalp decorated with an intricate green and brown Celtic braid, pulled himself toward Olmy and extended a paper certificate.

"We're going to vacuum in an hour," he said. "I hope everybody's here before then. I'd like to seal the ship and check its integrity."

Olmy applied his sigil to the document, transferring its command from borehole management and the construction guild to Way Defense.

"Two others were here earlier," the dock manager said. "Twins, young women. They carried the smallest clavicles I've ever seen."

Olmy looked back along the dock and saw three figures tracting toward them. "Looks like we're all here," he said.

"No send-off?" the manager asked.

Olmy smiled. "Everyone's much too busy," he said.

"Don't I know it," the manager said.

As a rule, gate-openers had a certain look and feel that defined them, sometimes subtle, usually not. Rasp and Karn were little more than children, born (perhaps *made* was a better word) fifteen years ago in Thistledown City. They were of radical Geshel ancestry, and their four parent-sponsors were also gate-openers.

They tracted to the flawship and introduced themselves to Olmy. Androgynous, ivory-white, slender, with long fingers and small heads covered with a fine silvery fur, each spoke with identical resonant tenor voices. Karn had black eyes, Rasp green. Otherwise, they were identical. To Olmy, neither had the air of authority he had seen in experienced gate-openers.

The dock manager picted a coded symbol and dilated the flawship entrance, a glowing green circle in the hull. The twins solemnly entered the ship.

Plass arrived several minutes later. She wore a formal blue suit and seemed to have been crying. As she greeted Olmy, her voice sounded harsh. She addressed him as if they had not met before. "You're the soldier?"

"I've worked in Way Defense," he said.

Gray eyes small and wary, surrounded by puffy pale flesh, face broad and sympathetic, hair dark and cut short, Plass today reminded Olmy of any of a dozen matrons he had known as a child: polite but hardly hesitant.

"Ser Flynch tells me you're the one who died on Lamarckia. I heard about that. By birth, a Naderite."

"By birth," Olmy said.

"Such adventures we have," she said with a sniff. "Because of Ser Korzenowski's cleverness." She glanced away, then fastened her eyes on him and leaned her head to one side. "I'm not looking forward to this. Have they told you I'm a little broken, that my thoughts take odd paths?"

"They said your studies and experiences have influenced you," Olmy said, a little uncomfortable at having to re-establish an acquaintance already made.

Rasp and Karn watched from the flawship hatch.

"She's broken, we're young and inexperienced," Rasp said. Karn laughed, a surprising watery tinkle, very sweet. "And you've died once already, Ser Olmy. What a crew!"

"I presume everyone knows what they're doing," Plass said.

"Presume nothing," Olmy said.

Olmy guided Plass into the ship. The dock manager watched this with dubious interest. Olmy swung around fields to face him.

"I take charge of this vessel now. Thanks for your attention and care."

"Our duty," the dock manager said. "She was delivered just yesterday. No one has taken her out yet—she's a virgin, Ser Olmy. She doesn't even have a name."

"Call her the *Lark*!" Rasp trilled from inside.

Olmy shook hands firmly with the manager and climbed into the ship. The entrance sealed with a small beep behind him.

The flawship's interior was cool and quiet. With intertial control, there were no special couches or nets or fields; they would experience only simulated motion, for psychological effect, on their journey: at most a mild sense of acceleration and deceleration.

Plass introduced herself to Karn and Rasp. Since she wore no pictor, only words were exchanged. This suited Olmy.

"Ser Olmy," Plass said, "I assume we are in privacy now. No one outside can hear?"

"No one," Olmy said.

"Good. Then we can speak our minds. This trip is useless." She turned on the twins, who floated like casual accent marks on some unseen word. "They've chosen you because you're inexperienced."

"Unmarked," Rasp said brightly. "Open to the new."

Karn smiled and nodded. "And not afraid of spooks."

This seemed to leave Plass at a loss, but only for a second. She was obviously determined to establish herself as a Cassandra. "You won't be disappointed."

"We visited with Number 2," Rasp said, and Karn nodded. "Ser Ry Ornis insisted we study it."

Olmy remembered his own encounter with the vividly glowing figure in the comfortably appointed darkened room. It was not terribly misshapen, as he had anticipated before the meeting, but certainly far from normal. Its skin had burned with the tiny firefly deaths of stray metal atoms in the darkened room's air. It had stood out against the shadows like a nebula in the vastness beyond *Thistledown's* walls. Its hands alone had remained dark, ascribing arcs against its starry body as it tried to speak.

It lived in a twisted kind of time, neither backwards nor forwards, and its words had required special translation. It had spoken of things that would happen in the room after Olmy left. It had told him the Way would soon end, "in the blink of a bird's eye." The translator relayed this clearly enough, but could not translate other words; it seemed the unknown figure was inventing or accessing new languages, some clearly not of human origin.

Plass said, "It'll be a mercy if all that happens is we end up like *him*."

"How interesting," Rasp said.

"We are fiends for novelty," Karn added with a smile.

"Monsters are *made*," Plass said with a grimace, clasping her Bible, "not born."

"Thank you," Karn said, and produced a forced, fixed smile, accompanied by a glassy stare. Rasp was obviously thinking furiously to come up with a more witty riposte.

Olmy decided enough was more than enough. "If we're going to die, or worse, we should at least be civil." The three stared at him, each surprised in a different way. This gave Olmy a bare minimum of satisfaction. "Let's go through our orders and manifest, and learn how to work together."

"A man who wants only to die again—" Karn began, still irritated, her stare still glazed, but her twin interrupted.

"Shut up," Rasp said. "As he says. Time to work." Karn shrugged and her anger dissolved instantly.

At speed, the flawship's forward view of the Way became a twisted lens. Stray atoms and ions of gas within the Way piled up before them into a distorting, white-hot atmosphere. Rays of many colors writhed from a skewed vertex of milky brightness; the flaw, itself a slender geometric distortion, now resembled a white-hot piston.

Stray atoms of gas in the Way were becoming a problem, the result of so many gates being opened to bring in raw materials from the first exploited worlds.

The flawship's status appeared before Olmy in steady reassuring symbols of blue and green. Their speed: three percent of c', the speed of light in the Way, slightly less than c in the outside universe. They were now accelerating at more than six g's, down from the maximum they had hit at 4 ex 5. None of this could be felt inside the hull.

The display showed their position as 1 ex 7, ten million

kilometers beyond the cap of the seventh chamber, still almost three billion kilometers from the Redoubt.

Olmy had a dreamlike sense of dissociation, as always when traveling in a flawship. The interior had been divided by its occupants into three private compartments, a common area, and the pilot's position. Olmy was spending most of his time at the pilot's position. The others kept to their compartments and said little to each other.

The first direct intimation of the strangeness of their mission came on the second day, halfway through their journey. Olmy was studying what little was known about the Redoubt, from a complete and highly secret file. He was deep into the biography of Deirdre Enoch when a voice called him from behind.

He turned and saw a young woman floating three meters aft, her head nearer to him than her feet, precessing slightly about her own axis. "I've felt you calling us," she said. "I've felt you studying us. What do you want to know?"

Olmy checked to make sure this was not some product of the files, of the data projectors. It was not; no simulations were being projected. Behind the image he saw the sisters and Plass emerging from their quarters. The sisters appeared interested, Plass bore an expression of shocked sadness.

"I don't recognize her," Plass said.

Olmy judged this was not a prank. "I'm glad you're decided to visit us," he said to the woman, with a touch of wry perversity. "How is the situation at the Redoubt?"

"The same, ever the same," the young woman answered. Her face was difficult to discern. As she spoke, her features blurred and re-formed, subtly different.

"Are you well?" Olmy asked. Rasp and Karn sidled forward around the image, which ignored them.

"I am nothing," the image said. "Ask another question. It's amusing to see if I can manage any sensible answers."

Rasp and Karn joined Olmy. "She's real?" Rasp asked. The twins were both pale, their faces locked in dread fascination.

"I don't know," Olmy said. "I don't think so."

"Then she's used her position on the Redoubt's timeline to climb back to us," Rasp said. "Some of us at least do indeed get to where we're going!"

Karn smiled with her usual fixed contentment and glazed eyes. Olmy was beginning not to like this hyper-intelligent twin.

Plass moved forward, hands clenched as if she would hit the figure. "I don't recognize you," she said. "Who are you?

"I see only one of you clearly." The young woman pointed at Olmy. "The others are like clouds of insects."

"Have the Jarts taken over the Redoubt?" Rasp asked. The image did not answer, so Olmy echoed the question.

"They are alone in the Redoubt. That is sufficient. I can describe the situation as it will be when you arrive. There is a large groove or valley in the Way, with the Redoubt forming a series of bands of intensely ranked probabilities within the groove. The Redoubt has grown to immense proportions, in time, all possibilities realized. My prior self has lived more than any cardinal number of lives. Still lives them. It sheds us as you shed skin."

"Tell us about the gate," Karn requested, sidling closer to the visitor. "What's happened? What state is it in?" Again, Olmy relayed the question. The woman watched him with discomforting intensity.

"It has become those who opened it. There is an immense head of Issa Danna on the western boundary of the gate, watching over the land. We do not know what it does, what it means."

Plass made a small choking sound and covered her mouth with her hand, eyes wide.

"Some tried to escape. It made them into living mountains, carpeted with fingers, or forests filled with fog and clinging blue shadow. Some waft through the air as vapors that change whoever encounters them. We've learned. We don't go outside, none for thousands of years..."

Rasp and Karn flanked the visitor, studying her with catlike focus.

"Then how can you leave, return to us?" Olmy asked.

The young woman frowned and held up her hands. "It doesn't speak. It doesn't know. I am so lonely."

Plass, Rasp and Karn, and Olmy stood facing each other through clear air.

Olmy started, suddenly drawn back to the last time he had seen a ghost vanish—the partial of Neya Taur Rinn.

Plass let out her breath with a shudder. "It is always the same," she said. "My husband says he's lonely. He's going to find a place where he won't be lonely. But there are no such places!"

Karn turned to Rasp. "A false vision, a deception?" she asked her twin.

"There are no deceptions where we are going," Plass said, and relaxed her hands, rubbed them.

Karn made a face out of her sight.

"No one knows what happened to the gate opened at the Redoubt," Rasp said, turning away from her own session with the records. Since the appearance of the female specter, they had spent most of their time in the pilot cabin. Olmy's presence seemed to afford them some comfort. "None of the masters can even guess."

Karn sighed, whether in sympathy or shame, Olmy could not tell.

"Can either of you make a guess?" Olmy asked.

Plass floated at the front of the common space, just around the pale violet bulkhead, arms folded, looking not very hopeful.

"A gate is opened on the floor of the Way," Rasp said flatly, as if reciting an elementary lesson. "That is a constraint in the local continuum of the Way. Four point gates are possible in each ring position. When four are opened, they are supposed to always cling to the wall of the Way. In practice, however, small gates have been known to rise above the floor. They are always closed immediately."

"What's that got to do with my question?" Olmy asked.

"Oh, nothing, really!" Rasp said, waving her hand in exasperation.

"Perhaps it does," Karn said, playing the role of thoughtful one for the moment. "Perhaps it's deeply connected."

"Oh, all right, then," Rasp said, and squinched up her face. "What I might have been implying is this: if Issa Danna's gate somehow lifted free of the floor, the wall of the Way, then its constraints would have changed. A free gate can adversely affect local world-lines. Something can enter and leave from any angle. In conditioning we are made to understand that the world-lines of all transported objects passing through such a free gate actually shiver for several years backward. Waves of probability retrograde."

"How many actually went through the gate?" Olmy asked.

"My husband never did," Plass said, pulling herself into

the hatchway. "Issa Danna and his entourage. Maybe others, after the lesion formed...against their will."

"But you didn't recognize this woman," Olmy said.

"No," Plass said

"Was she extinguished when the gate became a lesion?" Olmy continued. "Was her world-line wiped clean in our domain?"

"My head hurts," Rasp said.

"I think you might be right," Karn said thoughtfully. "It makes sense, in a frightening sort of way. She is suspended... We have no record of her existence."

"But the line still exists," Rasp said. "It echoes back in time even in places where her record has ended."

"No," Plass said, shaking her head.

"Why?" Rasp asked.

"She mentioned an *allthing*."

"I didn't hear that," Rasp said.

"Neither did I," Olmy said.

Plass gripped her elbow and squeezed her arms tight around her, pulling her shoulder forward. "We heard different words." She pointed at Olmy. "He's the only one she really saw."

"It looked at you, too," Rasp said. "Just once."

"An allthing was an ancient Nordic governmental meeting," Olmy said, reading from the flawship command entry display, where he had called for a definition.

"That's not what she meant," Plass said. "My husband used another phrase in the same way. He referred to the Final Mind of the domain. Maybe they mean the same thing."

"It was just an echo," Rasp said. "We all heard it differently. We all interacted with it differently depending on... Whatever. That means more than likely it carried random information from a future we'll never reach. It's a ghost that babbles...like your husband, perhaps."

Plass stared at the twins, then grabbed for the hatch frame. She stubbornly shook her head. "We're going to hear more about this allthing," she said. "Deirdre Enoch is still working. Something is still happening there. The Redoubt still exists."

"Your husband told you this?" Rasp asked with a taunting smile. Olmy frowned at her, but she ignored him.

"We'll know when we see our own ghosts," Plass said, with a kick that sent her flying back to her cabin.

Plass calmly read her Bible in the common area as the ship prepared a meal for her. The twins ate on their own schedule, but Olmy matched his meals to Plass's, for the simple reason that he liked to talk to the woman, and did not feel comfortable around the twins.

There was about Plass the air of a spent force, something falling near the end of its arc from a truly high and noble trajectory. Plass seemed to enjoy his company, but did not comment on it. She asked about his experiences on Lamarckia.

"It was a beautiful world," he said. "The most beautiful I've ever seen."

"It no longer exists, does it?" Plass said.

"Not as I knew it. It adapted the ways of chlorophyll. Now it's something quite different, and at any rate, the gate there has collapsed... No one in the Way will ever go there again."

"A shame," Plass said. "It seems a great tragedy of being mortal that we can't go back. My husband, on the other hand...has visited me seven times since I left the Redoubt." She smiled. "Is it wrong for me to take pleasure in his visits? He isn't happy—but I'm happier when I can see him, listen to him." She looked away, hunched her shoulders as if expecting a blow. "He doesn't, can't, listen to me."

Olmy nodded. What did not make sense could at least be politely acknowledged.

"In the Redoubt, he says, nothing is lost. I wonder how he knows? Is he there? Does he watch over them? The tragedy of uncontrolled order is that the past is revised—and revisited—as easily as the future. The last time he returned, he was in great pain. He said a new God had cursed him for being a counter-revolutionary. The Final Mind. He told me that the Eye of the Watcher tracked him throughout all eternity, on all world-lines, and whenever he tried to stand still, he was tortured, made into something different." Plass's face took on a shiny, almost sensual expectancy and she watched Olmy's reaction closely.

"You denied what the twins were saying," Olmy reminded her. "About echoes along world-lines."

"They aren't just *echoes*. We *are* our world-lines, Ser Olmy. These ghosts...are really just altered versions of the originals. They have blurred origins. They come from many different futures. But they have a reality, an independence. I feel this...when he speaks to me."

Olmy frowned. "I can't visualize all this. Order is supposed to be simplicity and peace... Not torture and distortion and coercion. Surely a universe of complete order would be more like heaven, in the Christian sense." He pointed to the antique book resting lightly in her lap. Plass shifted and the Bible rose into the air a few centimeters. She reached out to grasp it, hold it close again.

"Heaven has no change, no death," she said. "Mortals find that attractive, but they are mistaken. No good thing lasts forever. It becomes unbearable. Now imagine a force that demands that something last forever, yet become even more the essence of what it was, a force that will accept nothing less than compliance, but *can't communicate.*"

Olmy shook his head. "I can't."

"I can't, either, but that is what my husband describes."

Several seconds. Plass tapped the book lightly with her finger.

"How long since he last visited you?" Olmy asked.

"Three weeks. Maybe longer. Things seemed quiet just before they told me I could return to the Redoubt." She closed her eyes and held her hands to her cheeks. "I believed what Enoch believed, that order ascends. That it ascends forever. I believed that we are made with flaws, in a universe that was itself born flawed. I thought we would be so much more beautiful when—"

Karn and Rasp tracted forward and hovered beside Plass, who fell quiet and greeted them with a small shiver.

"We have ventured a possible answer to this dilemma," Karn said.

"Our birth geometry, outside the Way, is determined by a vacuum of infinite potential," Rasp said, nodding with something like glee. "We are forbidden from tapping that energy, so in our domain, space has a shape, and time has direction and a velocity. In the universe Enoch tapped, the energy of the vacuum is available at all times. Time and space and this energy, this potential, are bunched in a tight little knot of incredible density. That is what your husband must call the Final Mind. That our visitor renamed the allthing."

Plass shook her head indifferently.

"How amazing that must be!" Karn said. "A universe where order took hold in the first few nanoseconds after creation, controlling all the fires of the initial expansion, all the shape and constants of existence..."

"I wonder what Enoch would have done with such a domain, if she could have controlled it," Rasp said, hovering over Plass, peering down on her. Plass made as if to swat a fly, and Rasp tracted out of reach with a broad smile. "Ours is a pale candle indeed by comparison."

"Everything must tend toward a Final Mind. This force blossoms at the end of Time like a flower pushed up from all events, all lives, all thought. It is the ancestor not just of living creatures, but of all the interactions of matter, space, and time, for all things tend toward this blossom."

Olmy had often thought about this quote from the notes of Korzenowski. The designer of the Way had put together quite an original cosmology, which he had never tried to spread among his fellows. The original was in Korzenowski's library, kept as a Public Treasure, but few visited there now.

Olmy visited Rasp and Karn in their cabin while Plass read her Bible in the common area. The twins had arranged projections of geometric art and mathematical figures around the space, brightly colored and disorienting. He asked them whether they believed such an allthing, a perfectly ordered mind, could exist.

"Goodness, no!" Karn said, giggling.

"You mean, *Godness*, no!" Rasp added. "Not even if we believed in it, which we don't. Energy and impulse, yes; final, perhaps. Mind, no!"

"Whatever you call it—in the lesion, it may already exist, and it's different?"

"Of course it would exist! Not as a mind, that's all. Mind is impossible without neural qualities—communication between separate nodes that either contradict or confirm.

If we think correctly, a domain of order would reach completion within the first few seconds of existence, freezing everything. It would grasp and control all the energy of its beginning moment, work through all possible variations in an instant—become a monobloc, still and perfected, timeless. Not eternal—eviternal, frozen forever. Timeless."

"Our universe, our domain, could spin on for many billions or even trillions more years," Karn continued. "In our universe, there could very well be a Final Mind, the summing up of all neural processes throughout all time. But Deirdre Enoch found an abomination. If it were a mind, think of it! Instantly creating all things, never being contradicted, never *knowing*. Nothing has ever frustrated it, stopped it, trained or tamed it. It would be as immature as a newborn baby, and as sophisticated—"

"And ingenious," Rasp chimed in.

"—As the very devil," Karn finished.

"Please," Rasp finished, her voice suddenly quiet. "Even it such a thing is possible, let it not be a mind."

For the past million kilometers, they had passed over a scourged, scrubbed segment of the Way. In driving back the Jarts from their strongholds, tens of thousands of Way defenders had died. The Way had been altered by the released energies of the battle and still glowed slightly, shot through with pulsing curls and rays, while the flaw in this region transported them with a barely noticeable roughness. The flawship could compensate some, but even with this compensation, they had reduced their speed to a few thousand kilometers an hour.

The Redoubt lay less than ten thousand kilometers ahead.

Rasp and Karn removed their clavicles from their boxes

and tried as best they could to interpret the state of the Way as they came closer to the Redoubt.

Five thousand kilometers from the Redoubt, evidence of immense constructions lined the wall of the Way: highways, bands connecting what might have been linked gates; yet there were no gates. The constructions had been leveled to thin lanes of rubble, like lines of powder.

Olmy shook his head, dismayed. "Nothing is the way it was reported to be just a few weeks ago."

"I detect something unusual, too," Rasp said. Karn agreed. "Something related to the Jart offensive..."

"Something we weren't told about?" Plass wondered. "A colony that failed?"

"Ours, or Jart?" Olmy asked.

"Neither," Karn said, looking up from her clavicle. She lifted the device, a small fist-sized sphere mounted on two handles, and rotated the display for Olmy and Plass to see. Olmy had watched gate-openers perform before, and knew the workings of the display well enough—though he could never operate a clavicle. "There have never been gates opened here. This is all sham."

"A decoy," Plass said.

"Worse," Rasp said. "The gate at the Redoubt is twisting probabilities, sweeping world-lines within the Way to such an extreme... The residue of realities that never were are being deposited."

"Murmurs in the Way's sleep, nightmares in our unhistory," Karn said. For once, the twins seemed completely subdued, even disturbed. "I don't see how we can function if we're incorporated into such a sweep."

"So what is this?" Olmy asked, pointing to the smears of destroyed highways, cities, bands between the ghosts of gates.

"A future," Karn said. "Maybe what will happen if we fail..."

"But these patterns aren't like human construction," Plass observed. "No human city planner would lay out those roadways. Nor does it match anything we know about the Jarts."

Olmy looked more closely, frowned in concentration. "If someone else had created the Way," he said, "maybe this would be their ruins, the rubble of their failure."

Karn gave a nervous laugh. "Wonderful!" she said. "All we could have hoped for! If we open a gate here, what could possibly happen?"

Plass grabbed Olmy's arm. "Put it in our transmitted record. Tell the Hexamon this part of the Way must be forbidden. *No gates should be opened here, ever!*"

"Why not?" Karn said. "Think what could be learned. The new domains."

"I agree with Ser Plass," Rasp said. "It's possible there are worse alternatives than finding a universe of pure order." She let go of her clavicle and grabbed her head. "Even touching our instruments here causes pain. We are useless...any gate we open would consume us more quickly than the gate at the Redoubt! You *must* agree, sister!"

Karn was stubborn. "I don't see it," she said. "I simply don't. I think this could be very interesting. Fascinating, even."

Plass sighed. "This is the box that Konrad Korzenowski has opened for us," she said for Olmy's benefit. "Spoiled genius children drawn to evil like insects to a corpse."

"I thought evil was related to disorder," Olmy said.

"Already, you know better," Plass rejoined.

Rasp turned her eyes on Olmy and Plass, eyes narrow and full of uncomfortable speculation.

Olmy reached out and grasped Rasp's clavicle to keep

it from bumping into the flawship bulkheads. Karn took charge of the instrument indignantly and thrust it back at her sister. "You forget your responsibility," she chided. "We can fear this mission, or we can engage it with joy and spirit," she said. "Cowering does none of us any good."

"You're right, sister, about that at least," Rasp said. She returned her clavicle to its box and straightened her clothing, then used a cloth to wipe her face. "We are, after all, going to a place where we have always gone, always will go."

"It's what happens when we get there that is always changing," Karn said.

Plass's face went white. "My husband never returns the same way, in the same condition," she said. "How many hells does he experience?"

"One for each of him," Rasp said. "Only one. It is different husbands who return."

Though there had never been such this far along the Way, Olmy saw the scattered wreckage of Jart fortifications, demolished, dead and empty. Beyond them lay a region where the Way was covered with winding black and red bands of sand, an immense serpentine desert; also unknown. Olmy felt a spark of something reviving, if not a wish for life, then an appreciation of what extraordinary sights his life had brought him.

On Lamarckia, he had seen the most extraordinary variations on biology. Here, near the Redoubt, it was reality itself subject to its own flux, its own denial.

Plass was transfixed. "The next visitors, if any, will see something completely different," she said. "We've been caught up in a sweeping world-line of the Way, not necessarily our own."

"I would never have believed it possible," Rasp said,

and Karn reluctantly agreed. "This is not the physics we were taught."

"It can make any physics it wishes," Plass said. "Any reality. It has all the energy it needs. It has human minds to teach it our variations."

"It knows only unity," Karn said, taking hold of Plass's shoulder.

The older woman did not seem to mind. "It knows no will stronger than its own," she said. "Yet it may divide its will into illusory units. It is a tyrant..." Plass pointed to the winding sands, stretching for thousands of kilometers beneath them. "This is a moment of calm, of steady concentration. If my memories are correct, if what my husband's returning self...selves...tell me, is correct, it is usually much more frantic. Much more inventive."

Karn made a face and placed her hands on the bars of her clavicle. She rubbed the grips and her face became tight with concentration. "I feel it. There is still a lesion..."

Rasp took hold of her own instrument and went into her own state. "It's still there," she agreed,. "It's bad. It floats above the Way, very near the flaw. From below, it must look like some sort of bale star..."

They passed through a fine bluish mist that rose from the northern end of the desert. The flawship made a faint belling sound. The mist passed behind.

"There," Plass said. "No mistaking it!"

The gate pushed through the Way by Issa Danna had expanded and risen above the floor, just as Rasp and Karn had felt in their instruments. Now, at a distance of a hundred kilometers, they could see the spherical lesion clearly. It did indeed resemble a dark sun, or a chancre. A glow of pigeon's blood flicked around it, the red of rubies and enchantment. The black center, less than the width of a fingertip at this distance, perversely seemed to fill Olmy's field of vision.

His young body decided it was time to be very reluctant to proceed. He swallowed and brought this fear under control, biting his cheek until blood flowed.

The flawship lurched. Its voice told Olmy, "We have received an instructional beacon. There is a place held by humans less than ten kilometers away. They say they will guide us to safety."

"It's still there!" Plass said.

They all looked down through the flawship's transparent nose, away from the lurid pink of the flaw, through layers of blue and green haze wrapped around the Way, down twenty-five kilometers to a single dark, gleaming steel point in the center of a rough, rolling land.

The Redoubt lay in the shadow of the lesion, surrounded by a penumbral twilight suffused with the flickering red of the lesion's halo.

"I can feel the whipping hairs of other world-lines," Karn and Rasp said together. Olmy glanced back and saw their clavicles touching sphere to sphere. The spheres crackled and clacked. Karn twisted her instrument toward Olmy so that he could see the display. A long list of domain "constants"—pi, Planck's constant, others—varied with a regular humming in the flawship hull. "Nothing is stable out there!"

Olmy glanced at the message sent from the Redoubt. It provided navigation instructions for their flawship's landing craft; how to disengage from the flawship, descend, undergo examination, and be taken into the pyramid. The message concluded, "We will determine whether you are illusions or aberrations. If you are from our origin, we will welcome you. It is too late to return now. Abandon your flawship before it approaches any closer to the allthing. Whoever sent you has committed you to our own endless imprisonment."

"Cheerful enough," Olmy said. The ghastly light cast a fitful, abbatoir glow on their faces.

"We have always gone there," Rasp said quietly.

"We have to agree," Plass said. "We have no other place to go."

They tracted aft to the lander's hatch and climbed into the small, arrowhead-shaped craft. Its interior welcomed them by fitting to their forms, providing couches, instruments, tailored to their bodies. Plass sat beside Olmy in the cockpit, Rasp and Karn directly behind them.

Olmy disengaged from the flawship and locked the lander onto the pyramid's beacon. They dropped from the flawship. The landscape steadily grew in the broad cockpit window.

Plass's face crumpled, like a child about to break into tears. "Star, fate and pneuma, be kind. I see the opener's head. There!" She pointed in helpless dread, equally horrified and fascinated by something so inconceivable.

On a low, broad rise in the shadowed land surrounding the Redoubt, a huge dark head rose like an upright mountain, its skin like gray stone, one eye turned toward the south, the other watching over the territory before the nearest face of the pyramid. This watchful eye was easily a hundred meters wide, and glowed a dismal sea green, throwing a long beam through the thick twisted ropes of mist. Plass's voice became shrill. "Oh Star and Fate..."

The landscape around the Redoubt rippled beneath the swirling rays of rotating world-lines, spreading like hair from the black center of the lesion, changing the land a little with each pass, moving the bizarre landmarks a few dozen meters this way or that, increasing them in size, reducing them.

Olmy could never have imagined such a place. The Redoubt sat within a child's nightmare of disembodied human limbs, painted over the hills like trees, their fingers grasping and releasing spasmodically. At the top of one hill stood a kind of castle made of blocks of green glass, with a single huge door and window. Within the door stood a figure—a statue, perhaps—several hundred meters high, vaguely human, nodding its head steadily, idiotically, as the lander passed over. Hundreds of much smaller figures, gigantic nevertheless, milled in a kind of yard before the castle, their red and black shadows flowing like capes in the lee of the constant wind of changing probabilities. Olmy thought they might be huge dogs, or tailless lizards, but Plass pointed and said, "My husband told me about an assistant to Issa Danna named Ram Chako... Duplicated, forced to run on all fours."

The giant in the castle door slowly raised its huge hand, and the massive lizards scrambled over each other to run from an open portal in the yard. They leaped up as the lander passed overhead, as if they would snap it out of the air with hideous jaws.

Olmy's head throbbed. He could not bring himself out of a conviction that none of this could be real; indeed, there was no necessity for it to *be* real in any sense his body understood. For their part, Rasp and Karn had lost all their earlier bravado and clung to each other, their clavicles floating on tethers wrapped around their wrists.

The lurid glare of the halo flowed like blood into the cabin as the lander rotated to present points of contact for traction fields from the Redoubt. Olmy instructed the ship to present a wide-angle view of the Redoubt and the land, and this view revolved slowly around them, filling the lander's cramped interior.

The perverse variety seemed to never end. Something had dissected not only a human body, or many bodies, and wreaked hideous distortions on its parts, but had done the same with human thoughts and desires, planting the results over the region with no obvious design.

Within the low valley—as described by the female visitant—a large blue-skinned woman, the equal of the figure in the doorway of the castle, crouched near a cradle within which churned hundreds of naked humans. She slowly dropped her hand into the cauldron of flesh and stirred, and her hair sprayed out from her head with a sullen cometary glow, casting everything in a syrupy green luminosity.

"Mother of geometries," Karn muttered, and hid her eyes.

Olmy could not turn away, but everything in him wanted to go to sleep, to die, rather than to acknowledge what they were seeing.

Plass saw his distress. Somehow she took strength from the incomprehensible view. "It does not need to make sense," she said with the tone of a chiding schoolteacher. "It's supported by infinite energy and a monolithic, mindless will. There is nothing new here, nothing—"

"I'm not asking that it make sense," Olmy said. "I need to know what's behind it."

"A sufficient force, channeled properly, can create anything a mind can imagine—" Karn began.

251

"More than any mind will imagine. Not a mind like our minds," Rasp restated. "A unity, not a *mind* at all."

For a moment, Olmy's anger lashed and he wanted to shout his frustration, but he took a deep breath, folded his arms where he floated in tracting restraints, and said to Plass, "A mind that has no goals? If there's pure order here—"

Karn broke in, her voice high and sweet, singing. "Think of the dimensions of order. There is mere arrangement, the lowest form of order, without motive or direction. Next comes self-making, when order can convert resources into more of itself, propagating order. Then comes creation, self-making reshaping matter into something new. But when creation stalls, when there is no mind, just force, it becomes mere elaboration, an endless spiral of rearrangement of what has been created. What do we see down there? Empty elaboration. Nothing new. No understanding."

"She shows some wisdom," Plass acknowledged grudgingly. "But the allthing still must exist."

"And all this...elaboration?" Olmy asked.

"Spoiled by deathlessness," Plass said, "by never-ending supplies of resources. Never freshened by the new, at its core. Order without death, art without critic or renewal, the final mind of a universe where only riches exist, only joy is possible, never knowing disappointment."

The lander shuddered again and again as they dropped toward the pyramid. Its inertial control systems could not cope with the sweeping rays of different world-lines.

"Sounds like a spoiled child," Olmy said.

"Far worse," Karn said. "*We're* like spoiled children,

Rasp and I. Willful and maybe a little silly. Humans are silly, childish, always learning, full of failure. Out there—beyond the lesion, reaching through it..."

"Perpetual success," Rasp mocked. "Ultimate maturity. It cannot learn. Only rearrange."

"Deirdre Enoch was never content with limitations," Plass said, looking to Olmy for sympathy. "She went searching for what heaven would really be." Her eyes glittered with her emotion—exaltation brought on by too much fear and dismay.

"Maybe she found it," Karn said.

5

"I can't welcome you," Deirdre Enoch said, walking heavily toward them. Behind Olmy, within a chamber high in the Redoubt, near the tip of the steel pyramid, the lander sighed and settled into its cradle.

Olmy tried to compare this old woman with the portraits of Enoch in the records. Her voice was much the same, though deeper, and almost without emotion.

Rasp, Karn, and Plass stood beside Olmy as Enoch approached. Behind Enoch, in the lambency of soft amber lights spaced around the base of the chamber, wavered a line of ten other men and women, all of them old, all dressed in black, with silver ribbons hanging from the tops of their white-haired heads. "You've come to a place of waiting where nothing is resolved. Why come at all?"

Before Olmy could answer, Enoch smiled, her deeply wrinkled face seeming to crack with the unfamiliar expression. "We assume you are here because you think the Jarts could become involved."

"I don't know what to think," Olmy said, his voice hoarse. "I recognize you, but none of the others..."

"We survived the first night after the lesion. We formed an expedition to make an escape attempt. There were sixty of us that first time. We managed to return to the Redoubt before the Night Land could change us too much, play with us too drastically. We aged. Some of us were taken and... You see them out there. There was no second expedition."

"My husband," Plass said. "Where is he?"

"Yes... I know you. You are so much the same it hurts. You escaped at the very beginning."

"I was the only one," Plass said.

"You called it the Night Land," Rasp said, holding up her hands, the case with her clavicle. "How appropriate."

"No sun, no hope, only *order*," Enoch said, as if the word were a curse. "Did you send yourselves, or were you sent by other fools?"

"Fools, I'm afraid," Plass said.

"And you... You came back, knowing what you'd find?"

"It wasn't like this when I left. My husband sent ghosts to visit me. They told me a little of what's happened here...or might have happened."

"Ghosts try to come into the Redoubt and talk," Enoch said, her many legs shifting restlessly. "We refuse them. Your husband was caught outside that first night. He hasn't been changed much. He stands near the Watcher, frozen in the eyebeam."

Plass sobbed and hid her face.

Enoch continued, heedless. "The only thing left in his control—to shed ghosts like dead skin. And never the same... are they? He's allowed to take temporary twists of space-time and shape them in his own image. The allthing finds this sufficiently amusing. Needless to say, we don't let the ghosts bother us. We have too much else to do, just to keep our place secure, and in repair."

"Repair," Karn said with a beatific smile, and Olmy turned to her, startled by a reaction similar to his own. Karn did a small dance. "Disorder has its place here, then. You have to *work* to *fix things?*"

"Precisely," Enoch said. "I worship rust and age. But we're only allowed so much of it and no more. Now that you're here, perhaps you'll join us for some tea?" She smiled. "Blessedly, our tea cools quickly in the Redoubt. Our bones grow frail, our skin wrinkles. Tea cools. Hurry!"

"Don't be deceived by our bodies," Deirdre Enoch said as she poured steaming tea into cups for all her guests. "They are distorted, but they are sufficient. The *allthing* can only perfect and elaborate; it knows nothing of real destruction."

Olmy watched something ripple through the old woman, a shudder of slight change. She seemed not as old and wrinkled now, as if some force had turned back a clock.

"I'm not clear about perfection," Olmy said, lifting the cup without enthusiasm. "I'm not even clear on how you come to look old."

"We're not unhappy," Enoch said. "That isn't within our power. We know we can never return to *Thistledown*. We know we can never escape."

"You haven't answered Ser Olmy's question," Plass said gently. "Are you independent here?"

"That wasn't his question, Ser Gena Plass," Enoch said, an edge in her voice. "What you ask is not a *polite* question. I said, we were caught trying to escape. Some of us are out there in the Night Land now. Those of us who returned to the pyramid...did not escape the enthusiasm of the allthing. But it's influence here is limited. To answer one question at least: We have some independence." Enoch nodded as if falling asleep, her head dropping briefly to an angle with her shoulders...an uncomfortable angle, Olmy would have thought. She raised it again with a jerk. "The universe I discovered...there is nothing else. It is all."

"The Final Mind of the domain," Plass said.

"I gather it regards the Way and the humans it finds here as objects of curiosity," Olmy said. Rasp and Karn fidgeted.

"Objects to be recombined and distorted," Enoch said. "We are materials for the ultimate in decadent art. The allthing is beyond our knowing." She leaned forward on her cushion, where she had gracefully folded her legs into an agile lotus, and rubbed her nose reflectively with the back of one hand. "We are allowed to resist, I suspect, because we are antithesis."

"The *allthing* has only known thesis," Rasp said with a small giggle.

"Exa-a-a-ctly," Enoch said, drawing out the word with pleasure. Struck by another sensation of unreality, Olmy looked around the group sitting with Enoch and himself: Plass, the twins, a small woman with a questing, feline expression behind Enoch who had said nothing. She carried the teapot around again and refilled their cups.

The tea was cold.

Olmy turned on his sitting pillow to observe the other elderly followers, arrayed around the circular room, still, subservient. Their faces had changed since his arrival, yet no one had left, no one had entered.

It had been observed for a dozen generations that *Thistledown's* environment and culture bred followers with proportionately fewer leaders, often assigned much greater power. Efforts were being made to remedy that—to reduce the extreme schisms of rogues such as Deirdre Enoch. *Too late for these,* he thought. *Does this allthing want followers?*

He could not get his bearings long enough to plan his course of action. He felt drugged, but knew he wasn't.

"Can it tolerate otherness?" Karn asked, her voice high and sweet once more, like a child's.

"No," Enoch said. "Its nature is to absorb and disguise all otherness in mutation, change without goal."

"Like the Jarts?" Rasp asked, chewing on her thumb

with a coyness and insecurity that was at once studied and completely convincing.

"Not like the Jarts. The Jarts met the allthing and it gave them their own Night Land. I fear it won't be long until ours is merged with theirs, and we are both mingled and subjected to further useless change."

"How long?" Olmy asked.

"Another few years, perhaps."

"Not so soon, then," he said.

"Soon enough," Enoch said with a sniff. She rubbed her nose again. "We've been here already for well over a thousand centuries."

Olmy tried to understand this. "Truly?" he asked, expecting her to break into laughter.

"Truly. I've had millions of different followers here. Look around you." She leaned over the table to whisper to Olmy, "Waves in a sea. I've lived a thousand centuries in a thousand infinitesimally different universes. It plays with all world-lines, not just the tracks of individuals. Only I am relatively the same with each tide. I appear to be the real nexus in this part of the Way."

"Tea cools...skin wrinkles... But you experience such a length of time?"

"Ten thousand lengths cut up and bundled and rotated." She took a scarf from around her thin neck and stretched it between her fists. "Twisted. Knotted. You were sent here to correct the reckless madness of a renegade...weren't you?"

"A Geshel visionary," Olmy said.

Enoch was not mollified. She drew herself up and returned her scarf to her neck, tying it with a conscious flourish. "I was appointed by the Office of Way Maintenance by Ry Ornis himself. They gave me two of the best gate-openers in the guild, and they instructed me, specifically, to find a gate into total order. I wasn't told why. I can guess now, however."

"I remember two openers," Plass said. "They don't."

"They hoped you would find me transformed or dead," Enoch said. "Well, I'm different, but I've survived, and after a few thousands of centuries, one's personality becomes rather rigid. I've become more like that Watcher and its huge gaping eye outside. I don't know how to lie anymore. I've seen too much. I've fought against what I found, and I've endured atrocities beyond what any human has ever had to face. Believe me, I would rather have died before my mission began than see what I've seen."

"Where is the other opener?" Olmy asked.

"In the Night Land," Enoch said. "Issa Danna was the first to encounter the *allthing*. He and his partner, master Tolby Kin, took the brunt of its first efforts at elaboration."

Rasp walked over to Olmy and whispered in his ear. "There never was a master opener named Tolby Kin."

"Can anybody else confirm your story?" Olmy asked.

"Would you believe anyone here? No," Enoch said.

"Not that it matters," Plass said fatalistically. "The end result is the same."

"Not at all," Enoch said. "We couldn't close down the lesion now even if we had it in our power. Ry Ornis was correct. The rift had to be opened. The infection is not finished. If we don't wait for completion, our universe will never quicken. It'll be born dead." Enoch shook her head and laughed softly. "And no human in our history will ever see a ghost. A haunted world is a living world, Ser Olmy."

Olmy touched his tea cup with his finger. The tea was hot again.

The living quarters made available were spare and cold.

Most of the Redoubt's energy went to keeping the occupants of the Night Land at bay; that energy was derived from the wall of the Way, an ingenious arrangement set up by Issa Danna before he was caught up in the lesion; sufficient, but not a surfeit by any means.

For the first time in days, Olmy had a few moments alone. He cleared a window looking south, toward the lesion and across about fifty kilometers of the Night Land. Enoch had provided him with a pair of ray-tracing binoculars.

Beyond a tracting grid stretched to its limits, and a glowing demarcation of complete nuclear destruction, through which nothing made of matter could hope to cross, less than a thousand meters from the pyramid, lay the peculiar vivid darkness and the fitful nightmare glows of the allthing's victims.

Olmy swung the lightweight binoculars in a slow steady arc. What looked like hills or low mountains were constructions attended by hundreds of pale figures, human-sized but only vaguely human in shape. They seemed to spend much of their time fighting, waving their limbs about like insect antennae. Others carried loads of glowing dust in baskets, dumping them at the top of a hill, then stumbling and sliding down to begin again.

The giant head modeled after the opener stood a little to the west of the Green Glass Castle. Olmy could not tell whether the head was actually organic material—human flesh—or not. It looked more like stone, though the eye was very expressive.

From this angle, he could not see the huge figure standing in the door of the castle; that side was turned away from the Redoubt. Nothing that he saw contradicted what Plass and Enoch had told him. He could not share the cheerful nihilism of the twins. Nevertheless, nothing that he saw could be fit into any philosophy or web of physical laws he had ever encountered. If there was a mind here, it was incomprehensibly different—perhaps no mind at all.

Still, he tried to find some pattern, some plan to the Night Land. A rationale. He could not.

Just before the tallest hills stood growths like the tangled roots of upended trees, leafless, barren, dozens of meters high and stretching in ugly, twisted forests several kilometers across. A kind of pathway reached from the northern wall of the Redoubt, through the demarcation, into a tortured terrain of what looked like huge strands of melted and drawn glass, and to the east of the castle. It dropped over a closer hill and he could not see where it terminated.

The atmosphere around the Redoubt was remarkably clear, though columns of twisted mist rose around the Night Land. Before a wall of blue haze at some fifty kilometers distance, everything stood out with complete clarity.

Olmy turned away at a knock on his door. Plass entered, wearing a look of contentment that seemed ready to burst into enthusiasm. "Now do you doubt me?"

"I doubt everything," Olmy said. "I'd just as soon believe we've been captured and are being fed delusions."

"Do you think that's what's happened?" Plass asked, eyes narrowing as if she had been insulted.

"No," Olmy said. "I've experienced some pretty good delusions in training. This is real, whatever that means."

"I must admit the little twins are busy," Plass said, sitting on a small chair near the table. These and a small mattress on the floor were the only items of furniture in the room. "They're talking to anybody who knows anything about Enoch's gate openers. I don't think you can talk to the same person twice here in an hour—unless it's Enoch."

Olmy nodded. He was still digesting Enoch's claim that the Office of Way Maintenance had sent an expedition with secret orders... In collusion with the opener's guild.

Perhaps the twins knew more than he did, or Plass. "Did you know anything about an official mission?" he asked.

Plass did not answer for a moment. "Not in so many words. Not 'official.' But perhaps not without...support from Way Maintenance. We did not think we were out-laws."

"You've both talked about completion. Was that mentioned when you joined the group?"

"Only in passing. A theory."

Olmy turned back to the window. "There's a camera obscura near the top of the pyramid. I'd like to look over everything around us, try to make sense of our position."

"Useless," Plass said. "I'd wait for a visitation first."

"More ghosts?"

Plass shrugged her shoulders and stretched out her legs, rubbing her knees.

"I haven't been visited," Olmy said.

"It will happen," Plass said flatly. She appeared to be hiding something, something that worried her. "I wouldn't look forward to it. But then, there's nothing you can do to prepare."

Olmy laughed, but the laugh sounded hollow. He felt as if he were slowly coming unraveled, like Enoch's bundle of relived world-lines. "How would I know if I've seen a ghost?" he asked. "Maybe I have—on *Thistledown*. Maybe they're around us all the time, but don't reveal them-selves."

Plass looked to one side, then said, with an effort, her voice half-choking, "I've met my own ghost."

"You didn't mention that before."

"It came to visit me the night after we left *Thistledown*. It told me we would reach the pyramid."

Olmy held back another laugh, afraid it might get loose and never stop. "I've never seen a ghost of myself."

"We do things differently, then. I seemed to be working backward from some experience with the allthing. A ghost lets you remember the future, or some alternate of the future. Maybe in time I'll be told what the allthing will do to me. Its elaborations."

Olmy considered this in silence. Plass's somber gray eyes focused on him, clear, child-like in their perfect gravity. Now he saw the resemblance, the reason why he felt a tug of liking for her. She reminded him of Sheila Ap Nam, his first wife on Lamarckia.

"Your loved ones, friends, colleagues... They will see you, versions of you, if you meet the allthing." Plass said. "A kind of immortality. Remembrance." She looked down and clutched her arms. "No other intelligent species we've encountered has a history of myths about spirits. No experience with ghosts. You know that? We're unique. Alone. Except perhaps the Jarts...and we don't know much about them, do we?"

He nodded, wanting to get rid of the topic. "What are the twins planning?"

"They seem to regard this as a challenging game. Who knows? They're working. It's even possible they'll think of something."

Olmy aimed the binoculars toward the Watcher, its single glowing eye forever turned toward the Redoubt. He felt a bone-deep revulsion and hatred, mixed with a desiccating chill. His tongue seemed frosted. Perversely, the flesh behind his eyes felt hot and moist. His neck hair pricked.

"There's—" he began, but then flinched and blinked. A curtain of shadow passed through the few centimeters between him and the window. He backed off with a groan and tried to push something away, but the curtain would not be touched. It whirled around him, swept before Plass, who tracked it calmly, and then seemed to press against and slip through the opposite wall.

The warmth behind his eyes felt hot as steam.

"*I knew it*!" he said hoarsely. "I could feel it coming! Something about to happen." His hands trembled. He had never reacted so drastically to physical danger.

"That was nothing," Plass said. "I've seen them many times, more since I first came here."

Olmy's reaction angered him. "What is it?"

"Not a ghost, not any other version of ourselves, that's for sure," she said. "A parasite, maybe, like a flea darting around our world-lines. Harmless, as far as I know. But much more visible here than back on *Thistledown*."

Trying to control himself was backfiring. All his instincts rejected what he was experiencing. "I don't accept any of this!" he shouted. His hands spasmed into fists. "None of it makes sense!"

"I agree," Plass said, her voice low. "Pity we're stuck with it. Pity you're stuck with me. But more pity that I'm stuck with you. It seems you try to be a rational man, Ser Olmy. My husband was exceptionally rational. The allthing adores rational men."

6

Rasp and Karn walked with Olmy on the parapet near the peak of the Redoubt. Their work seemed to have sobered them. They still walked like youngsters, Karn or Rasp lagging to peer at something in the Night Land and then scurrying to catch up; but their voices were steady, serious, even a little sad.

"We've never experienced anything like the lesion," Karn said. The huge dark disk, rimmed in bands and flares of red, blotted out the opposite side of the Way. "It's much more than just a failed gate. It doesn't stop here, you know."

"How do you mean?" Olmy asked.

"Something like this influences the entire Way. When the gate got out of control—"

Rasp took Karn's hand and tugged it in warning.

"What does it matter?" Karn asked, and shook her twin loose. "There can't be secrets here. If we don't agree to do something, the allthing will get us soon anyway, and then we'll be planted out there...bits and pieces of us, like lost toys."

Rasp dropped back a few steps, folded her arms in pique. Karn continued. "When the lesion formed, gate-openers felt it in every new gate. Threads trying to get through, like spider-silk. We can see the world-lines being twirled here... But they bunch up and wind around the Way even where we can't see them. Master Ry Ornis thought—"

"Enough!" Rasp said, rushing to catch up.

Karn stopped with tears in her eyes and glared over the parapet wall.

"I can guess a few things," Olmy said. "What Deirdre Enoch says leaves little enough to imagine. You aren't failed apprentices, are you?"

Rasp stared at him defiantly.

"No," Karn said.

Her twin turned and lifted a hand as if to strike her, then dropped it by her side. She drew a short breath, said, "We act like children because of the mathematical conditioning. Too fast. Ry Ornis told us we were needed. He accelerated training. We were the best, but we *are* too young. It holds us down."

A sound like hundreds of voices in a bizarre chorus floated over the Night Land, through the field that protected the Redoubt's atmosphere. The chorus alternately rose and sank through scales, hooting forlornly like apes in a zoo.

"Ry Ornis thought the lesion was bending world-lines even beyond *Thistledown*," Karn said. Rasp nodded and held her sister's hand. "Climbing back along the *Thistledown's* world line...where all our lives bunch together with the lives of our ancestors. Using us as a ladder."

"Not just us," Rasp added. The hooting chorus now came from all around the Redoubt. From this side of the pyramid, they could see a slender obelisk the colors of a bright moon on an oil slick rising within an immense scaffold made of parts of bodies, arms and legs strapped together with cords. These limbs were monstrous, however, fully dozens of meters long, and the obelisk had climbed within its scaffolding to at least a kilometer in height, twice as tall as the Redoubt.

The region around the construction crawled with pale tubular bodies, like insect larva, and Olmy decided it was these bodies that were doing most of the singing and hooting.

"Right," Karn agreed. "Not just us. Using the branching lines of all the matter, all the particles in *Thistledown* and the Way."

"Who knows how far it's reached?" Rasp asked.

"What can it do?" Olmy asked.

"We don't know," Karn said.

"What can *we* do?"

"Oh, we can close down the lesion, if we act quickly," Rasp said with a broken smile. "That shouldn't be too difficult."

"It's actually growing smaller," Karn said. "We can create a ring gate from here... A cirque. Cinch off the Way. The Way will shrink back towards the source, the maintenance machinery in the sixth chamber, very quickly—a million kilometers a day. We might even be able to escape along the flaw, but—"

"The flaw will act weird if we make a cinch," Rasp finished.

"Very weird," Karn agreed. "So we probably won't get home. We knew that. Ry Ornis prepared us. He told us that much."

"Besides, if we did go back to *Thistledown*, who would want us now, the way we are?" Rasp asked. "We're pretty broken inside."

The twins paused on the parapet. Olmy watched as they clasped hands and began to hum softly to each other. Their clavicles hung from their shoulders, and the cases tapped as they swayed. Rasp glanced at Olmy, primming her lips.

"Enoch spoke of a plan by the Office of Way Maintenance," Olmy said. "She claims she was sent here secretly."

"We know nothing about that," Karn said guilelessly. "But that might not mean much. I don't think they would have trusted us."

"She also said that the allthing has some larger purpose in our own universe," Olmy continued. "Something that has to be completed, or our existence will be impossible."

Karn considered this quietly, finger to her nostril, then shook her head. "We heard her, but I don't see it," she said. "Maybe she's trying to justify herself."

"*We* do that all the time," Rasp said. "We understand that sort of thing."

They had reached the bottom of the stairs leading up to the peak and the camera obscura. Karn climbed two steps at a time, her robe swinging around her ankles, and Rasp followed with more dignity. Olmy stayed near the bottom. Rasp turned and looked down on him.

"Come on," she said, waving.

Olmy shook his head. "I've seen enough. I can't make sense out of anything out there. I think it's random—just nonsense."

"Not at all!" Rasp said, and descended a few steps, beseeching him to join her. "We have to see what happened to the openers' clavicles. What sort of elaboration there might be. It could be very important."

Olmy hunched his shoulders, shook his head like a bull trying to build courage. He followed her up the steps.

The camera obscura was a spherical all-focal lens, its principle not unlike that of the ray-tracing binoculars. Mounted on a tripod on the flat platform at the peak of the pyramid, it projected and magnified the Night Land for anyone standing on the platform. Approaching the tripod increased magnification in logarithmic steps, with precise quickness; distances of a few tenths of a centimeter could make objects zoom to alarming proportions. Monitors on the peripheral circle, small spheres on steel poles, rolled in and out with slow grace, tracking the developments in the Night Land and sending their results down to Enoch and the others inside.

Olmy deftly avoided the monitors and walked slowly, with great concentration, around the circle. Karn and Rasp made their own surveys.

Olmy stopped and drew back to take in the Watcher's immense eye. The angle of the hairless brow, the droop of the upper lid, gave it a sad and corpse-like lassitude, but the eye still moved in small arcs, and from this perspective, there was no doubt it was observing the Redoubt. Olmy felt that it saw him, knew him; had he ever met the opener, before his mission to Lamarckia, perhaps by accident? Was there some residual memory of Olmy in that immense head? Olmy thought such a connection might be very dangerous.

"The Night Land changes every hour, sometimes small changes, sometimes massive," Enoch said, walking slowly and deliberately up the steps behind them. She stopped outside the camera's circle. "It tracks our every particle. It's patient."

"Does it fear us?" Olmy asked.

"No fear. We haven't even begun to be played with."

"That out there is not elaboration—it's pointless madness."

"I thought so myself," Enoch said. "Now I see a pattern. The longer I'm here, the more I sympathize with the all-thing. Do you understand what I told you earlier? It *recognizes* us, Ser Olmy. It sees its own work in us, a cycle waiting to be completed."

Rasp held a spot within the circle and motioned for Karn to join her. Together, they peered at something in complete absorption, ignoring Enoch.

Olmy could not ignore her, however. He needed to

resolve this question. "The Office of Way Maintenance sent you here to confirm that?"

"Not in so many words, but... Yes. We know that our own domain, our home universe outside the Way, should have been born barren, empty. Something quickened it, fed it with the necessary geometric nutrients. Some of us thought that would only be possible if the early universe made a connection with a domain of very different properties. I told Ry Ornis that such a quickening need not have happened at the beginning. We could do it now. We had the Way... We could perform the completion. There was such a feeling of power and justification within the guild. I encouraged it. The connection has been made... And all that, the Night Land, is just a side effect. Pure order flowing back through the Way, through *Thistledown*, back through time to the beginning. Was it worth it? Did we do what we had planned? I'll never know conclusively, because we can't reverse it now...and cease to be."

"You weren't sure. You knew this could be dangerous, harm the Way, fatal if the Jarts gained an advantage?"

Enoch stared at him for a few seconds, eyes moving from his eyes to his lips, his chest, as if she would measure him. "Yes," she said. "I knew. Ry Ornis knew. The others did not."

"They suffered for what you've learned," Olmy said. Enoch's gaze steadied and her jaw clenched.

"I've suffered, too. I've learned very little, Ser Olmy. What I learn repeats itself over and over again, and it has more to do with arrogance than metaphysics."

"We've found one!" Karn shouted. "There's a clavicle mounted on top of the green castle. We can pinpoint it!"

Olmy stood where Rasp indicated. At the top of the squat, massive green castle stood a cube, half-hidden behind a mass of root-like growth. On top of the cube, a black pillar about the height of a man supported the unmistakable sphere-and-handles of a clavicle. The sphere was dark, dormant; nothing moved around the pillar or anywhere on the castle roof.

"There's only one, and it appears to be inactive," Rasp said. "The lesion is independent."

Karn spread her arms, wiggling her fingers. A wide smile lit up her face. "We can make a cirque!"

"We can't do it from here," Rasp said. "We have to go out there."

Enoch's face tensed into a rigid mask. "We haven't finished," she said. "The work isn't done!"

Olmy shook his head. He'd made his decision. "Whoever started this, and for whatever reason, it has to end now. The Nexus orders it."

"They don't know!" Enoch cried out.

"We know enough," Olmy said.

Rasp and Karn held each other's hand and descended the stairs. Rasp stuck her tongue out at the old woman.

Enoch laughed and lightly slapped her hands on her thighs. "They're only children! They won't succeed. What have I to fear from failed apprentices?"

The Night Land's atmosphere was a thin haze of primordial hydrogen, mixed with carbon dioxide and some small trace of oxygen from the original envelope surrounding the gate. At seven hundred millibars of pressure, and with a temperature just above freezing, they could venture out of the Redoubt in the most basic pressurized worksuits.

Enoch and her remaining, ever-changing people would not help them. Olmy preferred it that way. He walked through the empty corridors of the pyramid's ground floor and found a small wheeled vehicle that at one time had been used to reach the garden outside the Redoubt—a garden that now lay beyond the demarcation.

Plass showed him how the open vehicle worked. "It has its own pilot, makes a field around the passenger compartment."

"It looks familiar enough," Olmy said.

Plass sat next to Olmy and placed her hand on a control bar. "My husband and I used to tend our plot out there...flowers, herbs, vegetables. We'd drive one of these for a few hundred meters, outside the work zone, to where the materials team had spread soil brought through the first gate."

Olmy sat in the vehicle. It announced it was drawing a charge in case it would be needed. It added, in a thin voice, "Will this journey last more than a few hours? I can arrange with the station master for—"

"No," Olmy said. "No need." He turned to Plass. "Time to put on a suit."

Plass stepped out of the car and nervously smoothed her hands down her hips. "I'm staying here. I can't bring myself to go out there again."

"I understand."

"I don't see how you'll survive. "

"It looks very chancy," Olmy admitted.

"Why can't they open a ring gate from here?"

"Rasp and Karn say they have to be within five hundred meters of the lesion. About where the other clavicle is now."

"Do you know what my husband was, professionally? Before we came here?"

"No."

"A neurologist. He came along to study the effects of our experiment on the researchers. There was some thought our minds would be enhanced by contact with the ordered domain. They were all very optimistic." She put her hand on Olmy's shoulder. "We had faith. Enoch still believes what they told her, doesn't she?"

Olmy nodded. "May I make one last request?"

"Of course," Plass said.

"Enoch promised us she would open a way through the demarcation and let us through. She claimed we couldn't do anything out there but be taken in by the allthing, anyway..."

Plass smiled. "I'll watch her, make sure the fields are open long enough for you to go through. The guild was very clever, sending you and the twins, you know."

"Why?"

"You're all very deceptive. You all seem to be failures." Plass clenched his shoulder.

She turned and left as Rasp and Karn entered the storage chamber. The twins watched her go in silence. They carried their clavicles and had already put on their pressure suits, which had adjusted to their small frames and made a precise fit.

"We've always made her uncomfortable," Rasp said. "Maybe I don't blame her."

Karn regarded Olmy with deep black eyes. "You haven't met a ghost of yourself, have you?"

"I haven't," Olmy said.

"Neither have we. And that's significant. We're never going to reach the allthing. It's never going to get us."

Olmy remembered what Plass had said. She had seen her own ghost...

7

They cursed the opening of the Way and the change of the Thistledown's mission. They assassinated the Way's creator, Konrad Korzenowski. For centuries they maintained a fierce opposition, largely underground, but with connections to the Naderites in power. In any given year there might be only four of five active members of this most radical sect, the rest presuming to lead normal lives; but the chain was maintained. All this because their original leader had a vision of the Way as an easy route to infinite hells.

—Lives of the Opposition, Anonymous,
Journey Year 475

The three rode the tiny wheeled vehicle over a stretch of bare Way floor, a deeply tarnished copper-bronze colored surface of no substance whatsoever, and no friction at this point. They kept their course with little jets of air expelled from the sides of the car, until they reached a broad low island of glassy materials, just before the boundary markers that warned they were coming to the demarcation.

As agreed, the traction lines switched to low power, and an opening appeared directly ahead of them, a clarified darkness in the pale green field. This relieved Olmy somewhat; he had had some doubts that Enoch would cooperate, or that Plass could compel her. The vehicle rolled through. They crossed the defenses. Behind them, the fields went up again.

Now the floor of the Way was covered with sandy soil.

The autopilot switched off the air jets and let the vehicle roll for another twenty meters.

The pressure suits were already becoming uncomfortable; they were old, and while they did their best to fit, their workings were in less than ideal condition. Still, they would last several weeks, recycling gases and liquids and complex molecules, rehydrating the body through arterial inserts and in the same fashion providing a minimal diet.

Olmy doubted the suits would be needed for more than a few more hours.

The twins ignored their discomfort and focused their attention on the lesion. Outside the pyramid, the lesion seemed to fill the sky, and in a few kilometers, it would be almost directly overhead. From this angle, the hairlike swirls of spinning world-lines already took on a shimmering reflective quality, like bands sliced from a wind-ruffled lake; their passage sang in Olmy's skull, more through his teeth than through his ears.

The full character of the Night Land came on gradually, beginning with a black, gritty, loose scrabble beneath the tires of the vehicle. Olmy's suit readout, shining directly into his left eye, showed a decrease in air pressure of a few millibars beyond the demarcation. The temperature remained steady, just above zero degrees Celsius.

They turned west, to their left as they faced north down the Way, and came upon the path Olmy had seen from the peak of the pyramid. Plass had identified it as the road used by vehicles carrying material from the first gate Enoch had opened. It had also been the path to Plass's garden, the one she had shared with her husband. Within a few minutes, about three kilometers from the Redoubt, passing over the rise that had blocked his view, they came across the garden's remains.

The relief here was very low, but the rise of some fifty

meters had been sufficient to hide what must have been among the earliest attempts at elaboration. Olmy was not yet sure he believed in the allthing, but what had happened in the garden, and in the rest of the Night Land, made any disagreement moot. The trees in the southwest corner of a small rapid-growth orchard had spread out low to the ground, and glowed now like the body of Number 2. Those few trees left standing flickered like frames in a child's flipbook. The rest of the orchard had simply turned to sparkling ash. In the center, however, rose a mound of gnarled brown shot through with vivid reds and greens, and in the middle of this mound, facing almost due south, not looking at anything in particular, was a face some three meters in height, its skin the color of green wood, cracks running from crown to chin. The face did not move or exhibit any sign of life.

Puffs of dust rose from the ash, tiny little explosions from within this mixture of realities. The ash reformed to obliterate the newly-formed craters. It seemed to have some purpose of its own, as did everything else in the garden but the face.

Ruin and elaboration; one form of life extinguished, another imbued.

"Early," Karn said, looking to their right at a sprawl of shining dark green leaves, stretched, expanded, and braided into eye-twisting knots. "Didn't know what it was dealing with."

"Doesn't look like it ever did," Olmy said, realizing she were speaking as if some central director actually did exist. Rasp set her sister straight.

"We've seen textbook studies of gates gone wrong. Geometry is the living tissue of reality. Mix constants and you get a—"

"We've sworn not to discuss the failures," Karn said, but without any strength.

"We are being driven through the worst failure of all," Rasp said. "Mixed constants and skewed metrics explain all of this."

Karn shrugged. Olmy thought that perhaps it did not matter; perhaps Rasp and Karn and Plass did not really disagree, merely described the same thing in different ways. What they were seeing up close was not random rearrangement; it had a demented, even a vicious quality, that suggested purpose.

Above the rows of flip-book trees and the living layers of ash stretched a dead and twisted sky. From the hideous chancre of dead blackness, with its sullen ring of congealed red, depended curtains of rushing darkness that swept the Night Land like rain beneath a moving front.

"Mother's hair," Karn said, and clutched her clavicle tightly in white-knuckled hands.

"She's playing with us," Rasp said. "Bending over us, waving her hair over our crib. We reach up to grab and she pulls away."

"She laughs," Karn said.

"Then she gives us to the—"

Rasp did not have time to finish. The vehicle swerved abruptly with a small squeak before a sudden chasm that had not been there an instant before. Out of the chasm leaped white shapes, humanlike but fungal, doughy and featureless. They seemed to be expelled and to climb out equally, and they lay on the sandy black-streaked ground for a moment, as if recovering from their birth. Then they rose to loose and wobbling feet and ran with speed and even grace over the irregular landscape to the trees, which they began to uproot.

These were the laborers Olmy had seen from the pyramid. They paid no attention to the intruders. The chasm closed, and Olmy instructed the car to continue.

"Is that what we'll become?" Karn asked.

"Each of us will become *many* of them," Rasp said.

"Such a relief to know!" Karn said sardonically.

The rotating shadows ahead gave the ground a blurred and frantic aspect, like unfocused time-lapse photography. Only the major landmarks stood unchanged in the sweeps of metaphysical revision: the Watcher, pale beam still glowing from its unblinking eye, the Castle with its unseen giant occupant, and the obelisk with its scaffold and hordes of white figures working directly beneath the lesion.

Olmy ordered the vehicle to stop, but Rasp grabbed his hand. "Farther," she said. "We can't do anything here."

Olmy grinned and threw back his head, then grimaced like a monkey in the oldest forest of all, baring his teeth at this measureless madness.

"Farther!" Karn insisted. The car rolled on, jolting with the regular ridges some or other force had pushed up in the sand.

Above the constant sizzle of rearranged world-lines, like a symphony of scrubbing and tapping brooms, came more sounds. If a burning forest could sing its pain, Olmy thought, it would be like the rising wail that came from the tower and the Castle. Thousands of the white figures made thousands of different sounds, as if trying to talk to each other, but not succeeding. Mock speech, sing-song pidgin nonsense, attempts to communicate emotions and thoughts they could not truly have; protests at being jabbed and pulled and jiggled along the scaffolding of the tower, over the uneven ground, like puppets directed by something trying to mock a process of construction.

Olmy's body had up to this moment sent him a steady

bloodwash of fear. He had controlled this emotion as well as he could, but never ignored it; that would have been senseless and wrong, for fear was what told him he came from a world that made sense, that held together and was consistent, that *worked*.

Yet fear was not enough, could not be an adequate response to what they were seeing. This was a threat beyond anything the body had been designed to experience. Had he allowed himself to scream, he could not have screamed loudly enough.

The Death we all know, Olmy told himself, is an end to something real; death here would be worse than nightmare, worse than the hell one imagines for one's enemies and unbelievers.

"I know," Karn said, and her hands shook on the clavicle.

"What do you know?" Rasp asked.

"Every meter, ever second, every dimension, has its own mind here," Karn said. "Space and time are arguing, fighting."

Rasp disagreed violently. "No mind, no minds at all!" she insisted shrilly.

Light itself began to waver and change as they came closer to the tower. Olmy could see the face of oncoming events before they occurred, like waves on a beach, rushing over the land, impatient to reach their destinations, their observers, before all surprise had been lost.

They now entered the fringes of shadow. The revisions of their surroundings felt like deep drumming pulses. Caught directly in a shadow, Olmy felt a sudden rub of excitement. He saw flashes of colors, felt a spectrum of unfamiliar emotions that threatened to cancel out his fear. He looked to his left, into the counterclockwise sweep, anticipating each front of darkness, leaning toward it.

Ecstasy, followed by a buzz of exhilaration, suddenly a spasm of brilliance, all the while the back of his head crisping and glowing and sparking. He could see into the back of his brain, down to the working foundations of every thought; where symbols with no present meaning are painted and arrayed on long tables, then jerked and jostled until they become emotions and memories and words.

"Like opening a gate!" Karn shouted, seeing Olmy's expression. "Much worse. Dangerous! Very dangerous!"

"Don't ignore it, don't suppress," Rasp told him. "Just pay attention to what's in front! That's what they teach us when we open a gate!"

"These aren't gates!" Olmy shouted above the hideous symphony of brooms. The twins' heads jerked and vibrated as he spoke.

"They are!" Rasp said. "Little gates into directly adjacent worlds. They're trying to escape their neighboring realities, to split away, but the lesion gathers them, holds them. They flow back behind us, along our world-lines."

"Back to the beginning!" Karn said.

"Back to our birth!" Rasp said.

"Here!" Karn said, and Olmy brought the car to a stop. The two assistants, little more than girls, with pale faces and wide eyes and serious expressions climbed down from the open cab and marched resolutely across the rippled sand, leaning into the pressure of other streams of reality. Their clothes changed color, their hair changed its arrangement, even their skin changed color, but they marched until the clavicles seemed to lift of their own will.

Rasp and Karn faced each other.

Olmy told himself, with whatever was left of his mind, that they were now going to attempt a cirque, a ring gate, that would bring all this to a meeting with the flaw. Within the flaw lay the peace of incommensurable contradictions, pure and purifying. Within the flaw this madness would burn to less than nothing, to paradoxes that would cancel and expunge.

He did not think they would have time to escape, even if the shrinking of the Way was less than instantaneous.

He stood on the seat of the car for a moment, watching the twins, admiring them. *Enoch underestimates them. As have I. This is what Ry Ornis wanted, why he chose them.*

He hunched his shoulders: something coming. Before he could duck or jump aside, Olmy was caught between two folds of shadow, like a bug snatched between fingers, and lifted bodily from the car. He twisted his neck and looked back to see a fuzzy image of the car, the twins lifting their clavicles, the rippled and streaked sand. The car seemed to vibrate, the tire tracks rippling behind it like snakes; and for a long moment, the twins and the car were not visible at all, as if they had never been.

Olmy's thoughts raced and his body shrieked with joy. Every nerve shivered, and all his memories stood out together in sharp relief, with different selves viewing them all at once. He could not distinguish between present and future; all were just parts of different memories. His reference point had blurred to where his life was a flat field, and within that field swam a myriad possibilities. What would happen, what had happened, became indistinguishable from the unchosen and unlived moments that *could* happen.

This blurring of his world-line rushed backward. He felt he could sidle across fates into what was fixed and unfix it, free his past to be all possible, all potential, once more. But the diffusion, the smearing and blending of the chalked line of his life, came up against the moment of his resurrection, the abrupt shift from Lamarckia—

And could not go any further. Dammed, the tide of his life spilled out in all directions. He cried out in surprise and a kind of pain he had never known before.

Olmy hung suspended beneath the dark eye, spinning slowly, all things above and below magnified or made minute depending on his angle. The pain passed. Perhaps it had never been. He felt as if his head had become a tiny but all-seeing camera obscura.

There was a past in which Ry Ornis accompanied the twins; he saw them working together near a very different vehicle, tractor rather than small car, to make the cirque. Already they had forced the Way to extrude a well through the sand. A cupola floated over the well, brazen and smooth, reflecting in golden hues the flaw, the lesion.

Olmy turned his head a fraction of a centimeter and once more saw only the twins, but this time dead, lying mangled beside the car, their clavicles flaring and burning. Another degree or two, and they were resurrected, still working. Ry Ornis was with them again.

A memory: Ry Ornis had traveled with them in the flawship. How could he have lost this fact?

Olmy rotated again, this time in a new and unfamiliar dimension, and felt the Way simply cease to exist and his own life with it. From this dark and soundless eventuality, he turned with a bitter, acrid wrench and found a very narrow course through the gripping shadows, a course illumined by half-forgotten emotions that had been plucked like flowers, arranged like silent speech.

He had been carried to the other side of the lesion, looking north down the endless throat of the Way.

The gripping baleen of shadow from the whale's mouth of the lesion, the driving cilia whisking him between world-lines, drove him under and over a complex surface through which he could see a deep mountainous valley, its floor smooth and vitreous like obsidian.

Black glass, reflecting the lesion, the flaw behind the lesion, scudding layers of mist. The cilia that controlled Olmy's orientation let him drop to a few meters above the vitreous black floor.

Motion stopped. His thoughts slowed. He felt only one body, one existence. All his lines clumped back into one flow.

He tried to close his eyes, to not see, but that was impossible. He faced down and saw his reflection in the mirror-shiny valley floor, a small still man floating beneath the red-rimmed eye like an intruding mote.

On either side of the valley rose jagged glassy peaks, mountain ranges like shreds of pulled taffy. A few hundred meters ahead of him—or perhaps a few kilometers, mounted in the middle of the valley lay something he recognized: a Jart defensive emplacement, white as ivory, jagged spikes thrusting like a sea urchin's spines from a squat discus. Shaded cilia played around the spikes, but the spikes did not track, did not move.

The emplacement was dead.

Olmy held his hands in front of his face. He could see them, see through them, with equal clarity. Nothing was obscured, nothing neglected by his new vision.

He tried to speak, or perhaps to pray, to whatever it was that held him, directed his motion. He asked first if anything was there, listening. No answer.

He remembered Plass's comments about the allthing: that in its domain it was unique, had never learned the arts of communication, was *one* without other and controlled all by *being all*. No separation between mind and matter, observed and observer. Such a being could neither listen nor answer. Nor could it change.

He thought of the emotions arrayed along the path that had guided him here. Pain, disappointment, fear. Weariness. Had the allthing learned this method of communication after its time in the Way? Had it dissected and rearranged enough human elements to change its nature this much?

Why pain? Olmy asked, spoken but unheard in the stillness.

He moved north down the center of the valley, over the dead Jart emplacement. His reflection shimmered in the uneven black mirror of the floor. He looked east and west, up the long curves of the Way beyond the jagged mountains, and saw more Jart emplacements, the spiral and beaded walls of what looked like Jart settlements, all abandoned, all spotted with large, distorted shapes he could not begin to comprehend.

Olmy thought, *It's made a Night Land for the Jarts. It does not know any difference between us.*

As if growing used to the extraordinary pressure of the shadow cilia gripping him, his body once more sent signals of fear, then simple, childlike wonder, and finally its own exhaustion. Olmy's head rolled on his shoulders and he felt his body sleep, but his mind remained alert. All his muscles tingled as they went off-line and would not respond to his tentative urgings.

How much time passed, if it were possible for time to pass, he could not judge. The tingling stopped and control returned. He lifted his head and saw a different valley, this one lined with huge figures. If the scale he had assumed at the beginning of his journey was still valid, these monolithic sculptures or shapes or beings—whatever they might be—were fully two or three kilometers distant, and therefore hundreds of meters in height. They were so strange he found himself looking at them in his peripheral vision, to avoid the confusion of placing them at the points of his visual focus. While vaguely organic in design—compound curves, folds of what might have been a semblance of tissue weighted by gravity, a kind of multilateral symmetry—the figures simply refused to be analyzed.

Olmy had many times experienced a lapse of visual judgment, when he would look at something in his living quarters and not remember it right away, and because of dim lighting or an unfamiliar angle, be unable to judge what it was. Under those conditions, he could feel his mind making hypotheses, trying desperately to compare them with what he was looking directly at, to reach some valid conclusion, and so actually *see* the object. This had occurred to him many times on Lamarckia, especially with regard to objects unique to that planet.

Here, he had no prior experience, no memory, no physical training or familiarity whatsoever with what he looked at, so he saw *nothing* sensible, nameable, to which he could begin to relate. Slowly, it dawned on Olmy that these might be more trophies of the allthing's encounters with Jarts.

He was drifting down a rogue's gallery of failed models, failed attempts to duplicate and understand, much like the gallery of objects and conditions around the Redoubt that made up the Night Land.

Humans had approached from the south, Jarts from the north. The allthing had applied similar awkward tools to both, either to unify them into its being, or to find some new way to experience their otherness. Both had been incomprehensibly alien to the allthing.

Pain. One of the emotions borrowed from Olmy's mind

and arrayed along the pathway. A sense of disunification, unwanted change. The allthing had been disturbed by this entry; there was no evil, no enthusiastic destruction, in the Night Land. Olmy suddenly saw what Enoch had been trying to communicate to him, and went beyond her own understanding.

A monobloc of pure order had been invaded by a domain whose main character was that of disunity and contradiction. That must have been very painful indeed. And this quality of order was being sucked backward, like gas into a vacuum, into their domain.

Enoch and the guild of gate-openers had manufactured the tip of a tooth. They had thrust into this other domain the bloody predatorial tooth of a hungry universe seeking quickening, a completion at its own beginning.

But this hypothesis did not instantly open any floodgate of comprehension or communication. Olmy did not find himself suddenly analyzing the raw emotional outbursts of another mind, godlike or otherwise; the allthing was not a mind in any sense he could understand. It was simply a pure and necessary set of qualities. It gripped him, controlled him, but literally had no use for him. Like everything else here, it could neither analyze nor absorb him. It could not even spread back along his world-line, for Olmy's existence had begun over with this new body, with his resurrection.

That was why he had not met any ghosts of himself. Physically, he had almost no past. The allthing, if such existed, had flung him along this valley of waste and failure, another piece of detritus, even more frustrating than most.

He squirmed, his body struggling to break free like an animal in a cage. Panic overwhelmed him despite his best efforts. Olmy could not locate any point of reference within; not even a self was clearly defined.

Everything blurred, became confused, as if he had been smudged by an enormous finger and no outline remained. *I am no where, no here, no name, moving, no future*

He twisted, convulsed, trying to find his center. The figures mounted on the ranges of mountains to either side seemed interested in this effort. He could feel their attention and did not welcome it. He fancied they moved, however slowly, advancing toward him across astronomical time.

If this lump of conflicting order and chaos could define himself anew, perhaps these incomprehensible monoliths, these unworshipped gods and unrealized mockeries, could establish a presence as well.

The panic stopped. Signals stopped.

He had come to an end. That minimum condition he had wished for was now upon him. He cared nothing for past or future, had lost nothing, gained nothing.

I am or was a part of a society really no part of any
This name is Olmy Ap Sennen
Lover of many loved and loving by few
Contact nothing without
Without contact nothing
Uprooted tree

The lesion's inflamed rim began to brighten. The suspended and aimless figure in its gripping cilia of probabilities maintained enough structure and drive to be interested in this, and noted that compared to past memory, the lesion was much smaller, much darker, and the flaring rim much broader. It resembled an immense solar eclipse with a bloody corona.

Loyalties and loves uprooted

Language itself faded until the aimless figure saw only

images, the lushness of another world out of reach, closed off, the faces of old humans once loved once reassuringly close now dead and without ghosts.

Can't even be haunted by a past uprooted

The figure's motion down the valley slowed. No time passed. Eveternity, endless now. Naked, skinless, fleshless, boneless. Consumed, integrated.

Experiences stillness.

Mark this in an endless column: *experiences*

Experiences stillness

stillness

stillness

No divisions. A tiny place no bigger than a fist a womb. Tiny place of infinite peace at the heart of a frozen geometry. All elaboration, variation, permutation, long since exhausted; infinite access to unbounded energy contained in oneness.

You/I/We no difference. See?

See. Vidya. *All seeing. Eye of Buddha. Nerveless kalpas of some body. Nerve vanity.*

This oneness consumed. Many nows, peace past.

At peace in the past. Loved women, raised children, lived a long life on a world to which there is no returning.

Nothing one at peace in no past all completed no returning.

Point.

One makes possible all.

I see. Buddha, do not leave your student bound.

The eye is shrinking, closing, its gorgeous bloody flare dimming. It is pierced by a white needle visible behind the small dark center.

Small large no matter no time

Do not go. Take us with

Am your father/mother/food

THE WAY OF ALL GHOSTS

loved raised living longing no return
my own ghost

8

Ry Ornis, the tall insect-thin master, smiled down on him. Olmy saw many of the master opener, like an avatar of an ancient god. All the different masters merged.

They were surrounded by a glassy tent and a slow breeze cooled his face. Ry Ornis had wrapped him in a rescue field where he fell, carrying safe cool air to replenish what his worksuit could no longer provide.

Olmy rediscovered scattered rivers of memory and bathed his ancient feet there. He swallowed once. The eye, the lesion, had shut forever. "It's gone," he said.

Ry Ornis nodded. "It's done."

"I can never tell anybody," Olmy realized out loud.

"You can never tell anybody."

"We robbed and ate to live. To be born."

Ry Ornis held his fingers to his lips, his face spectral in a new light from the south. A huge grin was spreading around half the Way, a gorgeous brilliant electric light. "The ring gate. A cirque," the gate-opener said, glancing over his shoulder. "Rasp and Karn, my students, have done well. We've done what we came here to do, and we saved the Way, as well. Not bad, eh, Ser Olmy?"

Olmy reached up to grab the gate-opener, perhaps to strangle him. Ry Ornis had moved, however.

Olmy turned away, swallowed a second time against a competing dryness. There had been no need to complete the ring gate. The unfinished cirque had done its job and drained the final wasted remnants of the lesion, forcing a closure.

As they watched, the cirque shrank. The grin became a

smile became an all-knowing serene curve, then collapsed to a point, and the point dimmed on distant rippled sands.

"I think the twins are a little disappointed they can't finish the cirque. But it's wonderful," Ry Ornis enthused, and performed a small dance on the black obsidian of the valley floor. "They are truly masters now! When I am tried and convicted, they will take my place!"

The Way remained. Rolling his head to one side, Olmy could not see the Redoubt.

"Where's the pyramid?" he asked hoarsely.

"Enoch has her wish," Ry Ornis said, and shaded his eyes with one hand.

Plass, Enoch, the allthing.

Plass had seen her own ghost.

To east and west, the ruined mountains and their statues remained, rejected, discarded. No dream, no hallucination.

He had been used again. No matter. For an endless instant, like any gate-opener, only more so, he had merged with the eye of the Buddha.

9

"The Infinite Hexamon Nexus does not approve of risky experiments that cannot be documented or explained. How many were deceived, Master Ry Ornis?"

"All, myself included."

"Yet you maintain this was done out of necessity?"

"All of it. The utmost necessity."

"Will this ever be necessary again? Answer honestly; the trust between us has worn very thin!"

"Never again."

"How do you explain that one universe, one domain, must feed on another in order to be born?"

"I don't. We were compelled. That is all I know."

"Could it have gone badly?"

"Of course. As it is, in our clumsiness and ignorance, we have condemned all our ancestors to live with unexplainable presences, ghosts of past and future. A kind of afterbirth."

"You are smiling, Master Gate Opener. This is intolerable!"

"It is all I can do, Sers."

...

"For your disobedience and arrogance, what punishment do you choose, Master Ry Ornis?"

"Sers of the Nexus. This I swear. I will put down my clavicle from this time forward, and never know the grace again."

—Sentencing Phase of Secret Hearings Conducted by the Infinite Hexamon Nexus, "On the Advisability of Opening Gates into Chaos and Order"

*   *   *

Tracting through the weightless forest of the Wald in the rebuilt Axis Nader, reaching out to the trees to push or grab roots and branches, half-flying and half-climbing, in his mind's river-wide eye, Olmy Ap Sennen returned to Lamarckia, where he had once nearly died of old age, and retrieved a package he had left there, tied in neat pieces of mat-paper. His wives and children had kept it safe for him, and now they returned it. There was much smiling and laughter, then saying of farewells, last of all a farewell to his sons, whom he had left behind. Occupants of a different land, another life.

As they faded, in his mind's eye, he opened the package they had given to him and greedily swallowed the wonderful contents.

His soul.

ABOUT THE AUTHOR

GREG BEAR is the author of over twenty-seven books of science fiction and fantasy. He has been awarded two Hugo and five Nebula Awards for his fiction, one of two authors to win a Nebula in every category. He has been called the "best working writer of science fiction" by *The Ultimate Encyclopedia of Science Fiction*. His novel *Darwin's Radio*, published by Ballantine Books, won the Nebula Award for "Best Novel of 2000," and was honored with the prestigious Endeavor Award. He is married to Astrid Anderson Bear. They are the parents of two children, Erik and Alexandra.